Prairie Angel

By Reaona T. Hemmingway

Bodge House Press
Topeka, Kansas

Prairie Angel
A novel by Reaona Hemmingway

This novel is suitable for all teen and adult audiences.

ISBN-13: 978-1492739470
ISBN-10: 1492739472

Copyright © 2013 by Reaona Hemmingway

All rights reserved. Except for brief quotations in reviews, no part of this work may be reproduced in whole or in part by any form of electronic, mechanical, or other means, now known or later invented, including scanning, photocopying, and recording, or in any information storage or retrieval system such as the Internet without the written permission of the author, Reaona Hemmingway. For more information, contact Bodge House Press, P.O. Box 254, Topeka, KS 66601-0254.

This is a work of fiction. All characters and events in this book exist only in the imagination of the author. Any resemblance to real people or events is purely coincidental.

Printed in the U.S.A. by CreateSpace.com

Prairie Angel

Dedication

In 2006, I searched online for an affordable writing convention to attend within driving distance of my hometown of Topeka, Kansas. I stumbled upon the Tallgrass Writers Workshop at Emporia State University in Emporia, Kansas. For $60 I enrolled and mailed in ten pages of a manuscript for critique by one of the published authors, who were presenting at the breakout sessions.

The published author who received my ten critique pages was Don Coldsmith, author of the Spanish Bit series. Don was a retired doctor, who decided to hang up his stethoscope when his malpractice insurance premiums grew larger than his annual salary. His syndicated column "Horsing Around" was published in the Emporia Gazette as well as other newspapers and magazines across the Midwest.

My manuscript, *Prairie Angel*, happened to be a western and in the first ten pages my main character is confronted with delivering a baby. I was just a bit nervous having someone with his background read and critique my work, but things worked out pretty good. Don's first question was how I knew so much about birthing babies. I've never had children and my only experience with the birthing process comes from reading books and watching television. That amazed him because the details in Chapter 1 were quite right for what Angela does to act as a midwife.

Don then told me my pages were so well drafted they needed little editing to be publishable. Before our session ended, he asked to see the whole manuscript. I said sure and wrote down his address. I spent the next couple of week finishing the novel to mail to him.

It was several months before I heard back from Don. I finally called him in November and learned that he had suffered a heart attack not long after the workshop and didn't get around to reading my manuscript until fall. When he returned it, he said he had never read a first draft so well written and ready for publication.

I regret Don Coldsmith never saw this book in print because he believed in it so strongly.

I gratefully dedicate *Prairie Angel* to his memory.

Chapter 1

Nebraska, September 1874

"God, help me!"

My head rose up off the ground, as I cocked an ear into the night air to discern whether the woman's agony came from my turbulent dreams or a real life plea for help. Unsure, I glanced at Ruth. The white mare stood with her head up and her ears pricked.

"So you heard it, too?"

At the sound of my voice, she bobbed her head.

Convinced the woman existed in the real world, I sat up and tossed off my blankets. The woman needed help, and although the thought made my pulse quicken, my conscience took hold. A story about a Samaritan and an injured man fluttered through my mind. Where it came from, I don't recall, but the message of the story was the same: Do the right thing for your fellow man or, in this case, woman. Besides, out here in the middle of nowhere, the odds leaned toward the possibility I was the only help available.

I slid on my boots, tucked my shirt inside my trousers, and packed my camp gear into the saddlebags.

Several minutes passed before the scream came again.

"God, help me!" The woman's clear voice carried well in the crisp night air.

This time I identified the direction from which the scream came: North.

I saddled Ruth and guided her toward the woman's plea. In doing so, I ignored the anxious voice inside my head that warned, *Run! Go the other way!* That cautious voice had kept me safe and alive so far. But, for the first time since waking up four months ago unable to remember my own name, I listened to a calmer instinct, which told me to help the agonized woman.

A gentle pull on the reins brought Ruth to a halt at the top of a hill. Under a full moon, I surveyed the small homestead's run down sod cabin and out buildings. The field beyond the farmyard laid fallow with weeds and the stalk stubble remains of last year's harvest. In the corral, a lone nanny goat paced with quick, nervous steps. Next to the shed, a chicken coop stood empty. Like the field, the farmyard and garden were overrun with sunflowers, thistles, and sagebrush.

I urged Ruth down the hill. As we crossed the creek, the water soaked into my scuffed boots and the calves of my denim trousers.

Men's pants on a woman? Again, the quandary entered my mind's quest to figure out who I am. The inventory of my clothes included two pairs of pants and six flannel shirts. That was the count left after I burned the clothes I awoke in four months ago. That shirt and pair of trousers were too torn and stained with blood and bodily waste to save.

Why not dresses, corsets, and petticoats? Why not a bonnet instead of the battered light brown Stetson I found among the rocks on a slope not far from where I awoke?

Aren't those the clothes women are supposed to wear?

I rode into the farmyard, stopped Ruth beside the barn, and tied her to the corral rail. My hand grabbed the Colt Peacemaker from the saddle holster in an instinctive move left over from my forgotten past. The weight of the gun felt natural. Too natural. That made me wonder how often I had used the Colt before waking up with a cracked skull.

I reached up and touched the rough, jagged scar on the left side of my head. Beneath the scar was a slight ridge where the crack in my skull healed. Beneath the crack, my mind battled to put the broken pieces of my past into some explanation of my present. Fighting that battle produced headaches like the one forming now.

The pain urged me to stop thinking about it and accept the fact that I know how to use the Colt with the same skill as fishing and making coffee. Those things came easily without headaches. The Colt and the Winchester in Ruth's saddle scabbard were part of a life I might want to leave forgotten. But the voice in my head, the one that urged me to run away or hide from people, told me I needed to remember the past before I stumbled into danger.

I stopped at the sod cabin's window and peered in. There, in the middle of the floor lay a woman writhing in agony as she held her rounded belly with both hands.

Her leathered skin and graying blond hair made her appear much older than me. What little I knew of my age came from looking into the still water of a pond. What I learned from the watery image was that I'm not nearly as old as the woman inside the cabin. For one thing, I don't have gray strands in amongst the brown hair I comb and braid down to my waist every morning.

The woman screamed again and that anxious voice inside me tried to send doubts into my thinking. What did I know about birthing babies? I should ride fast and find a doctor. But in what direction would I go? And how far would I have to ride?

The calmer voice reminded me I would never find help in time. I must stay.

I gulped down the knot in my throat, walked the last few steps to the open door, and knocked. "Ma'am, I'm coming in to help you." Without waiting for a response, I entered.

She looked up and screamed as her body contorted from another contraction. Her eyes rounded with fear as they focused on the gun in my hand, so I set it down on the table.

In a quick swivel of my head, I surveyed the room. In the far corner stood a double bed with a cedar trunk at its foot. To one side of the bed stood a washstand with a green and white porcelain pitcher and bowl. Underneath the only window sat a crate filled with rags. Next to the fireplace, a rocking chair held a small blue blanket hanging over the back. In the kitchen area, two shelves held stacks of dishes above a wooden workbench, which held a washtub. The table with two chairs ended the inventory of furnishings except for the rag rug the woman lay on.

That rug put an inadequate barrier between her and the hard packed dirt floor.

"We have to get you onto the bed," I said, as I helped her to her feet.

Although laden with child, she felt light in my arms. Through her dress, my hands felt bones protruding through her skin. The term emaciated came to mind as I eased her onto the mattress. She no sooner lay down and another contraction seized her. Not more than a full minute went by, which meant the contractions were coming too fast for my comfort.

"Take short, quick breaths," I said.

I swung her feet up on the bed and removed her slippers and undergarments. With her skirt bunched up past her thighs, I checked between her legs. The dim light made it difficult to see, so I moved the lantern from the table to the cedar chest and turned up the wick. Sure enough, dark, matted, wet hair appeared in the birth canal.

"It shouldn't be much longer, ma'am. The head is crowning. Push real hard the next time you feel a contraction."

She nodded, as she gasped for air.

I wasn't sure if I told her the right thing to do, but it seemed important to sound like I did. Was it a woman's instinct to know what to do when birthing a child? Some maternal instinct we're born and raised with perhaps?

Pain gripped her again and she pushed. I wiped my hands on my pants and prepared to pull the baby out. But, just as I thought the infant would break free of the mother, it slipped back.

The woman screamed and almost passed out.

I placed my hand on her shoulder and shook her. "You have to stay with me now." She let out an exhausted sigh and nodded. "This time push real hard and I'll reach my fingers around the head and shoulders to pull it down and out."

Again she nodded as I pushed her bony knees further apart.

Sweat trickled down my face. I wiped my sleeve across my forehead. I was no more ready for this than she. The baby seemed to be the only one ready, providing it could get past its mother's small pelvis.

When the next contraction came and the head appeared, I forced my hands in around it and barely managed to loop my middle fingers under the baby's armpits before it tried to disappear again. The woman groaned at the extra pressure caused by the presence of my hands inside her already overburdened birth canal.

I held onto the baby and pulled.

"Push!"

"Arrgh!" Her shoulders came off the mattress as she bore down and used what little strength she possessed to force the child out.

Once the head and shoulders came free, the little girl slid easily out of her mother's womb. I lifted her gently into my arms and covered her mouth and nose with my lips. Sucking in, I cleared her airway and spit the mucus and fluids onto the floor. The baby wailed as she sucked the foreign air into her lungs. As she cried, her skin color changed from blue to red and finally a pinkish white.

To keep her warm, I laid her long thin body on top of her unconscious mother's stomach while I searched through the cedar chest. A sewing box held a spool of white thread and scissors. I also grabbed two towels and what looked like diapers made from bed sheets. Beneath those were baby sleepers made from used flannel.

I tied two lengths of thread around the umbilical cord and cut between the tie offs. Somehow birthing, washing, and dressing the baby came as natural as handling the guns.

I moved the rag-filled crate closer to the fireplace and laid the baby down in the makeshift cradle. She looked quite cozy swaddled in the blue blanket, but I didn't have time to admire her for long. My work was only half through at that point.

I tossed the afterbirth in a mixing bowl and did what I could to stop the woman's bleeding. My head throbbed, but I continued to bathe the woman, dress her in a clean nightgown, and at last bury the afterbirth. With those tasks accomplished, I carried her soiled dress outside and placed it and my own shirt to soak in a washtub that hung from a hook on the side of the soddy.

It was well after four in the morning when I put Ruth in a barn stall and filled the empty manger with a bushel basket of grass I cut from the overgrown yard.

I looked up at the stars, as a good feeling enveloped me. My presence made a difference here tonight. Because I survived my accident, a child has a chance to live.

Chapter 2

Late in the morning, after I returned from hanging out the laundry, the woman awoke. Her pale skin and the large dark circles around her eyes made her look haunted. Deep down, I sensed she would die. The best I could do was make her comfortable for as long as possible.

In a barely audible whisper she said, "Thank you."

She took a sip of water before I brought her the baby girl to hold. "She's fed twice upon you already and shouldn't be hungry for another hour." I helped her place her feeble arms in position to hold her daughter. "I'll fix you some soup."

"There is no food."

"I've got some. I'll boil buffalo jerky and mix in some goat's milk and wild onions."

I hung the kettle over the fire, and then left her alone to cuddle her child. I went outside to check on Ruth. After four months of living outdoors, the white mare appeared pleased to have a barn to live in.

There was no way to know how long we were out in the wilderness before I awoke. The passage of time came from watching the moon. Inside my saddlebags were five stones, one for each full moon since I awoke. On the stones I scratched a mark for each day since the last full moon. It wasn't the most perfect calendar in the world, but it served my needs.

As I stroked Ruth's neck, she nuzzled the side of my head as if to kiss the pain away. I owed my life to Ruth. The name I gave her was one my befuddled mind remembered from story about a woman who cared for her mother-in-law the same way Ruth took care of me. During the first few days after I awoke, Ruth kept me awake by nudging and nipping at me. She gave me water by taking mouthfuls of cool refreshing liquid from a nearby stream and dribbling it into my mouth. She stood over me and protected me against the rain and at night she lay beside me to share the warmth of her side and belly.

Two weeks passed before I rallied enough cognizance and strength to untie the cinch and pull on a stirrup to slide the saddle off her back. Covered with saddle sores, her white fur was stained red-brown and matted with scabs. Free of the saddle, Ruth ran to the stream and rolled around in the cool water, which washed away the redness.

While Ruth soaked in the creek, I rummaged through the saddlebags for clues to my identity. All I found were men's clothing, food, dishes, a hunting knife, ammunition, a copy of *The Prairie Traveler*, and a wallet with the initials JC McD embossed into the leather. The wallet contained $1,790 and a square piece of paper with a crude map drawn on it. The drawing showed a river, rock formations, hills, and an 'X'. No names, no measurements, just the 'X'.

The discovery of these items kept my mind pondering several questions. Why would I, a woman, travel out on the prairie alone? How did I get hurt? Who am I that I would carry a large sum of money, two guns, and a book on surviving in the wilds of the western frontier? And most of all: Where did the 'X' tell me to go? Or…was it some place I already went and wanted to return to at a later date?

For three full moons I pondered these questions while I stayed in what I refer to as my healing camp.

When I felt well enough to travel, I let Ruth pick our path in the hopes she knew the way home. So far she's followed the stream while I lived off the land by collecting berries, nuts, and roots. For meat, I shot rabbits, squirrels, and one lone, orphaned buffalo calf that I smoked and jerked two weeks ago. For the past month, Ruth acted as trail guide until last night when I turned her toward this farm.

I scratched Ruth's chin. "We'll have to stay here a while, my friend. Tomorrow we'll hunt some game and ride back to that onion patch we found yesterday. I also saw some berries growing on that knoll a few miles back just before the sun went down."

Ruth nodded. She seemed to know it would be a lot of hard riding to get the gathering done in a short time. I took a brush off a shelf and brushed her fur and then combed through her mane and tail. Her back healed faster than my head. There were only a few scars left behind from the saddle sores and a gash on her right foreleg. The white fur glistened from the attention I gave it last night and again this morning. After I put the brush away, I led her out into the corral where she stared down the goat.

That goat and I already tangled with each other earlier in the morning when I milked it. She was as ornery as any goat I ever saw, not that I remember seeing any until now. Even so, I was pretty sure that like geese, goats possessed a mean streak.

Somewhere from my mind came a memory about a goose chasing me. It was on a farm. Not a farm like this one, but one with well kept wooden buildings. There was a red barn, a green chicken coop, and a white, two-story house with a wraparound porch. There were tool sheds, hay barns, and farm equipment protected from the snow and rain by arbors. The corrals were filled with horses, mules, and other livestock. The farm was definitely prosperous and well maintained.

In the memory, I held a cinnamon bun in my hand when a goose waddled up from a pond and ran toward me. "Granma, help! Sossy wants my roll."

"Throw it on the ground," a woman on the porch said. "I'll give you another."

The memory ended with me running to the porch where the woman embraced me with strong, loving arms. She smelled of peaches and fresh baked bread.

Trying to remember more strengthened my headache, so I stopped in favor of heading back to the cabin where I added wild onions to the stew pot. While the soup simmered, I took a piece of paper from the woman's trunk and sat down at the table. Because my mind seemed to pick and choose what it remembered, I wanted to write down what I remembered about a goose named Sossy and a grandmother who smelled like peaches and baked bread.

On another sheet of paper, I drew the layout of the farm in the memory. With surprising artistic talent I sketched a picture of the woman and the goose. Like the woman in the soddy, Granma was much older than me with graying chestnut hair pulled back and pinned into a bun. Short, fluffy curls framed her face. I was trying to remember her eye color when the woman in the cabin spoke.

"What is your name?"

I glanced over at her. She held the baby to one of her small breasts. I wasn't sure what to tell her, so I shook my head.

"Don't you have a name, child?"

"I...I..." The words stuck in my throat. How could I forget something as simple as my own name? I rubbed the side of my head and felt the uneven ridge. "I had an accident, ma'am. I...I don't remember my name."

"Oh, dear. You poor child."

Why did she keep calling me 'child'? I went to the cedar chest and picked up the hand mirror that lay inside. Unlike the distorted reflections in the water, the mirror showed my blue eyes and a thin pink scar along my left jaw. The scar started an inch beyond my chin and traveled back and up toward my ear, which also bore a few small scars along the contours. Other than the scar, my skin was smooth and tanned by the sun.

"How old do you think I am?" I asked.

"My guess is about twenty. Not more than twenty-two."

"How old are you?"

"I'll be forty-six in December. Homer and I waited thirty years to have a child." She looked down at the baby with a sad smile. "He doesn't even know he finally became a father."

"Where is he?"

"He left to get supplies back in February. That was over seven months ago. It's about ninety miles to the nearest town. It should've taken him five or six days to get there with an empty wagon and a day or two more than that to come back with a loaded one. The longest he's ever been gone is two weeks."

I put the mirror away and closed the chest.

"I didn't have the strength to walk to town after I gave up hope of him returning." She peered down into the suckling child's face. "I put in as much of a garden as there was seed and stretched the food as best I could. One by one I ate the hens and the rooster," she looked up, "and Jane, the milk cow after she went dry. Coyotes broke into the smokehouse and took most of that meat the day I hung it. All that's left is that goat and she'll dry up soon if she's not mated in another month or so."

She rolled her eyes toward the ceiling and then back toward me. "She won't hardly let me near her after watching the other animals get butchered. It's been a bear trying to milk her in the condition I'm in. Milk, water, and an occasional fish from the creek is all I've lived on the last three weeks."

Her fevered brow glistened in the lamplight. I stood up and placed a cool cloth on her head. "You lost a lot of blood after the baby was born," I said. "I had to cauterize a tear in your birth canal with a stick from the fire."

"I'd say you've been around a midwife or a doctor sometime in your life."

I picked up the sleeping baby, burped her, and put her down to sleep in her makeshift crib. The soup was ready by then, so I sat on the edge of the bed and helped the woman eat.

"My name's Margie," she said. "Margaret Drummond to those who don't know me."

"What are you naming the baby?" I asked.

"Her name is Carol Anne Drummond, after my mother."

She finished her soup and then settled down into a fevered sleep. By the time morning came, her fever left her too weak to sit up, but she still insisted on breast-feeding Carol.

Before leaving the cabin to go foraging, I placed the lantern on the trunk and changed the dressing between Margie's legs. Then I moved the table closer to the bed with a pitcher of water, a jar of goat's milk, and a pan of broth on it. I hated leaving Margie alone, but I needed to gather more food while she was still alive to care for Carol.

Chapter 3

The sun hovered two hours above the horizon when I came up over the hill with a young deer slung across Ruth's back and two gunny sacks filled with wild vegetables and fruit. The berries were gone when I returned to the bush, but I found three apple trees near some graves left behind by a wagon train.

The name Lyndon was carved into a stone with the given names Albert, Myrtle, Pip, and Frances. Beneath the names, the headstone maker carved out the word Typhoid and the year, 1851. I decided the Lyndon family was taking saplings to Oregon when they died and that whoever buried them planted the trees to lighten the wagon load.

Seeing the marker made me think about how close I came to dying. All anyone would've ever found of me were bleached bones in a grove of pines, elms, and cottonwoods. The thought of dying alone without a proper grave sent a chill through me. As I crossed the creek, I spotted a piece of sandstone that would make a good headstone for Margie. Ruth could help me drag it out in the morning and I could use Homer's tools to chisel the words.

By the time I stabled Ruth, skinned the deer, and hung the meat in the smokehouse, the sky turned solid black with its countless white twinkling specks. I selected a small roast and carried it into the cabin where I lit the lantern on the table.

Margie slept with an arm wrapped around Carol to keep her from rolling. I moved the table back to the center of the room and put Carol in her rag box cradle. She woke up, but seemed content to just lie there while I took care of her mother.

Margie's forehead felt warmer than before I went foraging for food. I placed cold wet towels over her body. She drank a cup of water without waking. I gave her a second cup. She still slept.

I hung a pot with the meat in it over the fire to boil and then warmed a cup of goat's milk. Sitting at the table with Carol cradled in my lap, I used a clean white handkerchief dipped in the milk to feed her. She sucked the nectar from the linen. It took longer to feed her this way, but she endured the process with patience and made very little fuss.

Once the baby fell back to sleep, I fixed willow bark tea for Margie. Her fever came down some, but she didn't wake up until early the next morning while the moon still shined through the window.

"I'm going to join Homer soon," she whispered. I awoke from Homer's side of the bed and rolled toward her. She was sitting up, staring at Carol. "I want you to take Carol and raise her as your own." She pointed to the cedar chest. "Get out a sheet of paper. The Bible, too."

I did as she asked. Margie kept all of her clothes and personal items in that chest to keep the bugs from eating at them. I moved the table next to the bed again and she began to write. Where she found the strength, I don't know, but she wrote out her last will and testament. She gave everything she owned to Carol and named me the baby's guardian. In the document, she called me Angela Prairie. Startled, I looked at her, but before I could ask why, she gave me the answer.

"You came to me like a prairie angel from God to save Carol's life. I give you this name as my gift of thanksgiving for all you've done for me and all you will do for Carol." She slid down on the bed and nestled her head into the pillow. "Now sign it as a witness and if by chance you find Homer alive, tell him I love him."

Margie fell asleep and never woke up again. The coma lasted for three days before the fever finished pushing what little life remained out of her. I buried her in the garden bed where the soil turned up easily with the shovel. The headstone read, "Here lies Margaret Drummond, Wife to Homer, Mother of Carol, Born December 5, 1828, Died September 13, 1874." I saw her birth date in the Bible when she added Carol's name to the family tree page in the center. For the date of death, I added three days to the date she wrote on the last will.

Two weeks later I saddled Ruth, placed Carol on my back swaddled up like a papoose, and dragged the goat toward town. I really wanted to leave that old nanny behind, but Carol needed the milk, so I put up with her stubbornness and unsociable disposition toward Ruth.

Thankfully, the trail Homer blazed between the homestead and town pretty much followed the creek and made traveling easy. Carol rarely fussed unless she wanted to eat or needed changing. If I fed her at nine o'clock in the evening, she slept until five the next morning. The feeding schedule was about every four hours during the day and each time I stopped, I took time to wash her linens in the creek.

There were six regular campsites along Homer's trail. At each site, he made a stone fire ring, piled a stack of wood, and built a lean-to. Homer also hung signs asking travelers to please replace any firewood they used and to keep the campsites neat and in good repair. Apparently people obeyed the request because at the third site the firewood was freshly cut and at the fifth, a new support pole held up one corner of the lean-to.

I wish I'd asked Margie why she didn't go with Homer when he went to town. It seemed strange for a man to leave his woman out in the middle of nowhere by herself. That thought made me smile. After all, I was a woman out in the middle of nowhere and I was surviving by myself.

Patting Ruth on the neck, I thanked her again for helping me stay alive.

Late in the afternoon on the sixth day, I spotted the town and stared at it from a distance for almost an hour before kneeing Ruth forward. My pulse raced as that voice of anxiety, once again, tried to tell me to stay away from people.

I continued forward because Carol needed a wet nurse and I needed to find out what happened to Homer, providing he made it this far. Actually, I was pretty sure he did make it to town. I stayed to his trail the whole ninety miles and nowhere within view did I see an abandoned wagon, the remains of a human body, or a grave.

As I thought about where Homer may have disappeared, I finished riding into the town of Welcome, Nebraska. The hotel, if you could call it that, was easy to find. In a lot next to what now served as the hotel stood several stacks of lumber. A work crew was busy clearing away the charred remains of what I assumed used to be the actual hotel. The lot next door contained a one-story building with signs advertising a saloon and a restaurant. I peered through the central doorway and saw a hallway that separated the two businesses. Behind the building, the current hotel consisted of twelve cabin tents on platforms in a yard surrounded by a wooden fence. With the night air turning frigid, I needed better lodging than that for Carol.

Turning Ruth away from the hotel, I scanned the length of the street. At the far end, a new schoolhouse stood with paint so fresh and white it blinded the eyes. The progression of buildings included a church, a tailor's shop, which also doubled as a barbershop and undertaker's parlor, a general store, the bank, and across from the hotel, the sheriff's office, which stood next to the livery stable.

Moving on down the street from the hotel, I found Garrett's Feed & Seed, which also hauled freight and served as the stage depot, post office, and telegraph station. Next door was another saloon. Passing a hardware store, I rounded a street corner and found a few more shops, the courthouse, and, finally, a two-story boarding house with white clapboard siding and a wrap-around porch and balcony. Next door was a two story yellow house with brown shutters. The house was attached to a doctor's office.

Welcome was by no means a city, but a small, growing town of about three hundred people judging by the number of homes and businesses. A quarter mile north, the sun glinted off the railroad tracks. Grain silos were under construction and a water tower stood nearby. West of town, the town dammed up a creek to make a water reservoir. If the citizens continued to plan for their future in this manner, the town promised growth and prosperity to those who lived here.

I tied Ruth to the hitching rail outside the picket fence, which surrounded the boarding house's front yard. The gate swung easily on the hinges and the path to the porch was paved with bricks.

A chubby, gentle looking woman with auburn hair answered my knock. In height, she only came up to my nose, but in presence she seemed much taller.

"Do you have a vacancy?" I asked when she stepped out onto the porch.

She walked around me, her eyes missing nothing in my unladylike attire or the fact I carried Carol strapped to my back. Like everything else about my lost past, I knew nothing of why the only clothing I possessed besides my undergarments and kerchiefs were more suited to a man. For some reason, I didn't even have a coat or jacket.

Margie's clothes were too small and Homer's too big, not that there were many of his things left in the soddy. Margie had used most of his clothes to make gowns and diapers for the baby. From Margie's coat I made a second blanket for Carol and used her dresses and petticoats to make more baby clothes and diapers.

Before leaving the homestead, I packed and locked the chest with anything of value or use. That way, once I found a place to settle in town, all I needed to do was find an honest man who would drive out there and bring back the cedar chest, bed, table, and rocking chair.

"Where's the baby's father?" the woman asked when she finished her inspection.

"I don't know." I stood tall against her gaze, which accused me of being a loose, unwed mother. "Margaret Drummond asked me to take care of her."

Her wary expression changed into a puzzled look. "The only Drummond I know is Homer."

My pulse quickened with excitement. "Is he still in town?"

She shook her head. "He always stays here when he comes to town. Last time was eight months ago. Do you know him?"

"No. I found his wife all alone four weeks ago trying to give birth to Carol on her own."

"His wife?" Again she looked puzzled.

"Margaret Drummond. They homesteaded ninety miles from here about six years ago. Hasn't she ever been to town?"

"Don't recollect ever meeting her. Besides, Homer never mentioned having a wife." She cocked her head to one side and patted her bosom. "Funny, the things a man doesn't mention when he's sharing your bed."

The admiration I felt for Homer died a sudden death. No wonder he left Margie behind when he came to town. The man I thought was a devoted and loving husband led a secret life. The bastard never told anyone he was married.

The woman leaned in close. "You know, I always thought Homer was hiding something." She pointed down the street at the law office of James W. Talbourne, P.A. "Kimberly Talbourne disappeared eight months ago. She was only sixteen and came up pregnant after Homer's visit last fall. I bet they ran off together, leaving his poor wife alone carrying this sweet little babe." She tickled Carol under the chin and cooed at the baby.

Feeling an ache in my back and a throbbing in my temples, I tapped the woman on the shoulder. "Miss...uh..."

"Mrs. Chalk, dear."

"Mrs. Chalk, do you have a room available?"

"Oh, my, yes, and a barn for your animals," she said, pointing at Ruth and the goat. "It'll be two dollars a week for the room, a dollar for your animals, and four bits a day for meals. Having your laundry done is another ten cents per bag."

"That will be fine."

I followed her inside and up the stairs to the corner room at the end of the hall facing the street.

"Mr. Peabody next door to you is half deaf, so the baby shouldn't bother him." Mrs. Chalk unlocked the door and handed me the key. "What you have on is fine for breakfast and lunch, but I require my guests to come *dressed* for dinner when they share my table."

My cheeks heated. "I don't own a dress."

"Oh, dear." Mrs. Chalk hurried across the room and opened the window to let the fresh air in. "There isn't much time. The shops will close soon. I'll watch the baby and have Jarvis stable your animals while you run across the street to Paula's and tend to your wardrobe."

I removed Carol from my back and laid her on the bed. She whimpered as I untied the straps holding her to the baby board, but she quieted when I held her to my shoulder.

"You have a natural caring instinct for babies, dear," Mrs. Chalk said as she rubbed Carol's back. "She purrs like a kitten in your arms. Do you have many brothers and sisters?"

A lump formed in my throat. But then, in the back of my mind, I heard a boy yell at me, "Dad's gonna pickle your hide if you don't let go of my hair."

The boy whose back I sat on was older with the same color of hair as mine.

"I have an older brother." *I think.* I tried to drive the memory further along, but my temples ached and I felt dizzy. Afraid I might drop Carol, I handed her to Mrs. Chalk. "I'd best go get that dress," I said as I hurried out of the room. I needed air.

Chapter 4

Paula's Dress Shop would've felt cozy if it wasn't for the way my headache caused my stomach to feel nauseated from the smells of perfumes and bath oils. It took all my willpower not to run outside and vomit in the street.

"You should like it at Emma's," Paula said as she finished taking my measurements. She looped the measuring tape over her neck and walked to a rack of dresses. "She's a wonderful, dear soul, and a very good friend."

I couldn't quite decide how old Paula Klondike was, but she stood a half-inch taller than me with brown eyes and golden brown hair, which she wore in a brown, lacy snood. My best guess put her in her thirties with a complexion and figure that made her look much younger.

She picked out three dresses from the rack and looped them over the back of a chair upholstered in plum velvet. The dress on top was made of black taffeta.

"I don't think I want that one," I said. "My tastes are simple and I've never enjoyed wearing black."

Why didn't I enjoy wearing black? A vision of standing in front of two shiny, black lacquered coffins flashed through my mind. Unlike other images I tried to hang onto, I chased this one away as quickly as it came. Even so, I sensed the image came from a somewhat recent occurrence.

The second dress was made of royal blue cotton with white lace around a modest neckline and the cuffs of the long sleeves. The skirt was made in three split front tiers around a white lace-covered underskirt. It would be perfect for dinner and other social occasions.

"I'll take that one," I said.

"It will make your eyes look even bluer," Paula said as she showed me the third dress.

Simply styled, the third dress looked serviceable for everyday. Made of soft gray wool, it was trimmed with pink velvet piping around the high-buttoned collar, cuffs, and bodice yoke. Buttons made from seashells with a pink and silver glimmer ran from the top of the collar to the sloping waistline where the fullness of the unadorned skirt was gathered in small tucks.

"I'll take that one as well," I said.

"Do you need any petticoats or slippers to wear with them?"

I looked down at my current attire of blue flannel shirt, black jeans, and scuffed riding boots. "You're looking at what I have other than more of the same in my bedroll."

After selling me all the accoutrements that go with wearing a woman's wardrobe, Paula closed her shop and helped me carry the packages across the street. Mrs. Chalk greeted her with a kiss on the cheek when we entered my room where Carol now slept in a white wicker bassinet.

Mrs. Chalk answered the questioning look I gave her. "Jarvis carried it down from the attic after he put your animals in the barn." She walked over to the bassinet and brushed a finger along Carol's cheek. "Poor little dear. Ninety miles at such a young age, she deserves to live like a princess. My own darling slept many a peaceful night in this crib. Never could figure out why I dragged it with me when I moved here. It's good to see it in use again."

"Thank you, Mrs. Chalk." I spotted an empty baby bottle on the nightstand. "Thanks also for feeding her."

"It was a pleasure, dear."

I turned and found Paula putting my purchases away in the wardrobe. "I can do that."

"Nonsense," she said in a sisterly tone. "You're nearly about to drop yourself. Take a towel and go down the hall to wash up," she winked at Mrs. Chalk, "before Emma charges you double for the trail dust you're carrying around with you."

"We'll tend to the babe and get you all settled in," Mrs. Chalk said. She walked over to the wardrobe and pulled out the green flannel bathrobe I purchased. "You can put this on. I've already poured you a hot bath and there's a laundry bag with your room number marked on it hanging on the back of the door. Just throw it in the hamper when you get through."

As I carried the robe out the door, I ran into a short, stocky man in his mid-twenties carrying my Colt and Winchester. He looked at me with childlike innocence.

"I cleaned…your guns…and brushed…your white horse," he said. "Your goat…liked the carrots…I gave her."

"Thank you." I smiled. "Thank you also for bringing the bassinet down for Carol."

"Carol's a…pretty name…it's like…a song." He laid the guns on top of the bureau in my room. "Do you sing…pretty songs?" he asked when he turned back around.

"Jarvis, go set the table," Mrs. Chalk said.

"I don't know," I said in answer to his question.

"Tomorrow…we can go…to the church…and I'll play…a song …for you…to sing."

I didn't know what to say or do. Jarvis obviously suffered from some sort of disorder that slowed his speech. Mrs. Chalk wrung her hands together as though embarrassed. She ushered Jarvis out of the room and down the hall.

As I soaked in the hot water, I closed my eyes and tried to clear my mind in order to relieve the headache pounding against my brain. I thought about Jarvis and wished I could live a simple life. In many ways I envied him. How peaceful it must feel to have a childlike outlook on life with no hidden tormentors pressing against the mind.

That is how I felt, tormented, as though I balanced on a thin thread between rationality and uncertainty. It was like living in a dream where something obscures my vision while I stumble around trying to grasp an object that is always just out of reach.

It's like how I don't know whether I was leaving or returning when I got injured. If I was leaving, how much of a hurry was I in? Was my accident an accident? Or was it caused by someone chasing me? These questions gave root to my fear of being around people. Even in the daylight I stumble around in the dark, never knowing which destination leads to safety or peril.

There were many times during the past two months when I hid in gullies, behind boulders or bushes, or simply lay down in the tall prairie grass as people passed my location. Twice the people I saw traveled with wagon trains and once a lone wagon passed. Three times I saw cowboys and twice soldiers. The day before I shot the buffalo calf, I hid from a band of Indians toting the catch from their hunt back to their village. Not one person I saw looked menacing, but I stayed out of sight while I breathed deep to bring my anxiety under control.

I wore the blue dress to dinner and took the seat on Paula's right. Besides Paula and myself, there were four other boarders at the table. Paula lived in the room on the other side of Mr. Peabody, whom I learned was the old gentleman sitting across from me.

As soon as grace was said, Mrs. Chalk gestured toward me. "This is our new tenant, Angela Prairie. She and Carol Drummond will be staying in Room 5."

A young man to my right smiled. "My name is Neil Jones. I work at the bank." The cuffs of his tan dinner coat were frayed, but everything about him bespoke of someone with ambition. His hair looked soft and silky, and although he looked about five years older than me, there was a schoolboy charm about him I liked.

In contrast, the girl sitting across from Neil looked as timid as a mouse, ready to scurry away at the slightest sound. Her green eyes kept straying toward Jarvis and shifted in the opposite direction whenever he looked at her.

"This is…my friend, Sara," Jarvis said. He sat at the end of the table between Neil and Sara. "She reads to me…and teaches me…to write my name."

Sara's cheeks turned red.

"Sara is our new school teacher," Paula said. "She started this term."

The girl appeared younger than me and I couldn't picture someone that timid teaching school children. The schoolmaster back home spoke in a loud, stern voice and often needed to break up fights between the boys.

Back home. Where was back home? My temples started to throb again. What was the name of the bearded man who always carried a wooden pointer around the classroom and never hesitated to slam it down across a desk to keep my classmates in line?

Mr. Peabody smiled at me. "Who are you, my dear?" he asked as though he just realized I sat across from him.

"Angela Prairie, sir."

"Eh?" He cupped a hand to the back of his ear.

I repeated my name louder, taking great care to enunciate clearly.

"I knew an Angela once," he said. "She worked at a bordello in New Orleans. It was after we chased the British back to England in 1814. I finished my road into manhood that night. Oh, how I'd love to be sixteen again." He mumbled something incoherent about riding the saloon girl all night and disappeared into his own world while he began eating his supper.

Sara's cheeks turned a deeper shade of red when Mr. Peabody confessed his youthful indiscretions. Jarvis, on the other hand, didn't seem to understand what Mr. Peabody was talking about, while Neil fought to hold in a laugh. A glance at Paula showed that she chose to ignore the story as if hearing such comments from Mr. Peabody was normal.

Mrs. Chalk cleared her throat. "This is Reverend Joseph Alms, our preacher," she said, gesturing toward the man on her left. "He's Methodist, but will serve the needs of all Christians."

He looked to be about Margie's age with a dusting of gray around the temples. His hair was the same dark brown as mine, and his eyes just as blue. I felt uncomfortable under his gaze, but tried to smile to hide my ill ease.

"We are all God's children," he said. "The Lord called us to be a unified body in Christ and I refuse to let denominational background prevent anyone from being fed with God's word."

"You're talking about the Bible, aren't you?" I asked. "Mrs. Drummond had a Bible she asked me to keep for Carol when she gets old enough to read it."

Everyone stared at me as if I committed a grievous error. I reached for the bowl of peas and spooned some onto my plate. *What did I say?* I reached for the mashed potatoes. They still stared. I poured gravy over my potatoes and finally Jarvis said something.

"Don't you...go to church...Miss Angela?"

I wanted to run to my room. The last thing I wanted these people to know is that I didn't know anything about myself.

"It's been a long time," I said, as I forked a piece of ham onto my plate. They still looked stunned. "I've been traveling. This is the first time I've been in a town in several months."

Everyone except Reverend Alms relaxed.

"Don't you keep God's word with you at all times?" he asked.

"I don't have a Bible of my own at the moment." That explanation didn't appease him. "I do believe that God," *whoever He was*, "led me to the Drummond farm to save Carol's life. Margie even called me her angel sent by God."

He leaned back in his chair and stared more intently. It felt as though his eyes were drilling down into my soul to find what level of truth and goodness dwelt there.

Mr. Peabody looked up from his plate and gave me a surprised look.

"What's your name, my dear?"

Neil laughed and leaned close to my ear. "Be prepared to answer that question a hundred times until he finally remembers."

I repeated my name for the gentleman in a loud, clear voice.

"What happened to your husband?" he asked.

"I don't have one."

"Awful thing for a young girl to have a child when you don't have a husband. It's a shame how girls like you let any man under your skirts these days. Take that poor young thing last year. Barely sixteen years old and she got herself pregnant. She ran off to hide from the shame." He stopped talking long enough to butter his roll. When he looked up again, another surprised look came across his face. "What's your name, my dear?"

This time he talked about the girl in New Orleans again. By the time I finished eating, I had told him my name seven times, heard the story about Angela in New Orleans four times, Miss Talbourne's indiscretion twice, and finally, how wonderful he thought I was for taking care of another woman's orphaned child.

Every time he asked my name my head throbbed harder. I wanted to leave the table and go to my room. It didn't help that Reverend Alms kept eyeing me or that Neil tried to impress me with how prestigious his position as a clerk was at the bank.

Before excusing myself, I turned to Mrs. Chalk. "Is there a wet nurse in town?"

Mrs. Chalk exchanged an unspoken conversation with Paula before answering. "There's a Negro girl who launders for the hotel. She has a child about eleven months old she still nurses."

"Thank you. I'll look for her in the morning." Once again they stared at me. In retreat, I stood up and thanked Mrs. Chalk for a fine meal. Every eye followed me as I headed for the stairs and as I slowly walked up to my room I heard them talk.

"Surely she's not serious about letting a black woman nurse a white baby?" Sara asked.

"The baby needs milk," Mrs. Chalk said. "I'm sure Lucille's milk is no different from any white woman's and Lucille's the only woman with a baby in town at the moment."

"I don't see anything wrong with it," Paula said. "I think it takes spunk to throw caution to the wind the way she does. I've always dreamed of throwing on a pair of men's pants. It takes a lot of courage for a girl to do that. She's very refreshing."

By the time I reached my room, their voices became a muffled chatter. I locked the door and closed the window. Carol smiled when I peered into the crib after changing into the nightgown. I fed Carol the bottle of goat's milk I left sitting in a pan of warm water before going to dinner. After she burped, I spent the rest of the evening playing with her. Using a red kerchief, I kept her busy following the scarf with her eyes as I waved it above her head. When her eyes started to close, I put her to bed.

I found little resistance to sinking into my own sleep.

Chapter 5

In the middle of the night, something stirred in the room and woke me. Rising up on an elbow, I peered into the bassinet. Carol slept peacefully. My eyes scanned the room. A shadow moved near the open window. I closed that window, but now it was wide open with the curtain parted.

I reached under the second pillow on the double bed and pulled out the Colt. The shadow jerked when the double click of cocking the gun broke the silence.

"Who's there?" I asked.

Reverend Alms stepped into the moonlight.

"What are you doing here?" I asked.

Uninvited, he sat on the edge of the bed and for some reason didn't act concerned about whether I intended to shoot him.

"I'm here to save your soul, child." His soft, smooth voice floated across the space between us. "Put away the gun. You'll have no need for that devil's tool tonight."

I didn't trust him. "Get out of my room. You have no right to be in here."

"True. But you're hiding something and we should talk."

"You could've asked me to meet you at the church tomorrow." I pointed the gun at his skull. "Now, get out!"

He nodded and stood up. "You're right. It was wrong to sneak in here. It's just that you remind me of someone I knew a long time ago." He stepped toward the window. "But she and her husband were murdered last March during a train robbery. She had two children, a boy and a girl. I thought maybe you were the girl."

"Don't you know?"

"The most recent photograph I have was made when the girl was twelve. At the funeral, her face was covered with a black lace veil. After the service, she rushed away. I never spoke to her."

My temples throbbed again. "Why are you telling me this?"

"I think you're that girl. You look so much like Melinda and you're the right age. What is your real name?"

The name Melinda zinged through my head like a ricocheting bullet. I tried to shake it out, but the motion made my headache worse. "I told everyone my name."

"Yes, I heard you tell us several times during supper." He put his right foot through the window. "But I know it's not your real name because I saw it in your eyes that you're only using that name." As he lowered his head to duck out onto the balcony, he glanced back at me. "Be careful, Angela. There's a bounty offered for the girl I'm talking about."

"What happened to the brother?" I asked.

"After the funeral, he was taken back to jail. He beat the mayor's son half to death for molesting his sister." Alms leaned further into the room. "Along with other charges, the girl is wanted for breaking her brother out of jail."

Despite wanting him gone, I wanted to know more. "Where did this take place?"

"Wilmington, Illinois," he said and then disappeared.

I placed the gun back under the pillow and walked over to close the window. I thought about the gun and wondered when or why I put it under the pillow. The last time I remembered touching the Colt, I put it and the rifle inside the wardrobe before dinner. Having my mind play memory tricks like that sure was frustrating. The explanation I came up with was that maybe I woke up earlier and put it there to feel safer.

Before going back to bed, I wrote down what Reverend Alms told me. I then looked at the calendar on the desk. Melinda and her husband died in March. I found Margie in September. I woke up from my injuries four, almost five, months ago, which meant my accident was in May or late April. If I was the girl he spoke about, something happened to cause me to travel across three states during those two months between the funeral and when I cracked my skull.

Two questions went through my mind. If I was the girl Alms spoke about and broke my brother out of jail, why wasn't my brother with me? Why wasn't my brother there to keep me from getting hurt?

I sat thinking about these and other questions until Carol woke up at five in the morning. I took her down to the kitchen where I found Jarvis already preparing a bottle of goat's milk for her. I tested the temperature on my wrist and let him feed her while I took her diapers outside to give them a preliminary scrubbing before putting them in my laundry bag.

On my way back inside, I spotted Reverend Alms watching me from his bedroom window. When I glared back at him, he turned away.

The man was definitely going to test my ability to keep from giving in to that urge to run.

After breakfast, I walked to the hotel with Carol cradled in my arms. I chose to wear my jeans for this trek through town and the few people who were out on the street gave me the typical odd looks I expected. Carol smiled and took the experience in as if I were taking her to a circus.

At the tent hotel, I found Lucille hard at work washing sheets, blankets, and restaurant linens behind the building. She was about my height and age with a firm, large boned body. A bruise darkened her right cheek and her eyes kept checking the back door to the saloon.

Her infant son sat inside a copper bathtub near the wooden fence, which surrounded the hotel yard. I watched him play with a set of wooden blocks, which looked like a dozen children teethed on them before coming into his possession. He showed quite a talent for stacking two blocks on top of each other, but the third one always toppled. Not that he seemed to mind. He giggled at the avalanche. Apparently, he enjoyed watching them fall.

He looked up at me and pointed at Carol. I squatted down and sat her on my knee, so they could look at each other. He grabbed the tub's edge and pulled himself up. One little coppery-brown hand took hold of my other knee for support as he stood up straight. Just as he started to giggle and clap at his display of balance, he shifted a foot and tripped on a block. I reached out and grabbed the bib of his baby dress to keep him from hurting himself.

Protective of her son, Lucille rushed over. Unharmed, the eleven-month-old laughed and went back to playing with the blocks. I stood up with Carol cradled in both arms.

"He's a happy child," I said to break the tension and put her at ease.

"I give him lots of love," she said with a proud maternal smile. She wiped her soapy hands on her apron before holding one out to me. "I'm Lucille Drake."

I shifted Carol into one arm and took Lucille's hand. "Angela Prairie. I'm looking for a wet nurse. Carol's mother died a few days after she was born and the goat I've been milking is about dried up."

She took Carol into her arms. "She's a beautiful child. How old is she?"

I added it up, Margie died on the thirteenth, wrote her will on the tenth, which was three mornings after Carol was born, and then I stayed at the homestead for two weeks, took six days traveling, and this was another day. "Four weeks. I think."

She cocked her head to one side. "Don't you know?"

"There wasn't a clock, so I'm not sure if it was before or after midnight on the seventh. I'll have to look at what day Margie wrote in her Bible to know for sure."

Lucille's laugh was friendly. "Prob'ly doesn't really matter much, but I could've sworn she was twice as old by her size." It was close to nine o'clock and Carol began to nuzzle Lucille's breast and moving her little lips like a fish. Lucille unbuttoned her dress and sat down on a chopping block. "Simeon doesn't nurse as much as he used to before he started eatin' cooked veg'tables. I'd be happy to feed this little one when I'm not workin'."

"What hours do you work?"

"From before sunup to after sundown." She glanced at the back door of the saloon again and then looked back at me. "I usually finish with the laundry 'round ten and then I help in the kitchen 'til three, take a two hour break and then work in the kitchen 'til eight."

Lucille's schedule didn't quite match up with Carol's feeding habits, but maybe we could make some alterations to both their routines. As I contemplated what to do, I washed and hung the laundry so Lucille wouldn't fall behind schedule while she nursed

Carol.

"She usually eats at five, nine, one, five, and nine," I said. "Would your boss let me fill in for you and do your work while you fed her?"

She touched the bruise on her cheek. "I doubt it. He's short handed and short tempered. No white girls will work for him except as saloon girls. It's just me and Chen Sue who serve in the restaurant while Porky cooks."

The boardwalk between the two rows of tents led to a third center door to the building. A foul smelling pool of swill flooded the space between the boardwalk and the kitchen door. The question of how that swamp came into existence was soon answered when a fat man dumped a pot of sludge out the back door of the restaurant. He looked repulsive in his greasy clothes and heavily whiskered face. A cigar hanging out of his mouth flew across the yard when he went into an uncontrollable coughing fit.

"Is his cooking any good?"

"I'd as soon eat dirt," Lucille said.

I finished hanging the last of the sheets and threw two wet blankets over the top of the wooden fence. As I began to dump the washtub, a tall, slim man in a gray suit and a red silk vest exited the rear of the saloon. There wasn't any gray in his hair, but he appeared to be in his forties like Margie. His dark gray eyes were cold as steel as he gave Lucille a disapproving look.

"Get back to work! You've got no business feeding that white trash on my time."

I squared off against him. "Sir, I doubt you have much room to judge whether that child is white trash or carries royal blood."

"Who the hell are you?" he asked.

"The name's Angela Prairie and that child is under my care. I'm in need of a wet nurse and Lucille's the only one around." The edge in my voice cut through him and he stumbled back a step. I advanced toward him with a confidence that didn't match the anxious beat of my heart. But seeing that I somehow gained an advantage, I decided to use it for all it was worth.

"Now, since I'm going to be staying in Welcome for a while, you're going to fire that rotten cook you have and hire me. You're going to pay me two dollars a day and double that on Saturdays plus ten percent of the restaurant profits." Lucille looked nervous as she fumbled with her dress buttons. "You should also know that I don't work Sundays. You're going to treat me with respect and you won't slap Lucille around anymore. Do you understand?"

He gave Lucille a nervous glance. "Yes, ma'am. Anything you say is fine with me."

"Fine. I'll start tomorrow. Have my contract ready to sign in the morning."

I took Carol and walked back to the boarding house. Mrs. Chalk was in the middle of hanging out the laundry when I arrived. I noticed that the lines strung from the back of the house to a set of poles were numbered like the rooms and laundry bags. She was working on line five and it was filled with Carol's calico, gingham, and plaid diapers, some of which were double hung to conserve space.

"I need a baby sitter for a couple of hours," I said.

"Mrs. Miller is always the first one to go to." She pointed toward the yellow house with brown shutters next door. "She's Doc Miller's wife and loves taking care of babies."

"Thank you."

"How'd it go at the hotel?" she asked as she pinned the tail of the blue shirt I wore yesterday to the line.

"Lucille will feed Carol and I hired on as the new cook over at the restaurant starting tomorrow."

She looked dumbfounded. "Buford's a devil. He mistreats the girls he hires. You'd better be careful."

"Don't worry. I can handle him."

Could I handle him? It might've been a fluke that I overpowered him, but he made me mad when he called Carol "white trash." I remembered reading somewhere that only a person without sin could cast the first stone and he certainly looked like a very sinful man.

Chapter 6

After I left Carol with Mrs. Miller, I went back to Mrs. Chalk's and put on the gray dress. I coiled my long, dark hair into a French roll and dug my wallet out from beneath the mattress. With the ease in which Reverend Alms entered my room, I decided to make the bank my first stop because I didn't want to leave that much money laying around for someone to steal.

When I arrived at the bank, Neil stood at the teller window.

"Good morning, Miss Prairie," he said with a schoolboy grin that made him look fifteen rather than twenty-five.

"I'd like to open an account," I said.

His grin disappeared. "Uh, step this way."

He led me to a desk behind the counter where a gentleman with thinning hair and gold-rimmed eye glasses sat. As Neil slumped back to his teller window, I realized he wanted to be the one who helped me. Instead, he wound up deferring my business into the hands of Mr. Isaac Newman, the account manager and one of the bank's owners.

Mr. Newman gave me a wide smile. "It's not every day a pretty young lady opens an account with us."

"You do have women customers, don't you?" I asked.

"Oh, yes. There's Emma Chalk, Paula Klondike, and the new schoolmistress, Sara Hauser."

"And you give them the same interest rates as your gentlemen customers?"

"Of course," he said without losing his smile. "We also advise them on how to efficiently manage their money." He pulled a ledger and an account book out of his desk drawer. "Our regular account holders receive one percent interest on their savings and those who keep a balance over five hundred dollars receive two percent."

"What type of a return does the bank receive on its investments?" I asked.

He pushed his glasses up onto the bridge of his nose and gave me a thoughtful look. I seemed to possess a knack for making men uncomfortable. His voice was filled with pride when he answered. "On average, we make about a fifteen percent return on our investments. The stock market fluctuates considerably and we've made from as little as two-tenths of a percent to as high as forty."

He opened the ledger and began reaching for his pen as though he thought I was through asking questions.

"What type of investments do you make?"

He cleared his throat. "Naturally, we keep a certain amount in cash. We then invest twenty percent of our holdings in government bonds, treasury bills, and commodities. Another forty percent is invested in stocks."

"Which stocks?" Where I came up with these questions I don't know, but they seemed to come forth as though I knew about such things.

"Well, there's the U.P. Railroad, various shipping companies, steel mills, mining interests, pharmaceuticals, lumber, freight, and the like." He began reaching for the pen again.

"Could I see a list?"

He gave up on the pen and opened a drawer from which he handed me a piece of paper with a list of stock companies on it. Next to each company was the number of shares, a twelve-month tracking of price per share, and the stock values for the previous five years. Scanning the list, I was impressed with the number of companies with long histories of growth the bank invested in. But why were the names of the companies familiar?

"You certainly do your homework on which companies are worthy of your investment," I said as I handed the list back to him. "I didn't see a single company I would object to."

"You've done some investing yourself, then?" he asked.

My knowledge of the list impressed him, but I didn't know what to say as to why. "I have some experience in tracking stocks." I covered my uncertainty with a bright smile.

He leaned back in his chair with that thoughtful look on his face. "Then, I assume, we meet with your approval?"

"Oh, most adequately. But I would like to receive a higher interest rate on my savings."

He leaned forward. "How much are you planning to deposit?"

I laid the leather wallet on his desk. "Seventeen hundred dollars." I decided to keep some of my money to cover my immediate expenses.

His eyebrows rose. "Well," he said, "give me a moment to confer with my brother."

He walked over to a desk in the opposite corner of the bank and spoke to a man a few years older than himself with slightly thicker hair. The other man looked up at me so I gave him a confident smile, which contradicted the fluttering sensation in my stomach.

Interacting with people sorely tested that voice inside me that kept telling me to get away from here. It especially told me that partnering up with Buford earlier was a bad idea. But for Carol's sake, I ignored my intuition.

The other man stood up and walked over with Mr. Newman.

"This is my brother, Jacob," Isaac Newman said.

I stood up and shook his hand as I curtsied. "It's a pleasure, sir."

"My brother says you have a good understanding of investments and wish to achieve a higher rate of interest on your account," Jacob Newman said.

"Yes. Understanding that the stock market fluctuates, what I would like to propose is that as long as I keep a thousand dollars or more in my account, you give me an annual interest rate of four percent. In addition, I'd like an extra one percent bonus during any month that the bank's returns are greater than twenty percent. Whenever my account falls below a thousand dollars, you give me the standard percentage everyone else receives."

A pleasant smile crossed his face. "I might consider three percent."

"Three and a half," I countered.

Jacob Newman picked up the wallet and opened it. "How much did you say was here?"

"Seventeen hundred."

"It's a good sum, but I have depositors with far more than this who only get the two percent interest rate." It didn't appear Jacob

Newman intended to back down.

"It's not my fault they don't understand the rate of return you make on *their* money," I said, using that confident smile again.

He laughed. "Very well, four percent plus a half percent bonus. But your account can't fall below the thousand." He laid the wallet down. "Open her up an account, Isaac."

"You'll naturally put our agreement in writing," I said as I sat down to pull the money out of the wallet and place it on Isaac Newman's desk in piles by the denominations on the bills.

"I'm going over to my desk to do just that, Miss Prairie," Jacob said.

Before leaving the bank, I stopped at Neil's window. "Thank you very much for your assistance, Mr. Jones. I was hoping you could direct me to where I might hire someone with a wagon to retrieve some items that belonged to Carol's mother."

His face beamed with importance. "The feed store hires out wagons to haul freight. Paul Garrett is my…uh…I mean, he's a friend of mine. Just tell him I sent you."

"Thank you, very much, sir."

He looked down at his hands for a moment. When he looked up, his cheeks were red. "Miss Prairie, you can call me Neil."

"Please call me Angela, then."

"Thank you, Angela," he said with a shy smile.

I nodded and curtsied before turning and heading out the door.

At the feed store, a ten-year-old boy directed me to Paul Garrett's office. I watched the boy for a few minutes as he lifted a heavy bag of oats onto a wagon. He was much too young to do that type of heavy work, but he looked determined to keep up with the men who were also loading the wagon. He turned from the wagon and smiled when he saw me watching him.

"You can go on in, ma'am," he said as he grabbed hold of another grain sack. "A gal as pretty as you has no need to be bashful. Besides, I think he'd much rather look at you than his account ledgers."

My cheeks warmed up as I turned and reached for the doorknob. As soon as I stepped into Paul Garrett's office, my heart nearly forgot how to pump. No man I met thus far looked as strong and handsome as Paul Garrett did when he looked up from his ledger. The deep brown goatee on his sun-bronzed face gave him a handsome, dignified appearance in contrast to Neil's boy-like charm.

It took several moments for me to remember my task. During that time, I sensed from the way Paul Garrett stared back at me that he didn't mind the delay. The boy knew him all too well.

After I did finally tell him Neil sent me to do business with him, he offered to send someone to pick up Margie's chest and furnishings for five dollars.

"Do you have a place to store the furniture?" he asked.

"I'll have to ask Mrs. Chalk if I can use her attic or the loft in the barn," I said. The smaller items would fit in my room.

"I'm sure she will for a fee." He paused for a moment while his eyes probed deep beyond my smile and what men and boys apparently considered a pretty face. "If not, I've got a storeroom I can let you use for no charge."

"I'll keep that in mind." I took the five dollars out of my wallet and handed it to him.

As he reached out to accept the money with his left hand, sunlight through the window gleamed off the surface of a gold wedding band. He must've seen where my eyes fell because he pulled his hand back and placed the money in a drawer to his desk.

"Never knew Ole Homer had himself a wife," he said as he wrote out a receipt.

"You knew him?"

"He bought his seed and oats from me." After handing over the receipt with his right hand, he escorted me out of his office and toward the main entrance of the warehouse. "I probably shouldn't say such a thing, but I'm pretty sure he's the one who ran off with Kimberly Talbourne. I saw them come out of Mrs. Chalk's barn together the night of the Harvest Dance last year. He wasn't in town more than a day last February when they both disappeared."

"Everyone else seems to be under the same impression." I glanced at the ring on his finger again. I didn't even know Paul Garrett and my heart felt broken. He stuffed his hand in his pocket and I turned my eyes away to watch the boy. "Poor Margie. I'm glad she never found out about this. It would've broken her heart more than not knowing what happened to him."

"Guess it shows that you just don't know about folks," he said.

Wasn't that the truth? I didn't even know about myself. I could be engaged or even married. From the absence of stretch marks, I felt pretty sure I didn't have children. If I did have a man waiting somewhere for me, he probably wasn't rich since I didn't have a ring. But that wouldn't fit with the money I just deposited in the bank.

As I left the feed and seed, I overheard Paul Garrett tell the boy to get to school as soon as the wagon was loaded. The boy complained, but a few minutes later he rushed down the street carrying his schoolbooks. He was already three hours late. I started thinking about what kind of man Paul Garrett could be if he allowed his son to go late to school and, despite being married, openly show interest in another woman. My heart wished I was wrong, but that ring on his finger definitely told me he belonged to another woman, a woman who gave him at least one son. After all, the boy looked too much like Paul Garrett not to be his son.

It bothered me even more that he tried to hide that he was married after the way he talked about Homer. What's more, his son didn't seem too concerned about him taking an interest in me, either. The boy even smiled when Paul Garrett walked out of the office with me and escorted me to the street. It was almost as if he didn't mind whether or not his father fooled around with another woman.

The best thing I could do was stay away from Paul Garrett. Besides, until I knew whether my life was in danger or if I had a beau waiting for me, it made no sense to take interest in a man, especially not a married one.

Chapter 7

The sound of piano music caught my attention and lured me toward the church. The tune sounded familiar and brought to life the image of a woman with auburn hair pulled tightly into a French roll. She sat in a large, elegant parlor playing a piano. Her fingers moved across the keys in a fluid motion. When she finished the piece she smiled.

"Come, dear, let me hear the song I taught you yesterday."

I climbed up beside her on the piano bench and plunked out a stiff little song, one note at a time, with small fingers that barely stretched from one key to the next.

As soon as I entered the church I sat down beside Jarvis at the piano.

"Hello, Miss Angela," he said as he ended his song. "Are we going…to sing now?"

"In a moment," I said. "I want to play a song first."

I tested several keys until I found the note I wanted. Placing my right thumb over the key, I counted five steps to the left to find the position for my left hand. Closing my eyes, I began to play the song my mother played in the vision. Jarvis scooted to the far end of the piano bench and played along, adding in the notes I either didn't remember or never learned how to play.

Suddenly, without much thought, I knew the name of the song. "*Hymn to Joy*, by Beethoven."

"Yes, Miss Angela." Jarvis started singing, "Joyful, joyful, we adore thee, God of glory, Lord of love…"

He sang the whole song without a pause. Gone was the slowness in his speech and in its place came forth a rich, pleasant tenor voice.

I sang and played the song with him over and over. For the first time in months I felt joyfully happy as in the song. It felt good to remember something from my past without a headache or a fit of anxiety. Most important, I remembered what it felt like to be loved and to feel safe and secure.

I don't know how long we sat there playing the song before Reverend Alms slammed through the door. Jarvis jumped off the piano bench and headed for the door in a stumbling run.

"How dare you scare him like that?" I scolded the preacher after Jarvis disappeared. I refrained from mentioning that my own pulse took off on a sprint. It took every ounce of courage I possessed not to follow Jarvis in a race home.

"You've stirred up this town enough for one day without making a spectacle of yourself," he said. "Couldn't you see the crowd your caterwauling produced through the windows?"

I stood up and slammed the piano cover shut—a move which created a discordant clatter. "I'd think you'd want a crowd drawn to your church. Isn't bringing people into the presence of God the main mission of your job?" In long, echoing steps across the wooden floor, I advanced on him. I pointed at the Bible in his hand. "Make a joyful noise unto the Lord, doesn't that Bible of yours say? Praise the Lord with harp and lyre and voice." As I closed the gap between us, he stepped backward in retreat until the door blocked his way. "Go apologize to Jarvis, right now!"

"Y-yes, ma'am." He turned quickly and fumbled with the door.

Somehow my yelling scared him more than having my Colt pointed at his head.

He finally opened the door and exited the church. I watched him hurry down the street to Mrs. Chalk's. The crowd he spoke of slowly dispersed. It wasn't until after I closed the door I realized my hands were shaking.

While I waited for Reverend Alms to return, I searched through the church for a pencil and paper. I wanted to write down what I remembered about the woman playing the piano.

The search led me into Reverend Alms' office where I found a pile of plain white paper, a pen, and an inkbottle on the corner of his desk. I sat down and wrote out every detail of what I saw in the memory. As I drew a sketch of the woman, I realized her features were similar to the woman I called Granma in my goose memory.

When I finished, I realized Reverend Alms stood silently behind me, looking over my shoulder. I felt uncomfortable in his presence. I tried to stand, but he placed his hand on my shoulder and pushed me back down into the chair.

"So Melinda *is* your mother," he said as he walked around to the other side of the desk and sat across from me.

"Who is this Melinda you keep talking about?"

His eyes narrowed. "You know who she is or you wouldn't have drawn her picture."

I knew he was right, but my mind retreated behind waves of throbbing pain set loose by his inquisition.

"How do you know her?" I asked.

He stared at me and I stared right back, deep into his eyes until he looked away. "We went to school together," he finally said, "and..." He looked down at his left hand and rubbed his empty ring finger.

"And what?"

"It was a long time ago." He turned his face toward me, but refused to look me in the eyes. "Why do you pretend not to know her? Why are you using a fake name?"

Damn his hide. I didn't want to take him into my trust by telling him that I didn't know, but I needed to know anything he knew about my past. I took a deep breath to calm my nerves. "Have you heard anything about the older brother you mentioned last night?"

"He turned himself in to the governor of Illinois about four months ago. After receiving a pardon, he disappeared again. His grandmother thinks he's looking for you." He reached behind him and pulled open a cabinet door. I watched as he mixed white powder into a glass of water he poured from the pitcher on his desk. He handed it to me. "Take this," he said, "it will help your headache."

I stopped rubbing my temples and greedily reached for the glass. The medicine tasted bitter, so I chased it down with another glass of plain water.

"Thank you." I handed the glass back to him and took a good look around the room for the first time. On a bookcase in the corner and near the window, I spotted a picture of a woman. She was the same woman in my drawing.

I stood up and walked over to the photograph. I picked it up. "You knew her pretty well."

"I did once." He took the picture from my hands and looked warmly into the woman's face. "Melinda was a very kind and loving soul. I could've spent my whole life with her."

I sat back down and rested my head against the back of the chair while I listened to him lament about how Melinda made his life golden during the years they courted and the short time they were married before her father came and tore them apart. Joseph Alms wasn't good enough for the daughter of a moderately wealthy farmer with a seat in the United States Senate. The man used his influence to have their marriage discreetly annulled two days after it began.

"He hid her from me by placing her in a convent. That's why I went to seminary school. I thought maybe I could find her again through the church. Only because I'd been married, the Catholic Church refused me ordination. It wasn't until after the Methodists accepted me and assigned me to a church five miles out of Wilmington that I found out Melinda gave birth to a son four months after she was hastily married to a banker who owed her father a favor. Apparently, her father helped her husband's first wife's nephew get a partnership in a very successful brokerage firm in Chicago."

He laughed and I opened my eyes to see him still gazing into the photograph.

"Melinda kept the pregnancy hidden from them until one of the nuns stepped in on her while she was drying off after a bath. Her father was informed right away and she was whisked away to a wedding the following week. They falsified the wedding date so that there wouldn't be a scandal and told everyone that right after the wedding Melinda went to nurse a sick aunt."

He shook his head and stared out the window at the children playing in the schoolyard during their lunch recess next door. "Nathaniel was five years old by the time I saw him the first time. Melinda brought him to the church I was working in and we told him he needed to keep a really big secret from everyone. Every chance she found, Melinda brought him to see me until I was transferred too far away for her to make the trip without causing suspicion. The last night we saw each other I made love to her as though we were still married."

I heard the pain in his voice and watched the tears run down his cheeks as he continued his confession.

"I committed adultery with a married woman; a woman who should've been *my* wife. She belonged to me, not that old man." His face was red and I knew then this was the first time he ever told his story to anyone. For over twenty years, he kept it locked away. "Afterward I left, never to see her again. We frequently wrote to each other and she told me about how she gave birth to our daughter…" my mind spun again, pounding against my skull "…nine months after I left. A year later, her husband died and she married his nephew who raised…" his finger pounded against his chest "…*my* children."

He stopped and drank a glass of water before telling me how for a time, he tried to run away from his love for Melinda. But in his heart, she would always be his wife and he couldn't continue ignoring her letters.

"It wasn't until I spent a summer in Mexico helping the poor children down there that I realized God truly did call me into the ministry and would forgive me for committing adultery and take away the bitterness in my heart. When the war started, I came back north and joined the Army as a chaplain. I wrote Melinda about my newfound love for my work and she wrote back that it made her happy that I found joy in my life again." He fumbled in one of the desk drawers and pulled out a newspaper article. "I was on my way here when I read this in a St. Louis newspaper that I found lying in a train station in Iowa." He handed me the article and I read it:

> "Late yesterday afternoon, a train bound for St. Louis was boarded and robbed. Five passengers were killed during the robbery. Among the reported dead were the Chicago, Illinois finance wizard, Ely McDonald, and his wife, Melinda. The McDonalds were on their way to St. Louis for the Union Pacific Stockholder's Meeting being held next week…"

"I immediately traded in my ticket and went to Wilmington where Melinda was buried in the family plot with her father and two husbands. I could tell that Nathaniel recognized me right away and after I missed trying to visit with you, I went to the jailhouse. I was speaking to him about coming to live with me after he was released from jail when the news came that you disappeared from your grandmother's farm just moments before the mayor arrived with the marshal's posse. They planned to arrest you for taking the mayor's personal property from your stepfather's office. A week after I arrived here, I read in the paper that you broke Nathaniel out of jail the night after the funeral."

He looked me straight in the eyes. "So, Josephine, what did you take from your father's office that has the mayor of Wilmington hunting for you all over the country?"

Just like hearing the name Melinda the first time, the name Josephine echoed through my mind. I tried to shake it out, but it kept repeating over and over. How in the world could the woman at the piano name me after a man I didn't want to trust?

"My name is Angela," I said as I gathered up the pages I wrote about the piano playing memory and the sketch of my mother. "Quit accusing me of being someone I'm not."

I rolled the papers up and started to walk out of the office, but his hand grabbed my arm.

"Whether you believe me or not, you are my daughter and I want to help you and your brother. I just need to know what's really going on, so that I'll know how to help."

I yanked my arm free from his grasp. "Don't ever touch me like that again or you'll spend the rest of your days wishing you never met me."

"Very well." He stepped back. "I'll not bother you again. Eventually you'll realize that all I want to do is be your father and give you the love I was denied giving you for twenty-two years."

Chapter 8

An hour after leaving the church, I sat at the writing desk in my room transcribing everything Reverend Alms told me. As I set the pen down, I wondered what power I possessed that caused men to back away when I challenged them. It wasn't like I was tall and muscular like a man. After all, Paula only measured my height at five-six. The only man I met so far who wasn't taller than me was Jarvis, whom I approximated to stand five-two.

Lucille sat on the edge of my bed nursing Carol while she ate the sandwich Mrs. Chalk made for her. Jarvis sat on the floor playing with Simeon and the blocks, which were repeatedly stacked in pyramids and then knocked down, much to Simeon's giggling delight.

"Jarvis, do I scare you?" I asked.

He looked up and grinned at me. "Oh, no...Miss Angela. I think...Reverend Alms ...he's afraid...of you."

"Why do you think that?"

"He told me...he was sorry...for slamming...the door...and that you...made him...come apologize." He laughed. "Kind of like...how I do things...Mommy tells me to do...unless I get sent...to my room."

"Surely you're not afraid of your mother?"

"Oh, no...but I don't...want her... mad at me."

"You are very wise to please her," I said.

"Pleasing her...is the best way...to get...oatmeal cookies," he said with a grin.

Lucille laughed. "I'll have to remember that when Simeon gets older and I want him to behave." The blocks went tumbling again, and, on cue, Simeon giggled. "He enjoys destruction."

I went downstairs to eat my lunch. When I returned to my

room, Carol was sound asleep. The others were gone, which pleased me because my head still throbbed. After hanging up my dress, I slid into bed and fell asleep until Lucille returned at five to feed Carol again.

"Why you in bed, Miss Angela?" she asked.

"How'd you get Buford to let you off long enough during the dinner hour to feed Carol?"

She smiled. "I think he's afraid that if he doesn't, you'll come and castrate him. Now tell me, why you all in bed?"

"I get headaches and sometimes sleep is the only way to get rid of them."

"You should go see Doc Miller. You're not gonna be feelin' much like workin' at Buford's iffin you go 'round with your head poundin' you all the time."

She was right. The days on the trail were unbearable when my head ached. Working in a noisy kitchen would be twice as agonizing. Nevertheless, I contracted to do it six days a week.

Oh, how I wish I could crawl into my mother's arms. But if Reverend Alms spoke the truth, my mother was dead and he, as painful as the thought might be, was my father.

The first thing I did the next morning when I showed up at Buford's to cook the morning meal was close the place for "renovations." The kitchen looked slimier than a greased pig, and Lucille, Chen Sue, and I spent the whole day scraping and scrubbing the kitchen and dining room until the whole place smelled of pine oil.

I also convinced the construction workers from next door to shovel ashes from the charred remains of the hotel into the swill puddle behind the restaurant. Later in the day, they shoveled up the wet ashes and filled in the shallow area with gravel they hauled in from a nearby quarry.

Buford complained until I convinced him he would reap higher profits for both the restaurant and hotel if people found the place pleasing enough to return.

The following morning we opened up with fresh linens on the tables, a new menu, and clean dishes. The surprising thing came in finding out I really did know how to cook and remembered recipes without thinking about them.

At the end of the week, I helped Buford total the profits, which added up to more than he normally made in a month. My ten percent gave me an extra twelve dollars on top of my weekly pay to put in the bank.

Throughout the following week, Buford frequently calculated his profits as word spread throughout the county about the improved service and good food at his place. He was so captivated in his growing wealth that he barely took notice when the news came that Porky died Saturday afternoon.

"Are you going to the funeral tomorrow, Mr. Buford?" Lucille asked as she picked up her pay envelope after we closed.

"What funeral?" he asked.

"Mr. Porky died this afternoon," Chen Sue said.

He stopped counting his money for a moment and looked directly at me. "It's a good thing you came along when you did." He handed me an envelope with forty-seven dollars in it. "I'd be in big trouble next week if you weren't here to cook and manage the restaurant."

"You should go to the funeral, Mr. Buford," Lucille said.

He stood up from the table and closed the cash box. "I've got important business to take care of in Kearney tomorrow. Why don't you pay my respects to his widow for me?"

"He's got a wife?" I asked.

"Not the best looking thing around, but she does cook for my hotel guests on Sundays." He picked up the cash box and ledger as he looked at me. "Make sure she comes to work tomorrow. She doesn't have to fix anything fancy, just feed the hotel guests."

He seemed pleased with his generosity toward Mrs. Porky as he left the restaurant.

"Kind hearted fellow, isn't he?" Lucille said more as a statement than a question.

As much as I felt sorry for Mrs. Porky, I needed rest. "Look, I'm beat and can't deal with this right now. Chen Sue, go over to Porky's and check in on his wife. Let her know that Buford wants her to come to work as usual. She's to make sandwiches and nothing else. Get in and get out. And ask her to come see me Monday morning before we open."

"Sure, boss," Chen Sue said as she headed for the door. "I let her know."

Lucille glared at me like a mother getting ready to punish a child. "You haven't gone to see Doc Miller yet, have you?"

I stuffed the money envelope into my boot. "I've been busy."

"I'm telling you, Sis," she said, "I know you've been havin' more than just headaches. You've got female problems, too. So even if I have to drag your butt there myself on Monday, you're gonna see him after the lunch crowd clears out."

"Yes, ma'am," I said, giving her the best military salute I knew how to make. Then I smiled. "Come on, those kids of ours are probably wondering where their dinner is by now. It's nearly time for Carol's nine o'clock feeding."

I stretched out on my bed and fell asleep long before Lucille finished feeding Carol. On Sunday morning, I awoke to the suckling sounds of Lucille nursing Carol for her five o'clock feeding. I was still dressed in the clothes I wore the day before.

"You slept clean through the night, Sis," Lucille said. "I was startin' to wonder if you were ever gonna wake up."

"You stayed here all night?"

"Yes'm. You kept mumblin' things about evidence and needin' to find some feller named Nathaniel." She moved Carol to her shoulder for burping. "What you got yourself all tangled up in?"

I pulled off my dirty socks. "I have no idea. All I remember is waking up in the woods covered in blood and unable to move without my head feeling like it would bust apart."

I pulled the green bathrobe out of the wardrobe.

"That's why you have them headaches, isn't it?" she asked.

I nodded and left the room. The hot bath felt good, but the view I saw of my back in the new full-length mirror Mrs. Chalk bought the day before scared me. Three whipping scars crisscrossed my back. From the faded burgundy color, I judged they weren't too much older than the scar on my jaw. Somebody definitely tried to hurt me last spring. That constant urge to run away was making more sense every time I found out something new about myself.

I quickly dried off and put on my robe. Taking a deep breath, I exited the washroom and felt relieved to find the hallway empty at this time of the morning. In long, hurried strides I returned to my room.

"My Lord, you look like you've seen a ghost," Lucille said as I slammed the door shut a little harder than intended.

"What do you make of these?" I asked after I lowered the robe off my shoulders.

"Somebody sure had it in for you," she said. "Those marks cut you deep. Probably came from a bull whip like Master Jessup used on Pa the time he was out past curfew when Ma was dyin'. All Pa wanted to do was get a doctor, but Ole Jessup dang near killed Pa with that whip."

"What happened to your ma?" I asked.

"She died of the measles," Lucille said. "Pa and I, we came here after the war. Then four years ago when I was sixteen, I married Michael Drake. Last spring he hired out with a trail crew headed for Montana and should be comin' home soon. I got a letter from him last week sayin' he made it up to the Northern Rockies and couldn't wait to get back here to Simeon and me."

I pulled the robe back up around my shoulders. Even with the warm flannel around me, my whole body shivered. "I'm scared," I said, sitting down on the bed. "I have no idea who to trust and who to run away from."

"Maybe you should talk to Reverend Alms again," Lucille said. I raised my eyes to meet hers. "You also muttered somethin' about him tellin' you he was your pa."

"I don't trust him."

"Have you told him 'bout not knowin' who you are?"

The floorboards outside my door creaked and I put a finger to my lips. I tiptoed over and yanked the door open. Reverend Alms tried to dash away down the hall, but I grabbed his belt and yanked him around. When I let go to pull my robe together as the tie belt started to come undone, he tried to back away.

"Don't be going anywhere, mister!" I warned. I jerked my head toward my door and waited until he entered before following him back into my room.

After I shut the door, he turned around and looked at me with eyes held well above my shoulders. "Maybe we should wait to have this discussion after you get dressed."

Lucille laid Carol in the bassinet. "Maybe you should quit sneakin' 'round this room," she said. "It's no wonder the poor girl doesn't trust you."

"Do you know anything about why someone would whip me?"

I asked.

The surprised look on his face told me he didn't know about it.

"What's wrong with you?" he asked. "You keep saying you're someone you're not and now you don't even know why someone would…would…" Tears filled his eyes as the words caught in his throat. He put his hands on my shoulders and slowly turned me around. My body trembled as he lowered the robe off my shoulders just far enough to see the marks and then raise it again. "My God!" He sank to his knees. "I'm sorry I wasn't there to protect you."

While he knelt on the floor crying into his hands, Lucille held a blanket up for me to stand behind while I changed into my clothes. When I came out wearing the blue dress, he stared at me as he rose to his feet.

"What did you do to deserve such horrors in your life?" he asked.

I scowled at him. "What makes you think *I* did something to deserve this? Maybe somebody deserves to be punished because they did this to me."

"I wish you would quit playing these games with me," he said.

"She's not playin' games," Lucille said. "She really doesn't know."

"How could that be?"

Despite my trepidations about the man, I took his hand in mine and pressed his fingers against the scar and ridge on my skull. "I don't remember," I said, "because of this."

He turned me so that the left side of my head was toward the lamp on the nightstand and parted my hair to look at the scar. "When did this happen?"

"I think it happened about five and a half months ago," I said. "I'm not completely sure because for a long time I couldn't stay awake for more than five minutes at a time."

"I've told her to see Doc Miller, but she hasn't gone yet," Lucille said with that mother hen scowl of hers.

He sat on my bed with a stunned look on his face. "You have amnesia."

Simeon whimpered and Lucille picked him up off the folded quilt she used to make him a pallet on the floor last night. "I'd best get home and fix breakfast for Pa. I'll see you in a few hours."

She opened the door and found herself face to face with Mrs.

Chalk. "Mornin', ma'am," Lucille said as she left the room.

"What's going on in here?" Mrs. Chalk asked as she entered the room.

Reverend Alms reached into the bassinet and laid a hand on Carol's forehead. "I just wanted to find out if Miss Prairie wanted to have Carol baptized during church this morning."

"Shouldn't we wait until the adoption papers are signed by the circuit judge in two weeks?" I asked. "Mr. Talbourne said that if the judge chooses, he could order a search for Mr. Drummond or demand that I be married before giving me legal custody."

"I'm sure Mr. Talbourne will do everything in his power to keep this child from going back to Homer," Mrs. Chalk said. "After what happened, he hates the man."

"Besides," Reverend Alms said, "in the baptism ceremony, I christen new members of Christ's church by their Christian name, not their surname."

Although he was using the baptism as an excuse for being in my room, it sounded like he intended to do it for real and that made me nervous. Talbourne was right: Homer could claim Carol and take her away. That scared me because it meant I would be alone again.

I paced the room, not sure what to do.

My head throbbed again as a memory jumped in and blocked out the present. A fire burned on a dark night. My hands were tied above my head to a tree limb.

"Where'd you hide them?" a man demanded.

"Go to hell," I said and then I felt a deep burning pain across my back. I gulped down a scream and twisted around to face my attacker.

"Where are they?" He stepped closer and snaked the whip off to the side.

I spat in his face just before raising my legs up and kicking him in the jaw with my boot heels. He staggered, cursed, and then came toward me again. A layer of skin was missing from his jaw. He wiped at the blood with the back of his hand before he punched me in the stomach.

"Swing her back around," he said, "and this time hold her feet down."

A young man about my age approached out of the darkness and

twisted me around. The scars on his face looked to be about three weeks old.

"Maybe after you tell us what we want to know," the young man said as his hand slid down the front of my jeans, "we can finish where we left off the last time we were together."

"You can do that after I'm through with her," the older man said.

The scar-faced man removed his hand and sat down on the ground while holding my knees. Twice more I felt the whip against my back. Again I refused to scream and prepared to feel a fourth strike, but a gunshot silence the whizzing sound of the whip.

"Dad, are you all right?" the scar-faced man asked as he scrambled to his feet and disappeared behind me.

"Bastard shot the whip out of my hand," the older man said in a pain-strained voice.

A running horse halted beside me. The rider cut through the ropes and grabbed my belt to help me climb up on the horse behind him. We rode off into the night.

The memory ended and I immediately sat down at the writing desk and pulled two sheets of paper and a pencil out of the drawer. Writing fast, I recorded everything I saw in the vision and then drew pictures of the man with the whip and the scar-faced young man.

"What's she doing?" Mrs. Chalk asked.

"We should leave her alone," Reverend Alms said. "I'll discuss this with her when she's not upset."

I heard them leave the room, but didn't look up until I finished and put the pages into the leather document envelope I purchased and kept in the desk drawer. As I thought about the memory and what Reverend Alms told me about Nathaniel and Josephine, I came to the conclusion that the two men must be the mayor and his son from Wilmington, Illinois. But I couldn't remember what they wanted or why I took what they sought. The man on the horse might've been Nathaniel, but in the memory, I never saw his face.

The more I tried to force the memory to continue, the more my head throbbed until the room spun and everything went black.

Chapter 9

"Joseph, she's awake," a man wearing a white shirt, black vest, and a gray pin striped suit said when I opened my eyes.

"Where's Carol?" I asked after looking into the empty bassinet.

"Lucille took her downstairs." Reverend Alms stood at the foot of the bed, holding his Bible and wearing his black frock coat. It was then I recognized him from the memory of the funeral with the two caskets. "She found you on the floor when she came to feed Carol." He pointed to the other man. "This is Dr. Ronald Miller. You've met his wife, Catherine."

"Please don't tell anyone I passed out."

"Don't worry," he said. "Lucille came to my door just as I was heading for the church. I laid you on the bed and then told her to walk slowly to Ron's house. They waited until after the church doors were closed to come back."

"Do you remember what caused you to pass out?" Dr. Miller asked.

I looked up at Reverend Alms. "Before you left, I remembered the night I was whipped and the more I tried to remember who rescued me, the more my head hurt. It throbbed so hard, I got dizzy."

"Joseph told me what you told him about your accident," Miller said, "but I need you to tell me in more detail about your head injury."

I sat up and leaned against the headboard while I told him about waking up in the woods beside a stream and how Ruth kept me alive. I told him how it took two weeks before I could sit up and then nearly three more weeks to stand. At first I needed a thick branch to lean on when I tried to walk. After about five more weeks, I was able to discard the branch, and then came the painful and tiring process of saddling and riding Ruth.

Dr. Miller sat at the desk and wrote while I talked. When I finished, he examined the side of my head, ear, and jaw. Then he unbuttoned the back of my dress to look at the whip marks.

"Do you have any other injuries?" he asked.

I shook my head. "Just some cramping now and then. I only discovered the whip marks this morning."

"Ron," Reverend Alms said. His lips quivered as he looked at me. "I think you should...um...check...to see if she's been... raped."

Dr. Miller froze.

My hand reached under the pillow and wrapped around the Colt. Reverend Alms broke eye contact with Dr. Miller. His Bible hit the floor with a thud as he rushed to the other side of my bed. He grabbed the gun from my hand.

"Just what do you know about this girl, Joseph?" Dr. Miller asked as he picked up the Bible and lifted out a postcard from a page the book fell open to. He looked closely at the picture and then at me before reading the back of the card. His eyes focused on Reverend Alms again. "Is she really your daughter?"

Reverend Alms took a few steps back and leaned against the wall for a few seconds before sliding to the floor. He laid the gun beside him and removed a chain from around his neck that was hidden beneath his clergy shirt. Two gold wedding bands hung on the chain.

"I was married to her mother once." His pain-filled eyes turned toward me. "I told you the truth. I—"

Someone knocked at the door. "Angela, are you all right?" Mrs. Chalk asked.

"Yes, ma'am. I just dropped something is all."

"Do you want Lucille to bring Carol back up now that you're awake?"

"Ask her to wait about fifteen minutes while I straighten up the room a bit."

"I hope your stomach is feeling better. You missed a mighty fine sermon this morning. I think it was about the best I've ever heard. You should have Reverend Alms repeat it for you when he gets back from making rounds with Dr. Miller."

"Thanks for checking on me." I prayed she would go away.

As Mrs. Chalk's footsteps faded down the hallway, I looked at the two men in my room and wondered how they would leave without the whole town knowing.

"You two better get out of here," I said.

"He really should examine you," Reverend Alms said.

"The instruments I need for that type of exam are at my office," Dr. Miller said. "She'll need to come by tomorrow. That will give me time to study what my medical journals say about amnesia."

Doctor Miller handed the Bible and postcard back to Reverend Alms and then went over to the bureau. He pulled a bottle of white powder out of his medical bag. It looked like the same medicine Reverend Alms gave me in his office.

"When you get your headaches, mix a teaspoon of this with water and drink it," he said. "And I do want to see you tomorrow."

"I don't want the town knowing I need a doctor," I said.

"Bring Carol with you. The folks in town will just think you're bringing her for a check-up." He set the bottle on the desk as he looked at Reverend Alms. "Are you ready to sneak out of here yet?"

Reverend Alms rose from the floor and handed me the postcard and the rings. "See if these help conjure up any more memories. But don't try so hard that you pass out this time."

As I reached for the card, I saw in his eyes the same thing I remembered seeing in Melinda's eyes at the piano. It was the same thing Lucille's eyes showed when she looked at Simeon. And the same thing I saw in Mrs. Chalk's eyes when she looked at Jarvis. I knew what the love of a parent for a child felt like because it's the way I feel about Carol even though I'm not her real mother.

When I looked at the picture, I recognized the boy standing beside me. In the photograph, I looked to be about twelve and Nathaniel on the verge of becoming a man. "I remember sitting on his back and pulling his hair." I pointed to a mark on his jaw. "He scraped his jaw when I tripped him and Momma got mad because we were having photographs taken the next day."

"Did you just remember this?" Dr. Miller asked.

"Not all of it. I remembered the part about pulling his hair when Mrs. Chalk asked me if I had any brothers or sisters."

A satisfied smile curved on the doctor's lips. "It sounds like your memory isn't completely lost. You just need time to let it surface one piece at a time. What else have you remembered?"

I pointed to the desk. "In the drawer is a black leather envelope. Inside are the memories I've written down so far."

Reverend Alms walked over to the desk and pulled open the drawer. He lifted out the envelope and untied the string. Each page he finished reading, he handed to Dr. Miller.

"This is your grandmother, Julia Shepard," Reverend Alms said when he held up the picture of the woman in the memory about Sossy. He continued reading through the pages. "This is Melinda," he said when he showed the picture I drew in his office to Dr. Miller. When he read the last memory I wrote down before I passed out, he looked angry and his hands began to shake. "This is the mayor of Wilmington and his son, Conrad Cain."

Doctor Miller finished reading the last few pages and looked over at me. "I think he's right. Based on what he said about why your brother was in jail and what happened the night you were whipped, I do need to see if the boy harmed you." A chill came over me. I felt lost enough without having something horrible like that to plague my mind. "When can you come?"

"I already promised Lucille I'd see you tomorrow after the lunch crowd leaves the restaurant. It should be about two o'clock by the time I get the kitchen squared away."

The doctor looked very concerned. "I don't think working is a good thing for you to be doing right now."

"It keeps my mind busy on things that don't cause my head to hurt. Besides, I have to do it so that Lucille can feed Carol." I stood up when someone knocked at the door. "I also need to be there to keep Buford from mistreating Lucille and Chen Sue."

I walked unsteadily to the door and opened it a crack to look out before letting Lucille into the room. She laid Carol in the bassinet. Her eyes went from Reverend Alms to Dr. Miller and finally to me. "Sis," she said, "these two look ready to hunt bear."

Reverend Alms put my memory pages back into the envelope and returned it to the desk drawer. He pointed at the door and I looked out into the hallway.

"No one's out there," I said.

"There won't be," Lucille said. "I told them I'd stick around and give you some broth once you felt up to it and then they all went to Porky's funeral."

I looked at Reverend Alms. "Shouldn't you be going?"

"Porky was an atheist," he said. "The undertaker will preside over his funeral."

"With everyone headed out to the graveyard, this would be a good time to leave and go visit those patients Lucille told Mrs. Chalk we were seeing," Dr. Miller said.

He picked up his bag and I opened the door for the two men to leave, but Reverend Alms stopped. He wrapped his arms around me and kissed me on the forehead.

"Bless you, *my* child."

For the first time since meeting him, I didn't feel an urge to run. I wasn't completely ready to trust him, but next to Lucille, I knew I could turn to him for help.

I closed the door after they left and changed into a pair of pants and a shirt. The dress looked terribly wrinkled after lying in bed with it on all morning.

"I can clean and press that for you," Lucille said.

"Thank you." I walked over and picked my gun up off the floor.

"Why you carryin' that big gun 'round for?" she asked.

I slid the gun back under my pillow. "I don't know. But it feels so natural in my hand I think I've had it for a while." An image of riding Ruth came into my mind. She was running and I was firing the gun at a man. The man fired his gun at me. The image ended with the man falling from his horse. "And, God help me, I think I killed a man with it."

"Are you sure?"

"I fired it at someone chasing me and he fell off his horse."

"Maybe you just wounded him," she said.

I shrugged my shoulders. "Maybe."

Chapter 10

Porky's widow arrived at the restaurant before sunup on Monday morning. Unlike her slob of a husband, Agnes Hoggins looked clean and respectable in her black mourning dress. Her bright red hair hung down in ringlets, which were pulled back with a black velvet bow. I expected a much older woman, but she was thirty with a slightly plump, firm body. I understood how men like Buford considered her plain and unattractive, but if they were to look beyond the freckles, she was really quite handsome for a woman living in a prairie town.

She dabbed at bloodshot green eyes with a lace handkerchief. "I'm sorry to look like such a mess," she said as she sat down at the kitchen table where I stood stirring flapjack batter. "I just haven't had much sleep the past couple of nights."

I didn't know what to say as far as expressing sympathy for her loss. After meeting Porky, I figured she was better off without him.

"What are your plans now that he's gone?" I asked.

"I don't know," she said with a sniff. "He drank up what little savings we had after Buford fired him. I don't have any relatives, and what I make cooking on Sundays isn't enough."

"How much does Buford pay you for cooking on Sunday?" I asked.

"One dollar plus any tips the guests leave behind."

I thought about that for a moment. I knew Lucille and Chen were getting a dollar a day plus tips with Sundays off. With the growing number of customers, I needed help in the kitchen. Saturday nearly made me pass out from exhaustion, which was further hampered by a cramping pain I kept having in my lower abdomen whenever I worked too hard or stood on my feet for more than half an hour.

"Here's the deal," I said. "I need you to work Tuesday through Sunday for a dollar a day during the week and two dollars a day on the weekends. Can you do that?"

"Are you sure Buford will agree to it?"

"He'll have to. This place is starting to show a profit and he knows he needs us if he wants to see the money flow."

Agnes Hoggins gave me a questioning smile. "You've got something on him don't you?"

I didn't know what she was thinking, but I shook my head. "No. I just seem to have a way of getting men to do what I want."

She raised an eyebrow and I shook my head. "Not like that."

"No," Lucille said as she entered the back door.

"Then how?" Agnes asked.

"She scares the pants off them." Lucille pointed a thumb over her shoulder. "There were only four guests last night, so it won't take long to get the laundry done."

She picked up the basket of dirty kitchen linens and table cloths and headed back out the door just as Chen Sue came in.

"Mrs. Porky, how are you today?" Chen Sue gave her a hug.

"Much better now that I've talked with Miss Prairie," Agnes said. "At least Walter left me with a home to live in. He won it in a poker game, but it's mine free and clear. That's one thing I double-checked with the Newman brothers and the land agent at the funeral yesterday."

"You probably should check with the other businesses around town and make sure Walter didn't have any outstanding debts." I covered the bowl of flapjack batter with a damp dishtowel and then pulled a second mixing bowl out of the cupboard to start mixing another batch. "You don't want any surprises at the end of the month when people come collecting bills."

"That's good advice." Agnes stood up and held her hand out to me. "Thank you for asking me to come in today, Miss Prairie."

"You can call me Angela. I'll bring Buford's signed contract to you during the break."

She looked puzzled. "Contract?"

"It's just an insurance policy against him double crossing us," I said. "Lucille and Chen Sue each have one now and so do I."

Her face took on an odd expression as though she thought I really did know some hidden secret about Buford. "You do have a way of getting what you want, don't you?"

I shrugged. "Neil Jones thinks I have Amazon blood running through my veins. Something about Amazon women being fierce warriors and men in their tribes being subservient to them in some book he read once."

"He does like to read books about other parts of the world." Agnes gave Chen Sue a hug. "Thanks for helping me yesterday."

"I happy to do it," Chen Sue said. "Buford should not make you work yesterday."

Agnes left out the back door and Chen Sue began stacking dishes on the prep counter. By the time the sun came up, we were ready to handle a capacity crowd three times over.

When Buford stepped in during the half-hour lull between breakfast clean up and lunch preparation, he wasn't pleased about the deal I made with Agnes Hoggins. At least not until I explained how the growing crowds would require more help in order to maintain good customer service and achieve better profits. Only then did he sit down and write out Agnes' contract exactly as I dictated it to him.

After he signed two copies, he leaned back and stared at me while I sliced the first of twenty bread loaves. I tried to ignore him, but after each loaf, I looked up. What I saw in his eyes wasn't just the calculation of profits. There was something more. He seemed interested in me for some other purpose than to cook and manage the restaurant. My hand gripped the bread knife a little tighter because if it was lust I saw in his eyes, I intended to make it clear that I wasn't one of his saloon girls.

As I reached for the seventh loaf of bread, he finally spoke. "You know, Angela, with your head for business, I'm tempted to let you in on a business deal I'm about to wrap up in a few weeks."

"Running this restaurant is more than enough for me right now," I said.

"I must say that I appreciate how you've taken charge of the place. If it wasn't for the hotel guests needing meals, I would've closed it a long time ago. I never thought a young girl like you could do what you've done in such a short time." The expression on his face changed and I wasn't quite sure if he was undressing me with his eyes or deciding whether he approved of women wearing pants. "I kind of wish my ex-wife was more like you."

"In what way?"

He laced his fingers behind his head and leaned back with only two chair legs on the floor. "We're two birds of the same feather, Angela."

That comment lost me. After thirteen days of working for him, I was pretty sure Buford and I didn't share anything in common. "How so?"

"Oh, you know." He winked and then stood up. "That's why I think we could be great business partners on this deal. This business deal I'm working on requires people with a little grit in their craw and you certainly have that in spades."

"No thanks," was the first *decent* response I came up with. I took a deep breath while I set the bread knife far enough away that I couldn't throw it at him. "There's only one purpose for me even staying in this town and it has nothing to do with business."

Buford rubbed his chin. "Knowing the type of women who live in Welcome, I could understand that. I also know that for the right price, some girls like Dolly in the saloon will do anything with anyone when someone like you gets desperate."

He was definitely lucky I put that knife down. "Like I said, the work in this restaurant is plenty to keep me busy. Besides, I have a child to take care of and that's all that concerns me."

"Oh, yes, precious little Carol." He walked toward the door and paused. "I ran into Homer yesterday. You won't need to take care of her much longer and once that burden is off your hands, come talk to me. I know I can make it worth your while."

He disappeared, whistling a tune that intensified the anger I felt inside. It was bad enough he insinuated I was the type of girl who liked girls, but what really irked me was how sure he was I would give Carol up and still want to do business with him.

My eyes strayed to the knife. I helped my grandfather castrate a bull once, and I was pretty sure the same method worked on inhuman men like Buford.

After Carol's one o'clock feeding, I carried her to Dr. Miller's office. Another patient sat in the waiting room when I arrived, so I asked directions to Agnes Hoggins' house and left. By the time I returned with Buford's copy of Agnes' contract with her signature on it, Reverend Alms sat in the doctor's office with the Millers.

My nervousness over what Dr. Miller intended to look for increased and awoke that instinct to run. Mrs. Miller must've sensed my fear because she took my right hand in hers.

"Why don't you let Joseph take the baby?" she suggested. "I'll be with you the whole time. There's nothing to worry about."

Reverend Alms took Carol and sang Sunday school songs to her. His voice sounded so pleasant, I relaxed a little as I followed Mrs. Miller into the examining room.

She closed the door and told me to step behind a screen to change into a knee-length gown she handed me. I felt shaky when I came out from behind the screen. She pointed to the exam table and I laid down. Although she covered me with a sheet, I shivered.

Dr. Miller stood up from his desk. "Go put the closed sign in the window."

Mrs. Miller went out into the waiting room briefly. When she returned, she double checked that the lower curtains were drawn shut. I was about to ask why she didn't close the curtains on the upper windows when I realized that they were made of beveled glass. After she finished her task, she stood next to me and held my hand.

I fidgeted while Dr. Miller performed the examination. Mrs. Miller handed me a folded cloth and I bit into it to keep from screaming from the pain.

She pressed her cheek against my forehead. "There, there, now," she cooed. "Relax and breathe deeply while you concentrate on the song Joseph is singing to Carol."

I tried to do as she said, but my eyes watered and my head throbbed as I fought to relax. It seemed like an eternity before Dr. Miller finally placed his torturous instruments into a pan of water. The look on his face indicated he found something he didn't like.

"Angela, did you experience any pain down here when you woke up from your accident?" he asked as he pressed deeply upon my lower abdomen.

My eyes welled up with more tears. "Please…stop," I gasped. He removed his hands and waited for my answer. "I don't know. Maybe. My whole body hurt. I'm not sure what all was injured other than my head."

"Did you have a lot of bleeding?"

"I was so covered in blood, I'm surprised the wolves didn't sniff me out and eat me."

"How have your monthlies been since you woke up?"

Weren't men supposed to be shy when it came to talking about such things? "I haven't had any."

He pressed on my abdomen again. "How much pain have you experienced down here since you came here? And how often?"

"It comes and goes. Mostly when I'm working and standing on my feet a lot."

He patted my knee and told me to get dressed. While I waited for my head to quit spinning from the pain he put me through, I watched him sit at his desk and write up the results of the exam.

Five minutes passed before I found the strength to sit up. Mrs. Miller helped me off the table and guided me behind the screen. She handed me a pad of folded white rags to use until the bleeding between my legs stopped.

When I came out from changing into my clothes, Dr. Miller asked me to sit down in the chair next to his desk. Although the chair was cushioned, it hurt to sit. I squirmed without success to find a position that felt comfortable. He noticed my discomfort and pointed to a black leather chaise lounge across the room. "Let's go over there where you can lie down."

I followed him to the corner of the room.

"Do you want Joseph to come in?" Mrs. Miller asked.

I shook my head.

"Whether you like it or not, he is your father," Dr. Miller said. "He's very concerned about you."

I rubbed my temples. Dr. Miller went to his medicine cabinet and mixed a glass of the headache medicine. I drank it down with no concern for the bitterness.

"Do you want your father in here or not?" Dr. Miller asked.

I handed the glass back to him and rolled over to face the wall. The truth pounded in my head. I was afraid to hear what he discovered during the exam.

"You're acting like a child," Dr. Miller said. "Sooner or later you've got to admit to yourself that he's telling the truth. He's your father and he loves you."

"Leave me alone." I clasped both sides of my head and drew my knees up to my chest. I cried against the pain in my head.

"Why won't it stop?"

"I'm going to get Joseph," Mrs. Miller said.

A minute later I felt myself lifted up and then the sensation of coming back down to rest in someone's lap. I opened my eyes. Reverend Alms held me as he sat on the chaise with his back against the wall. He nestled my head against his shoulder and stroked my back. Mrs. Miller held Carol and Dr. Miller sat in the chair next to the chaise.

"When are they expecting you back at Buford's?" Dr. Miller asked.

"Four o'clock." I closed my eyes and listened to Reverend Alms sing a lullaby my mother used to sing to me. "Buford told Homer about Carol. He's coming to take her away. Everyone I love gets taken away."

"Ron, take Carol," Mrs. Miller said. "I'll ask Agnes to take over for her. I'll tell her Carol came down with a fever. Besides, Agnes could use something to take her mind off Walter."

I heard the door open and shut and then the bell on the outer door jingled. After that, all I heard was Reverend Alms singing softly. The calming vibration from his chest eased the throbbing in my head, allowing me to fall asleep.

Sometime later I awoke, covered by a blanket. Lucille sat in a chair next to the chaise, nursing Carol, while Reverend Alms played on the floor with Simeon.

"Hey, Sis," Lucille said. "How do you feel?"

"Exhausted," I said. "What time is it?"

"Almost five-thirty," she said. "Do you want me to fetch Doc?"

God no, I thought. But instead, I asked, "Where is he?"

Reverend Alms rose from the floor and sat down on the foot of the chaise. "He's outside talking to Homer."

"How long has Homer been here?"

"About an hour. He's demanding that we hand Carol over to him." He took hold of my hand. "Dr. Miller examined Carol. He thinks Margie's malnutrition and age may have attributed to Carol's deafness."

I sat up fast, too fast. My head dived into a new pool of dizziness. I swayed until Reverend Alms caught hold of me and eased me back down onto the chaise.

"Why does he think she's deaf?" I asked.

"She doesn't respond to sound."

"But she smiles when I sing to her."

"When you hold her against your chest, she probably feels the vibration of your voice."

That sounded logical. After all, the calm vibration of his voice helped me feel safe in his arms earlier.

"It's probably why she didn't jump like the rest of us when you dropped that big gun of yours on the floor yesterday," Lucille said. "Mrs. Chalk was afraid you'd fallen out of bed."

"Actually, it was my Bible that fell on the floor," Reverend Alms said.

"Mama," Simeon called, pointing to his stomach.

"In a minute, baby," Lucille said. "Carol's almost done with her supper." A minute later, Carol let go. Lucille burped her and then handed her into my arms.

"Thank you," I said. "Keep an ear out for anything Buford says tonight, will you?"

"Sure," she said. "Anything in particular?"

"He's got some business deal going on that he wanted to bring me in on. I told him I wasn't interested, but he seemed pretty sure I was going to be involved somehow."

She bent down and kissed me on the forehead. "My ears are open, Sis."

Lucille put Simeon's blocks into a leather bag and picked him up. When she opened the door, I heard a muffled argument coming from the front porch.

A few minutes later, Mrs. Miller came into the exam room and locked the door behind her. "Homer's mad. Lucille's going to send the sheriff over."

"What's he mad about?" Reverend Alms asked.

"He thinks we're lying about Carol's condition. Apparently, Kimberly's baby died in his sleep last month and he wants to take Carol back for them to raise."

"Poppa, go get Margie's last will from my room," I said.

A tear came to his eye. "What did you say?"

"Margie's last will and testament. It's inside her Bible."

"No," he said. "That's not what I meant." He leaned over and stroked my hair. "You called me 'Poppa'."

"No, I didn't."

"Yes, you did," Mrs. Miller said. Her smile confirmed they both told the truth.

"It must've been a momentary lapse of sanity," I said. "Please go get the will."

"I'll be back," he said.

Mrs. Miller unlocked the door and let him out.

Carol pulled on my hair. I looked down into her eyes. "You're a perfect little child and don't you ever forget that."

Chapter 11

A half hour later, Reverend Alms returned with Margie's will and James Talbourne. I stood in the waiting room and watched through the window while Homer, Dr. Miller, Sheriff Koker, Mr. Talbourne, and my father quarreled.

The acceptance of Joseph Alms as my father filled me with hope. I no longer felt alone. I had family and friends to help protect me from Mayor Cain and his son. I just needed to remember why they were chasing me.

The door and walls muffled the argument. As I strained my ears to hear each word, my pulse raced for wanting to go out and defend my right to Carol's guardianship. My hand itched to take hold of the doorknob, so I walked back into the examining room where Mrs. Miller sat on the chaise with Carol. It didn't matter that Homer was her father, I knew deep down in my heart I couldn't lose that child. With that thought in mind, I hurried out to the porch.

"You should go back inside, Miss Prairie," Mr. Talbourne said.

"This concerns me as well as Carol." I pointed to the number of bystanders lurking around. "We should take this over to the church or someplace else private."

Sheriff Koker stroked his mustache, which drooped down to his jaw. "She's right. Let's go over to the church where we can sit down and talk about this peaceably."

The urgency in my steps put me three paces ahead of the men. At the church, I took the four steps two at a time and opened the door for the others to enter before I followed. With the door secure behind me, I walked down the center aisle and stood in front of the pulpit. The men took seats in the front pews: Sheriff Koker and Homer on the left and Dr. Miller, James Talbourne, and my father on the right.

I reached my hand out and my father handed me the will. "Gentlemen, this here is Margaret Drummond's Last Will and Testament, signed by her, witnessed by me, and later read and duly recorded by Mr. Talbourne."

I showed the document to Sheriff Koker and gave him time to read it before I continued. "When I met Margie, she was malnourished and in labor. Her husband, Homer Drummond, went to town seven months earlier to get supplies, but never returned. Upon arriving in Welcome, I learned the reason he didn't return is that he ran off and married a teenage girl he impregnated on his previous visit." James Talbourne's face showed a mixture of anger and loss. The others squirmed in their seats. "Sheriff, based on these facts, I'm filing charges against Homer Drummond on Margie's behalf."

Homer came to his feet. "What charges?"

I looked straight into his eyes, which were a good foot above mine. Then, in what seemed to be my usual approach when dealing with men, I advanced toward him. "Adultery, statutory rape, polygamy, and murder."

"Murder!" The word came out of everyone's mouth at the same time.

"Yes, murder," I said with a nod. I jabbed a finger into Homer's chest. He retreated, tripping backwards into the pew. "You abandoned Margie and left her to die while you ran off with Kimberly Talbourne. In law, that's called negligent homicide."

Everyone sat silent for a minute except Homer, who rose awkwardly to his feet. His eyes searched the room for an escape. He tried to run for the front door, but I kicked up and out with my right foot and sent him tumbling into the pews again. He came up and took a swing at me. I ducked, shifted my weight, and kicked him again, in the jaw. My boot heel cut a deep gash across his cheek. He stumbled and fell to the floor. While he maneuvered to stand up, I moved to where I blocked his path to the door.

With fury in his eyes, he came forward again. I threw a spin kick at the side of his head and knocked him into another set of pews. He rolled to the floor in a limp heap. His closed eyelids didn't even try to flutter. He was out cold.

Sheriff Koker rushed forward and knelt beside him. "Doc, he's going to need stitches before I haul him off to jail." He stood up and looked at James Talbourne. "As prosecuting attorney in this county, do you support the charges Miss Prairie just made?"

"I do," Talbourne said. "I'll bring the paperwork to you first thing in the morning."

"Is that an objective decision?"

Talbourne nodded. "Even if Kimberly wasn't my daughter, I'd support the charges. I will, however, request an impartial attorney to sit in as prosecutor during the trial."

"Very well." Sheriff Koker gestured toward the door. "Get him over to Doc's to be patched up." The sheriff looked at me and shook his head.

After Dr. Miller and James Talbourne carried Homer outside, Koker closed the door behind them. He rubbed the back of his neck as though stalling while he figured out what he wanted to say. His eyes narrowed when he came to a decision.

"I have a wanted poster in my office for a gal fitting your description. It says she has deadly feet. It further says she's wanted for stealing the personal property of some feller back in Illinois and for breaking her brother out of jail. You wouldn't happen to know that gal, would you?"

I glanced at my father and shrugged. "I don't remember ever stealing anything from anyone or breaking anyone out of jail." I ran my fingers through my hair and felt the ridge beneath the scar. "And as far back as I can remember, I've never been in Illinois."

Although my father's face remained impassive, his eyes held admiration for how I answered with truth. After all, *he* was the one who told me the reason my life was in danger. I didn't remember it, and still hadn't conjured up the memory of what made me flee from home like a wanted criminal.

"Where'd you learn to kick like that?"

"A drifter who worked on my grandparents' farm when I was ten used to hang a gunny sack full of sand from the rafters in the barn and kick at it. I watched him and when no one was around, I'd lower the bag to my height and practice the same moves he used." The whole time I talked, I looked him straight in the eyes in order to read whether he believed me. "Until a moment ago, I didn't know I could still do it."

"I've heard a rumor that you're not afraid to face off against the men in this town," Koker said. "There're some who say you hate men. What do you say about that?"

I didn't know what to say. The only men I knew were those I met since coming to Welcome. Except for Buford, most of them acted like decent gentlemen. Granted, there were a few instances where I defended Lucille and Chen Sue against drunks who wandered into the restaurant at night looking for girls, but usually all I needed to do was talk sternly to them and send them back to the saloon. In the past two weeks, I turned down three marriage proposals on the grounds I wasn't interested in becoming anyone's wife. As for liking men, I knew that if Paul Garrett didn't have that wedding ring on his finger, I'd be spending more time around his feed store, but I wasn't about to tell Sheriff Koker that.

With another glance at my father, I answered. "Let's just say I don't trust men until I get to know them better."

Koker nodded. "Guess that's fair enough. Either way, I don't want you leaving town until I investigate that poster a bit." He reached for the knob and opened the door. "Besides, seeing as how you're the one charging Homer with his crimes, you can't go anywhere until after his trial." He stepped out onto the porch and looked back. "Reverend, I'm pretty sure she's who I think she is, so I'm placing her in your custody pending the outcome of my inquiry. She doesn't go anywhere outside of Mrs. Chalk's unless she's with you or working at the restaurant."

"What ever happened to innocent until proven guilty?" I asked.

"Let's just say you're under house arrest for protection against bounty hunters who might come after you for alleged criminal activities."

I stood with my fists clenched. I couldn't give in to the voice that told me to run. Carol needed me and I needed her. I needed to make sure Homer paid for what he did to Margie. I also needed my father.

"Don't worry, Sheriff," my father said. "I'll keep an eye on her and do my best to keep her safe."

"I knew I could trust you." The sheriff tipped his hat and left

I closed the door behind him. The sun set over half an hour ago and the interior of the church was dark except for the lantern on the altar. A shiver went down my spine. My whole body shook and tears trickled down my cheeks. My father wrapped his arms around me and pressed my head against his shoulder.

"It's okay. Koker's a good man and he'll keep quiet about his suspicions."

"I'm so scared. I don't know what I did. Lucille said I was mumbling something about evidence the other night, but I don't remember it." I lifted my head. "How can I defend myself if I don't know what I did or didn't do?"

His hand stroked my hair. "We'll take it one step at a time. I truly believe God led you here so you can get the help you need." He pushed me away far enough to lift my chin with a finger so he could gaze into my eyes. "Speaking of which, we still need to find out what Ron has to say about your exam."

"I'm scared, Poppa. I'm not sure I want to know."

"You have to stop running and you can't hide out in that locked up memory of yours forever." He brushed a strand of hair out of my face. "Besides, everything we find out about what happened to you puts us that much closer to knowing how to keep you safe."

I nodded and leaned into his shoulder. The warmth and strength of his arms comforted me. The distrust I felt over the past two weeks disappeared and in its place blossomed the love I needed during this tumultuous time in my life.

It was seven o'clock when I stopped shaking and felt in control again. After I helped my father reset the pews, we headed back to Dr. Miller's, together.

Chapter 12

Mrs. Miller waved for my father and me to come into the house rather than the doctor's office. We followed her into the parlor where Carol slept in a cradle next to the fireplace.

"Ron's still stitching up Homer's cheek," she said. "Mrs. Chalk came over earlier. I told her Carol's fever broke late this afternoon. I also told her I'd feed you."

My father shook his head as he leaned against the mantle. "I wonder which I'll get condemned to hell for most."

"What do you mean?" Mrs. Miller asked.

I sat in the rocking chair next to the cradle. "I thought God forgave our sins and the path to heaven came through believing in Jesus' salvation."

"For a girl who doesn't own a Bible, you sure seem to know enough of it to throw the Word at people when needed," he said.

Mrs. Miller shook her head and left the room. She returned holding a tray with two plates of food. She set it on the coffee table.

My father caught her arm as she started to leave the room again. "Catherine, I'm sorry. I didn't mean to ignore your question earlier."

She smiled. "It's okay. I know you were talking about lying to protect Angela's secret. I don't like it either, but I think for now we'll have to do what we can to protect the fact she has amnesia and the other problems she's dealing with."

I came to my feet. "What other problems?"

She placed a hand on my shoulder. "Well, besides finding out that Joseph is your real father and Homer showing back up, there's whatever caused you to get that crack on your head." She looked at my father and then back at me. "Ron will tell you the rest when he gets here."

"The rest of what?" my father asked.

She walked out of the room and left us alone with the food tray, which neither of us touched. My father paced the room while I sat in the rocking chair. I knew I should wake Carol and play with her so that she would sleep through the night, but I felt too drained.

Instead, I contemplated the questions Dr. Miller asked me earlier about whether I felt pain in my abdomen when I woke up and how much bleeding there was after the accident. My clothes were caked with dried blood that came from cuts and scrapes. I remembered the crotch and seat of my pants and underwear were heavily filled with blood, urine, and excrement. As a woman, the presence of vaginal blood didn't surprise me. I simply burned those clothes while I took a bath in the stream. Like Ruth's back after I removed her saddle, my hind end was so covered with sores and a rash that I lay on my stomach for several days wearing nothing but a shirt until it healed.

Dr. Miller arrived around eight-thirty. Looking rather haggard, he stopped in the archway to the parlor and looked at me. "Do you want Joseph to hear this?"

I thought about what my father said at the church earlier. We did need to learn everything we could about what happened to me. I just didn't know if I wanted to hear whether or not Conrad Cain raped me. Finding out that Mayor Cain whipped me was less scary than that.

My father knelt down at my feet and took my hand in his. "Do we do this together? Or do you fight through that jungle in your head alone?"

I looked up at Dr. Miller. "I've been thinking about it and there was a lot of blood and I did feel pain down there." I looked into my father's eyes. "Please stay; I need your strength."

He lifted my hands and pressed them to his lips. "Always."

Dr. Miller carried an armchair from across the room and placed it in front of the rocking chair, facing me. He sat down and looked at me as he shook his head. "By all my knowledge of medicine you should be dead right now. If not from that cracked skull, then by the internal injuries you suffered." He leaned forward and laid a hand on my abdomen. "The good news is you weren't taken."

My father gave my hands a gentle squeeze. In his eyes I saw the same kind of relief I felt.

"How would you be able to tell?" I asked.

"Until I performed the exam, your virginal skin was intact. That's rather miraculous, considering the trauma your body went through."

Dr. Miller's hand pressed more firmly against my abdomen and I felt a twinge of pain. Instinct told me he wasn't through. I put my hand over his and he stopped pressing.

"What's the bad news?" I asked.

"You have scarring that appears to go deep inside." He paused for a moment, rubbing his chin, his eyes focused on my abdomen. He glanced over at Carol and then looked directly into my eyes. "Given the amount of pain you feel when I pressed in on your womb and when you work too hard, I doubt you'll ever have children."

What little energy I still possessed from the day drained from my body until I felt empty. What is it men say? I need a drink. Did I have what it takes to drink a bottle of whisky and let the world go on without me while I drown myself in booze like Porky did?

The room remained quiet except for the crackling and hissing coming from the fireplace. The first person to make a sound was Carol as she stirred from her sleep. I reached down and picked her up. As I held her against my chest, she began rooting for her late evening meal. Without a word, I stood up and walked out of the house to go find Lucille.

I didn't notice the sound of footsteps behind me until I reached the gate at Mrs. Chalk's.

"Evening Miss Angela…Reverend Alms," Jarvis said. "Is Carol…feeling better?"

"Yes," I said. "Can you find Lucille for me? Carol's hungry."

"She's waiting…inside."

He opened the gate for me and I walked on up to the porch. My father moved in front of me and opened the door.

"We need to talk about this," he said as I rushed past him. He followed me up the stairs. Lucille came out of the kitchen and tagged along. "You need help to deal with the shock and the grief."

At the end of the hall, I pulled my key from my pocket. My hand shook so much I couldn't line it up with the hole. I dropped it on the floor. Lucille picked it up and opened the door. She took Carol from my arms and immediately went to work once she entered the room and sat down on the bed.

Neil and Paula stuck their heads out their doors. Thankfully, my father sidestepped toward his door.

"Is Carol all right, Miss Angela?" Neil asked.

"She's fine," I said as I retreated into the safety of my room until morning.

Chapter 13

My father looked at me from the other side of his desk. He showed up at the restaurant in time for my two-hour break and escorted me to the church. All the way over, he lectured me on not working so hard and getting rest. Dragging me into his office was one way to make sure I did just that. In this room, all I could do was sit and talk. No physical activity, just talk on the pretense of getting to know one another. Not that I could tell him anything about myself that he hadn't already read in the memory pages I wrote.

"You've been through a terrible ordeal, Angela," he said. "You're still going through it."

I just sat. I didn't know how to put into words the grief I felt from knowing I wouldn't have children. He expected me to cry, but there weren't any tears left. I used them up last night in my room. The consolation was I didn't have a husband expecting me to give him children.

"Damn it." I leaned forward and rubbed my temples.

In my mind, Conrad held my knees while his father whipped me. The shot rang out and the man on the horse came and rescued me. As we raced away, I sat on top of the man's bedroll while holding onto his waist. He took me to where Ruth stood tied to a fence outside a church. I switched horses, but before I could flee the man grabbed my arm.

"I can't let you go," he said.

I looked into the shadows of the man's face. "Who are you?"

"My brother was killed on that train and you know..."

The snapping pop of gun fire ended his explanation. The man fell to the ground, shot in the back. Conrad and his father rode out from the concealment of the trees. I kicked my heals against Ruth's sides and took off.

"Oh, God," I cried. "He's dead because of me."

"Who's dead?" my father asked.

"The man who saved me from being whipped."

He reached across the desk and grabbed my arm. Fear showed in his pale face. "Not Nathaniel?"

"No. It was someone else. He said his brother died on the train and then he was shot in the back by either Conrad or his father."

He let go of my arm and handed me a pencil and some paper. I wrote everything down and sketched a picture of the man. When I finished, I left the pages on his desk and rushed back to the restaurant even though the headache still pounded in my head.

The onions I chopped kept the others from asking why my eyes were red and watery. When I took a break to eat dinner, Paul Garrett came in and sat down across from me.

"Are you feeling all right, Miss Prairie?" he asked.

"I'm fine!" The few lingering patrons looked up. I stopped rubbing my temples and spoke softer. "Thank you for asking. Is there something you wanted?"

"I just came to let you know my driver returned with Margie's things. The rocker is in your room over at Mrs. Chalk's and I put the rest in a storeroom for you." He handed me the key. "It's the room behind the warehouse office. This will open the outside door if you need to get in there for anything."

Our hands touched as I took the key. The feel of his warm, calloused hand sent a tingling sensation through me. I pulled my hand back just as quickly as his left hand went beneath the table. My head hurt too much to care. He was married. That was all my heart needed to know to keep from fluttering every time I saw him out on the street.

"I should get back to work," I said.

He shook his head. "You need rest. Taking care of a sick infant and working twelve hours a day is wearing you out." He looked around the room before leaning forward and whispering. "I saw Doc Miller and Reverend Alms sneak out of Mrs. Chalks back door the other day. I also heard you were sick to your stomach that day. But I doubt that is what's really wrong with you. I also don't believe Carol was the one who was sick yesterday." He leaned in even closer. "If you need a place where you can stay rent free,

Lance can sleep in my room and you can have his bed."

I wanted to slap him for suggesting such an arrangement. For one thing, what would his wife think? Instead, I stood up and took a twenty dollar gold piece out of my pocket. "This is for the rent on the storage room, Mr. Garrett. You can send the receipt to Mrs. Chalk's in the morning. Let me know when I owe you more." Without giving him a chance to debate the matter, I returned to the kitchen.

Lucille came in a minute later and handed me the gold eagle. "Guess he didn't want your money. What'd he say to you?"

I shook my head. "He's been watching me."

"Him and every other man in town." She grinned and placed her hand on my arm. "But, Sis, he's the one you want. Don't go pushin' him away like you are."

I placed a steak in the skillet. "In case you haven't noticed, he's married."

She shook her head. "I know he wears a ring, but I ain't never seen no woman hangin' 'round with him. As far as I know, the only one livin' with him is his nephew, Lance, who he adopted after Miss Jenny died. She was his brother Wyatt's wife."

I turned the steak over and sprinkled pepper on it. "What happened to his brother?"

"Which one?"

"Wyatt."

"Well, he went back east somewhere to collect the body of their brother, Jared, who was killed durin' a train robbery. Wyatt was shot in the back while tryin' to find the men who killed Jared. From what I heard, the preacher who found him outside the church where he was shot mailed Miss Jenny a note Wyatt wrote her before he died."

Startled, I dropped the meat fork on the floor. I bent over to pick it up, but the movement caused my head to spin too fast at the same time as a sharp pain stabbed at my abdomen. I straightened up and the combination of my headache, the pain, and the sudden movements caused everything to spin faster. I ran out the back and puked up my supper.

"I'll go get Doc," Lucille said after I came back inside.

"No. I just need that headache medicine is all."

She mixed some up for me. After I drank it, I sat down with my head resting on the worktable in the kitchen. Agnes cooked and I just sat there waiting until we closed.

Feeling cold, I opened my eyes and stumbled to the window to close it. I didn't remember opening the window or going to bed. For that matter, I didn't remember leaving the restaurant. When I checked inside the basinet to make sure Carol didn't catch cold, she was gone.

"Carol!" Without putting on my robe, I rushed into the hallway. "Carol's gone!" Everyone except Mr. Peabody emerged from their rooms. "Where's Carol? I woke up and the window was open and she was gone. Where is she?"

Paula put her arms around me. "It's all right. She's over at the Millers'."

I tried to break away from her, but she held tight. "I need to go get her," I said. "I promised Margie I'd take care of her and raise her as my own. She needs me. Please let me go."

But she wouldn't let go and forced me to walk back into my room. Mrs. Chalk followed and they forced me to lie down. Paula pulled the covers over me while Mrs. Chalk mixed up some medicine in a glass. It wasn't the headache medicine. This medicine came from a different bottle.

Paula lifted my head and held the glass to my lips. I tried to shove it away, but Mrs. Chalk went to the other side of the bed and helped Paula hold me still while the bitter liquid went down my throat. When the glass was empty, Paula grabbed a cloth from the washstand and wiped my face and neck where some of the liquid dribbled around the edge of the glass.

"Now get some sleep," Mrs. Chalk said. "Carol will come back after breakfast. Dr. Miller just wants you to get a full night's rest and take the rest of the week off from work."

I didn't remember seeing Dr. Miller. "I-I can't. Carol needs Lucille to feed her."

"She will," Paula said. "Buford's out of town again." She brushed her hand over my hair. A strange look came over her face when her fingers felt the scar, but then she smiled. "I'll just sit here with you until the medicine helps you fall asleep."

It didn't take long for my eyes to close, but it was a troubled sleep. A couple of times I opened my eyes to find Paula lying in the bed beside me. She must've found the gun under the pillow because it lay on the nightstand.

"It's okay, Angela," she whispered. "I won't tell anyone. Just close your eyes and go back to sleep. You need to get well if you're going to take care of Carol."

I didn't open my eyes again until almost eight o'clock. Paula was gone and the gun was back under the pillow. When I returned from the washroom, a breakfast tray sat on the writing desk. While I ate, I read through my memory pages and tried to arrange them in some sort of chronological order—the earliest memory with Sossy and Granma, pulling Nathaniel's hair, tripping Nathaniel and having the picture taken, attending my parent's funeral, Mayor Cain whipping me, and then the one where the man who rescued me was shot.

Lucille brought Carol back after her nine o'clock feeding. I slid the pages back into the drawer and held Carol in my arms and kissed her. After Lucille left, I played with Carol and sang to her even though I knew she couldn't hear me. I was so captivated in watching her I didn't notice my father walk into the room.

"I truly do hope you get to keep her," he said. Startled, I reached for the gun, but stopped when he placed his hand on my shoulder. "How are you feeling this morning?"

"Tired."

"Are you ready to talk about what Ron told you the other night?"

I shook my head and chose a different subject. "I think the man who saved me from being whipped was Paul Garrett's brother, Wyatt. Lucille said he died at a church after trying to hunt down the men responsible for another brother being killed during a train robbery."

My father nodded. "That man was Wyatt. I recognized him in the sketch you drew, but you left so soon after finishing it, I didn't have a chance to tell you."

"Did you know him?"

He shook his head. "No. There's a picture of the three brothers at Paul's house. It was taken last winter before Jared went back east to purchase some new freight wagons. I arrived in town only days after Wyatt left to bring Jared's remains back here." He rubbed his forehead. "When I found out it was the same train Melinda was on, I somehow knew Wyatt wouldn't return."

I hugged my knees to my chest. Carol tugged at the hems of my jeans. It was amazing how much she had grown in the past six weeks. She was long to begin with, but even Lucille said Simeon didn't get to be Carol's size until he was three months old. There was no doubt Homer was her father. The man was over six feet tall and, except when faced with my flying feet, he was reportedly very strong. Carol possessed that strength and managed to use my jeans to pull herself into a sitting position. I laughed when she wobbled back over.

My father also laughed. "I better go. Sheriff Koker said he wanted to talk with me." He stepped over to the bed and kissed me on the forehead. "I know you cried the other night, but when I return later, we *will* talk about this."

At noon, Neil knocked on my door and gave me some magazines he found lying on a chair at the bank.

"What happened to you?" he asked. "You had us all very worried last night, especially after you passed out on your way back here from the restaurant."

I didn't want to lie to him, but I couldn't very well tell him the truth either. "It's not something I can talk about with a man."

"I understand." His cheeks turned red despite his reassuring smile. "I grew up with five sisters. I know all about female troubles. I hope you get to feeling better, Miss Angela."

He gave Carol a wooden rattle before he politely went downstairs to eat his lunch.

A few minutes later, my father returned with a tray of food. "Are you ready to talk about this?" he asked.

"I won't be able to have children. What's there to talk about?"

"Although it's not a topic normally discussed between men and women or even fathers and daughters, I think there's plenty to talk about. This isn't something your mind can block out like it has the rest of your life. It's real. It's now. You need to make peace with it and know that God has other plans for your life."

"That's the trouble," I said with an exasperated sigh. "I don't *know* God anymore."

He scowled and pointed to the Bible sitting on the nightstand. "You've been reading Margie's Bible, haven't you?

"Yes. But how can I know a God who lets everyone around me die?"

He sat silent while I ate my lunch. When I finished, he looked directly at me. "You know God whether you want to believe it or not." He pointed at Carol. "He brought you to Margie's to save Carol's life so that she could be the child you will never have on your own."

I moved the food tray to the foot of the bed and picked Carol up. "No man is ever going to want a woman who can't bear him a child. So why should I mourn about it?"

"I don't want you to mourn. I want you to come to peace with it." He looked out the window toward the church. "And with God." He walked over to the bed and picked up the tray. "I have an appointment that just showed up down the street. I want you to think about this and pray about it. We'll talk more later."

At one o'clock, Lucille came and fed Carol. When Carol fell asleep, Lucille placed her in the bassinet and sat in the rocker by the window.

"I hear Paul Garrett's doin' a lot of good freightin' business haulin' the harvest produce to Kearney," she said as she looked out the window. "He's payin' the farmers a discounted rate and sellin' the grain at a profit. He needs more drivers, so he said he'll hire—"

Lucille jumped up and rushed out of the room. I didn't see her again until she came for Carol's five o'clock feeding. The expression on her face said she just spent the last four hours in heaven instead of working at the restaurant.

"Michael's back, isn't he?"

"Yes," she said. "He said the homecomin' I gave him was better than he dreamed."

"Better than you dreamed too, I suspect."

She nodded. "I haven't felt this content in a long time."

I placed my hand over my abdomen. "I'll probably never feel the touch of a man. At least not without it being painful."

"Are you still in a lot of pain down there?"

"Only when I work too hard or when Dr. Miller presses on it or looks inside like he did Monday." I reached over and touched the bassinet. "He says I won't be able to have children."

After Carol finished nursing, Lucille placed her in the bassinet before sitting on the edge of the bed and unbuttoning my pants.

"Just relax now." Her hands were gentle while she felt my abdomen, but the pressure hurt and I panted against her touch. She stopped and shook her head. "One thing's for sure, Sis, you're gonna need to find yourself an awfully understandin' man who's willin' to take things slow with you."

"How slow?"

She buttoned my pants back up. "He'll need to be so slow that he's willin' to work you up with his hands rather than goin' in you." She stood up and wrapped her shawl around her shoulders. "Which means you'll have to take care of him with your hands. Then maybe, God willin', over time, the pain will go away and you'll be able to do it right."

"Do you think there's such an understanding man out there?"

She smiled as she opened the door. "Only one I can think of."

She left me alone with Carol. I stared up at the ceiling. "Lord, if there is such a man, I need to know and maybe that will help me know you better."

Chapter 14

On Thursday, the restaurant gave me a place to escape from the frustration of trying to remember what I couldn't and trying to forget what I could.

Lucille shook her head as I made the biscuit dough. She picked up the basket of kitchen linens and bumped the back door open with her hip. "Just remember to sit down once in awhile."

"Yes, Mom."

She chuckled as she headed toward the washstand.

While clearing tables after the lunch crowd disappeared, I saw Paul Garrett across the street. He went into the Sheriff's Office.

For some reason, a tear trickled down my cheek. I could very easily fall in love with a man like that, but he would never want a woman who was involved in the death of his brothers. And how could I let my heart fall for a man who was married? No matter what Lucille said, he wore that ring. There was a woman somewhere. Even if she didn't live here in town, he was married and taking an interest in me just like Homer did with Kimberly. A man like that couldn't be trusted and like Homer, he would seek out other wombs to bear his children.

A hand gently gripped my shoulder. I turned my head to see my father standing there.

"You'll have Carol," he said as he wiped tears off my cheeks.

"That is if Homer doesn't get her."

"Talbourne's pretty sure there's enough of a case to send Homer to prison with or without the murder charge."

"When will the circuit judge arrive?"

"Next Thursday. I thought you knew that."

As I shook my head, the door to the hallway between the restaurant and saloon opened. Paul Garrett stood there with Sheriff

Koker. My heart pounded in a mixture of emotions ranging from anxiousness about Paul to the fear of what the sheriff came to say about his investigation.

"I need to talk with you, Miss Prairie," Koker said.

I stood up straight and looked him in the eyes. "Not without a lawyer present, you don't."

He stepped into the room with Paul and closed the door. "Then you admit that you're Josephine McDonald?"

I glanced toward the kitchen door. Agnes, Lucille, and Chen Sue were back in the kitchen giggling about something while they washed dishes.

"I don't remember anyone ever calling me by that name until I came to this town," I said.

"What do you mean you don't remember?" Koker asked.

"I said I'm not saying anything without a lawyer."

"Your right," Koker said with a nod. "I'll go get Talbourne."

He left, but Paul stayed. "Can we go somewhere more private and talk alone?"

"I don't think it would be proper for us to be alone, but Reverend Alms could go with us to my room," I said.

The huff he made indicated he didn't like the idea of having an audience, but he nodded. "Very well."

I stepped into the kitchen to let the others know I would be starting my break early.

"You better lay down and take a nap while you're gone," Lucille said.

"I'll try."

When my father, Paul, and I entered my room, Paul pulled a letter out of his coat pocket. I closed the door and sat on the bed. He took a seat in the rocking chair while my father stood near the door.

"Wyatt wrote this letter before he died. Mostly it's his last will giving me full ownership of the property and businesses we own, but the rest is his deposition in which he relates how he rescued Josephine McDonald from being tortured by the same men who shot him. He also wrote about everything he found out concerning the train robbery and how our brother, Jared, was killed. I showed it to Sheriff Koker last spring and he mailed a copy of it to the attorney general in Illinois."

He glanced over at my father before he leaned forward and looked at me again. "One of the things I wanted to say is that if you are Josephine McDonald, I don't hold any blame against you for what happened to Wyatt. Even Jenny said it made her feel better knowing he died saving Josephine from those men."

"How did you find out who I really am?"

He looked down at his left hand and then slid it into his coat pocket. "I went to the church to talk with Reverend Alms yesterday. Although I've been in his office several times since my brothers and Jenny died, it was the first time I took a real good look at that picture of the woman on the bookcase. You look a lot like her." He glanced over at my father again. "Then, under a newspaper, I found a sketch of Wyatt and some pages describing what happened the night he was killed from Josephine's perspective. When Joseph walked in and caught me reading them, I asked him who wrote it. He wouldn't tell me, but then I was in Koker's office a bit ago when he received a telegram from Illinois in response to one he sent Monday to find out more information about Josephine. It didn't take much to put it together from there." He looked straight into my eyes. "Reverend Alms is your father, isn't he?"

I nodded. Right then, I decided he deserved to know more about why his brothers died. I told him everything from waking up in the woods beside the stream to the memories I managed to recover. Then just to see what his reaction would be, I told him what Dr. Miller told me about not being able to have children.

He turned his head to stare out the window. He looked pale and alone. When he turned his head back toward me, his eyes dripped with tears. "I'd marry you anyway." He looked down at the ring on his hand. "I already have one son because I jumped the gun too quick when I was seventeen. Wyatt and Jenny took Rose and me in when Pa threw me out of the house. Welcome wasn't much more than a stage depot eleven years ago, and there weren't any preachers or doctors here. We could've used both because we lived together unwed until Rose died giving birth to Lance. When the town grew, everyone assumed he was Wyatt and Jenny's son, so that's why after Jenny died, I *adopted* Lance."

"Does he know?" I asked.

"Yeah." Paul nodded. "He's always known."

My mouth felt dry and my heart pounded as I prepared to ask my next question. "Where'd the ring come from if you were never married?"

"After Wyatt left, Doc diagnosed Jenny with cancer. It took her quick after she found out he was dead. I think she just gave up. The night she died, she was pretty much out of her head and she thought I was Wyatt. The preacher who sent the letter also sent Wyatt's ring to her. It was lying on the nightstand when I came in to check on her that night. She thought I was him and told me to put it back on because she wasn't dead yet. She started to cry, so I let her put it on my finger and for twenty minutes I was Wyatt. We were still joined together when she died." He twisted the ring. "I tried to take it off to bury it with her, but it's stuck."

I didn't know what to say. We were both victims of the same crime and we were both searching for someone to hold onto.

My father was right. I needed to find peace with what happened to me. But could I find peace by falling in love with a man who lost two brothers because of the same crime that left me orphaned and fighting to remember what happened?

"Show him the scars on my back," I said.

"Are you sure?" my father asked.

I nodded. "If he's truly considering having me for a wife, he needs to see it."

I pulled the quilt up and covered my front while I unbuttoned my shirt and slid it off. My father walked over and lifted the back of my camisole. Paul walked over to the bed. He first looked at the whip marks and then the scar and uneven ridge on my skull. His fingers lightly caressed the smaller scars on my ear and the thin pink line along my jaw.

"I didn't even notice these until now," he said. "Trust me when I say they don't make you any less beautiful."

Hearing such words from him made me feel nervous, so I pointed to the writing desk. "In the drawer are the writings and sketches I made of the events I've remembered. If you see any of the people I've drawn, let my father know. I'm pretty sure Mayor Cain and Conrad are still looking for me, and I have a gut feeling they're not too far from finding me."

While he read the pages, I covered myself with the quilt and put my shirt back on. When I finished, I folded the quilt neatly across the foot of the bed.

Paul held up the pictures of Conrad and his father. "I saw these two with Buford in Kearney the week before you came here." He studied the map I found in my wallet after my accident. "I've seen these landmarks. I know it's a long shot, but I think I might be able to find the place and bring back whatever you hid there." He took the map and started to leave, but then he stopped and smiled at me. "When I get back, I'd be obliged if you would allow me to court you." He looked at my father. "That is if it's all right with you, sir."

My father smiled at Paul. "We'll discuss it when you return. I think we need to make sure she's safe and out of danger before any thoughts of courting are seriously considered."

"Take Ruth with you," I said. "She might be able to lead you to the exact spot."

After Paul left, my father sat on the bed. "I hate to say it, but I think whatever your brain is hiding will come to a climax whether you fully regain your memory or not."

I put my head on his shoulder. "Whatever it is, I'm pretty sure Buford's involved."

"I wouldn't put it past him. Have you ever met up with him before?"

"I don't know. But ever so often he'll say something that makes me think I've heard his voice somewhere before."

As hard as I tried not to, I yawned.

My father gently laid his hand on my cheek. "Take a nap. I'll bring Carol back from Ron and Catherine's in an hour."

Chapter 15

My room remained quiet for several minutes after I told James Talbourne everything I knew about what happened prior to waking up with amnesia. He read through the stack of pages I wrote. When he finished, he looked at my father and then at Dr. Miller, who had arrived while I was napping.

"Is she well enough to travel?"

"Surely, you won't let them extradite her back to Illinois?" my father asked.

"Sheriff Koker will have to wire Wilmington and the attorney general of Illinois," Talbourne said. "Given that she's under Dr. Miller's care, I might be able to delay the extradition temporarily, but I'll need to give them some sort of time frame."

Carol cried. I picked her up out of the bassinet. I laid her on the bed beside me and grabbed the red kerchief. She followed it with her eyes and grabbed it. I played tug-of-war with her while the others talked.

"Given the amount of trauma she's gone through, the frequent headaches, and abdominal pain, I'd say at a minimum, two more months," Dr. Miller said. He handed my medical chart to Talbourne. "If the headaches and abdominal pain don't lighten up, it could be longer."

As my lawyer, Talbourne read the chart thoroughly before nodding his head. He handed the folder back to Dr. Miller. "Hopefully by then, Miss Prairie will be able to remember what it was she took and we can get this cleared up by proving the real outlaws in this case are Mayor Cain and his son." He nodded to my father. "Go ahead and let Koker in."

My father opened the door and invited the sheriff to enter.

"Well?" Koker asked. "Is she Josephine McDonald or not?"

"Unless someone can provide a witness or photograph to verify the identity of the woman you seek," Talbourne said, "you have no grounds to hold Miss Prairie in custody."

"Look, it's not like I want to turn her in," Koker said. "But it's my duty to uphold the law and according to Marshal Becker in Wilmington, she matches Miss McDonald's description."

"So could half a dozen other women in this town," Talbourne said.

My head went on another rampage when Koker mentioned the name Becker. I dropped the kerchief and Carol started kneading it with her little fingers. I lay down while another onslaught of images took over my mind.

The night's darkness surrounded me as I lay on my stomach in a pasture, hiding among dairy cows while I waited for three men to ride by on horses. Ruth also lay there, staying quiet and still, hidden by five cows that were bunched together while they slept.

"Becker ain't gonna like this," one of them said.

"Then he should've stayed with us," another one said. "Why a lawman got mixed up with Cain's scheme sure beats the hell out o' me. Lord knows if anyone finds out he's the one who shot McDonald's wife, he'll hang before he even gets a trial."

"Shut up you two," the third man said. "Let's just find the girl and get it over with."

"I never signed on to kill no girls," the second one said. "All we were supposed to do was rob the train and kill the stockbroker. With this much blood on our hands, we'll all hang."

"The girl knows too much to stay alive," the third one said. "Besides, Cain's paying us double to get rid of her."

They kept riding and I waited until they were completely out of sight before standing up and mounting Ruth. I cut across the pasture where Ruth's tracks would blend in with those of the cattle. The barn was dark when I arrived and found Nathaniel's horse already in its stall. I started to open Ruth's stall, but Conrad stepped out of the shadows and grabbed me.

His face was smooth and handsome, but his eyes were a bit cocky when he laughed.

By the time my head stopped hurting enough to open my eyes,

everyone was gone except my father. Even Carol was missing. I reached my hand down into the empty bassinet.

"Where is she?"

"Over at Ron and Catherine's."

"What happened with Sheriff Koker?"

"You don't remember?"

I shook my head. "All I remember is watching three men ride past where I was hiding out after the train robbery. They said Marshal Becker was the one who shot Momma."

While he fought against his own emotions, I wrote down everything I remembered from the memory and drew the best pictures I could of the three men, considering it was dark.

"Koker's going to request that a picture of you be sent to him," he said after reading the pages. "Talbourne thinks that if they do identify you, he'll need to make a motion that you're incompetent to stand trial because of the amnesia. I'll give him this new information in the morning. But for now, I'll go down and ask Mrs. Chalk to warm up your supper."

Supper? I looked at the clock. It was almost seven o'clock. I should've returned to the restaurant three hours ago.

No matter how often my father told me I was safe, I couldn't shed the sense that my life was in danger. Unfortunately, I was stuck. I couldn't leave Carol, I needed to testify against Homer, and I let Paul take Ruth.

I thought about taking the train until I found out the spur line was incomplete and only provided passenger service once a month. The trains that passed through more regularly were supply trains hauling ties and rails to the work crews further up the tracks.

When I went to work on Friday, Buford was still gone. After the lunch crowd left, I entered his office while the bartender was in the outhouse. Luckily, it was also too early for the saloon girls to show up.

During my search, all I found were inventory sheets, ledgers, and orders for more beer and whiskey than Buford's customers consumed.

The invoice from the Milwaukee supplier showed an adequate supply for the number of customers the saloon served. The bottles and kegs were received and Buford shipped the empties back whenever there were enough to fill a boxcar on the train. In exchange for the empty kegs, the Milwaukee supplier gave him a discount on the liquor he ordered.

The Blue Mountain Liquor Company in Chicago only shipped kegs of beer. They apparently didn't offer a discount for empty kegs because Buford didn't have any records for returning them. He started dealing with the company in January and as far as I could tell, he received the beer, never sold an ounce, and yet the inventory sheets showed zero kegs in stock. I wasn't quite sure what to make of that information, especially since the ledgers showed he made a good profit from the saloon without selling one glass of the Blue Mountain beer.

As noise from the saloon started up, I decided to sneak out through the doorway that led into the storeroom. I glanced at the crates and kegs. Not one showed a Blue Mountain label even though the orders showed Buford received a shipment on Monday while I was at Dr. Miller's office.

I turned the knob on the back door, but it was locked. Five minutes into searching for a key, I heard someone turn the knob to the door that led to the saloon. I hid behind a pile of crates and watched as the bartender carried an empty keg in and set it on a stack next to the door. He lifted a full keg from another pile and carried it into the saloon.

He left the saloon door open, so I tiptoed over to it and removed the key from the lock. Staying in the shadows, I made my way to the rear door and tried the key in the lock. It worked. I slid outside into the dark night, hoping he wouldn't think anything about the key being in the wrong door when he locked up later.

Lucille was in my room feeding Carol when I returned a little after nine o'clock.

"Where've you been?" she asked with a scolding look.

I sat on the bed and pulled off my boots. "Trying to get my head blown off."

Chapter 16

On Saturday, Buford didn't look too pleased to hand over my share of the profits for the week. I teetered on my feet from working the full day without a break. My head throbbed and I wanted to sit in a nice hot tub of water. He gave me a passive look.

"I don't see why I should pay you when you haven't even put in a full day's work this whole week," he said.

Unable to stand any longer, I sat down. "I may not be here, but I'm working."

"Doing what?"

"Planning menus, counting the receipts, making out lists for ordering supplies." I looked at him. "You know; the managerial stuff you don't have time for when you're off ironing out business deals with those partners of yours in Kearney."

"What do you know about managerial stuff?"

"Plenty," I said. "I have a degree in business management and economics."

At least, I think I did. I halfway remembered receiving a rolled up piece of parchment from a man wearing a black robe. I was also wearing a black robe, but not quite as fancy as the one he wore with three velvet stripes on the sleeves. The image didn't make sense if Margie was right and I was only twenty years old, but maybe it was an associate's degree. But then I remembered my father saying something about giving me the love he was denied sharing with me for twenty-two years, so maybe the image did make sense.

"Maybe I should introduce you to my partners after all," he said. "A couple of them will be here next week."

A sick, cramping feeling took hold of my abdomen. "I need someone to help me home."

"I'm not taking you." He handed over my pay envelope and stood up. When he left, he locked the doors on his way back to the saloon.

I was in too much pain to stand up. Earlier in the day a rancher came through with his herd, headed for Kearney. His trail cook decided to take the day off since the restaurant was close at hand to feed the crew. Those thirteen men ate five times what all the other customers consumed. We wound up feeding them both lunch and dinner because the herd was still close enough to town for those cowboys to come back for more when evening came. Without Agnes, I never would have kept up.

The noise from the saloon across the hall intensified as the night wore on. I kept thinking sooner or later someone at Mrs. Chalk's would realize I was gone and come looking for me. But no one came until Sheriff Koker was making his rounds and checking doors.

He peered in through the window and I waved at him, but the door was locked and he couldn't come in. I stood up and shakily walked to the door and unlocked it.

"What are you still doing here?" he asked.

"Wore myself plumb out today," I said. "Buford refused to get someone to help me home and then he locked me in when I couldn't stand up any longer."

"He's definitely a low rung on the ladder."

I locked the door and sat down outside on the bench beneath the window. "Mind getting a buggy and driving me home?"

"Actually, I was planning on arresting you in the morning, Miss *McDonald*."

"Got that picture, did you?"

"Marshal Becker sent it by special courier. It arrived on the train twenty minutes ago."

"Can I see it?"

He pulled an envelope out of his back pocket and removed the photograph. I took it from his hand and looked at myself in the lantern light. It was a graduation photograph from the University of Illinois done up as a postcard. This particular copy was addressed to a Mrs. Willard Tannery whose name also drew out memories, all having to do with women belonging in the kitchen and not dirtying their hands plowing up fields. I read the note on the back.

"I told you she would amount to something. Ely is planning to take her into the brokerage when he returns from New York." It was dated May 30, 1873 and signed by my mother.

"Are you feeling all right?" Koker asked.

I was rubbing my temples again. "Yeah. It's just a headache. I need to go home and lay down. I worked harder today than I should. Dr. Miller's going to have a fit with me."

He helped me to my feet and I must've passed out because I woke up in a private cell with four brick walls and a wooden door. The peep door on the outside of the bars in the door was closed and the only light came in through a small barred window too far over my head to look through.

A foul stench in the cell drew my eyes to a bucket filled with vomit and other bodily emissions. I vaguely remembered arguing with Koker about the destination he took me to when we left the restaurant. His response to my telling him I needed to go to the outhouse was to hand me the bucket. The whole time I was puking, Homer laughed from one of the other cells.

Someone slammed the front door to the Sheriff's Office so hard I felt the vibration through my still-aching head.

"You can't keep her in there!" I sat up. James Talbourne came to my rescue.

"I have orders to extradite her back to Illinois," Koker said.

"She's in no condition to travel," Dr. Miller said.

"I don't see why not," Koker said. "With the way she busted Homer up Monday night, I'd say she's in better condition than half the men in this town."

"You said yourself you found her ill and nursing a headache last night," Dr. Miller said. "At least let us take her back to Mrs. Chalk's. If you have to, put a deputy outside her room."

"What's the bail?" Talbourne asked.

"There is no bail for murder," Koker said. "You know that."

Murder? I thought I was wanted for breaking Nathaniel out of jail and taking something belonging to Mayor Cain. I rushed to the cell door to try and hear the conversation better.

"Who is she accused of murdering?" my father asked.

"A man by the name of Kirk Muskie was found dead in April with a bullet in his head," Koker said. "A witness who was the last person to see Muskie alive said he was chasing a woman on a white horse and wearing men's clothing."

"Was he found with a gun in his hand?" Talbourne asked.

A drawer was opened and slammed shut. "There, read it yourself," Koker said. "His brother is the one who found him. There's no mention of him holding a gun or that there was a gun nearby."

The image of shooting a man off a horse came back. It went through my mind so fast I couldn't see what he looked like. I tried to slow it down, but it repeated at the same speed. Although my head spun, I brought the image back again anyway. Concentrating on what he wore, I remembered him wearing a brown hat, green coat, tan vest, and black pants, riding a brown horse. The fourth time the image went by I realized the man's hair was red.

"The man I shot wasn't Muskie!" I yelled. "Kirk Muskie had blond hair."

The cellblock door opened and Koker's face appeared in the hatch to the wooden door.

"I shot a man with red hair off of a brown horse," I said. "He was firing at me with a gun that fell into some rocks. Kirk Muskie had blond hair and was fired by my Dad for selling counterfeit stock certificates."

"Where?"

"Where what?" I asked.

"Where did you shoot the red-haired man?"

"I don't know."

He gave me a disgusted look and closed the hatch. A key turned in the lock and the door came open. "Get out here."

I followed Koker into the outer office. On the way, I saw Homer sitting on his cot. He stared at me with a stupid grin on his face. How could Margie ever love a man like that?

When I stepped out of the cellblock, my father walked toward me, but Koker waved him back. "No one gets close to her."

He sat me down at a table and put a tray of food in front of me. The eggs and bacon were cold and the milk smelled sour. I pushed the tray away without eating. Koker picked it up and carried it to his desk.

I looked at the clock. My father would have to leave soon for the church.

"You've remembered more?" my father asked.

"Yes."

He grabbed some paper and a pencil off Koker's desk and sat down on the opposite side of the table from me while I wrote out everything I remembered about Mrs. Tannery, the graduation ceremony, Muskie, and the man I shot. I drew a picture of Mrs. Tannery, the man in the black robe, Muskie, and the man with red hair.

My father looked at the picture of the man I shot. "He was at your parents' funeral. His father owns a bank in Wilmington. I think his name was Sorensen."

Sheriff Koker picked up a yellowed newspaper from his desk and pointed to an article at the bottom of the page. "The banker's son was found dead twenty miles east of Grand Island the same day Muskie was found dead in Illinois. According to this article his gun was half empty and found in some rocks about three feet from where he fell."

"See," Talbourne said. "There's no way she could have killed Muskie if she was east of Grand Island shooting Sorensen in self-defense at the same time Muskie was murdered in Illinois. Besides, according to the other article, Muskie's body was still warm when he was found."

"Sorensen was one of the train robbers," I said. "He was one of the men I hid from in the pasture. The one who said he didn't hire on to kill any girls. Obviously, something changed his attitude considering he tried to shoot me."

Hundreds of images flashed through my mind at such an overwhelming rate they didn't make sense. My stomach started to lurch from the dizziness the images caused. I looked around, but couldn't see a bucket or even a spittoon. I ran out the front door and reached the alley between the jail and the livery stable before I leaned over and heaved up nothing but stomach fluid. When I stopped heaving, Koker grabbed my arm and dragged me back inside.

"It's a good thing you didn't eat your breakfast," he said.

Dr. Miller fixed me a glass of bicarbonate. I sat back down at the table and drank it while he checked my pulse.

"I should take her to my office and examine her," he said. "She's been working too hard for someone in her condition."

"What condition?" Koker put his hands on his hips and stared at me. "I think it's about time someone told me what's going on here."

Talbourne pulled down the shades and locked the door. "Show him the whip marks Cain gave her the night he and Conrad shot Wyatt Garrett in the back."

With a towel held up to cover my front, I unbuttoned my shirt. Dr. Miller lifted the back and show Sheriff Koker the scars.

"Cain did that?" Koker asked.

"Yes," I said. "He wanted me to tell him what I did with whatever it was I took from Dad's safe. Wyatt Garrett came and cut me loose, but they shot him in the back. I escaped."

"What was it you took?"

"I don't know."

"Stop playing games!"

"She's not!" My father pounded his fist on the table. "At first I thought she was playing games too, but she has amnesia from having her skull cracked open." He waved the pages I just wrote into the air. "Everything she's remembered so far is written down on pages just like these in her room. The trouble is, every time she remembers something she gets headaches. The harder she tries to remember, the worse the headaches get."

Koker ran his fingers through his hair. "Go with Dr. Miller. I'm going to your room with Talbourne to look at those other sheets you've written."

I was lying on Dr. Miller's examining table wearing nothing but my shirt and covered with a sheet when Sheriff Koker barged in without knocking. My heels were in the table stirrups and Dr. Miller was preparing to do another female exam because the cramping wouldn't stop even after putting a bag of hot sand over my abdomen. He was also concerned because my temperature was 101 degrees. He quickly pulled the sheet further over my legs and Mrs. Miller stepped to the side of the table and fanned her skirt up to shield me.

"Get out of here!" Dr. Miller yelled.

Koker ignored them and walked over to stand close to my right shoulder.

I gave him a laudanum induced smile. "Hey, how the heck are you?"

"I just wanted to tell you I've telegraphed the Nebraska state governor's office to request a denial of extradition pending an investigation into charges that Mayor Cain tortured you, was involved in murdering Wyatt, and organized the train robbery. Tomorrow, I'll have Hollings over at the newspaper office print copies of those pages you wrote. When he's finished, I'll have you sign the copies before I mail a set to the governor as evidence to support the denial of extradition. Another set of copies will go to the attorney general of Illinois." With that said, Koker left the room. Next, I heard a chair creak out in the waiting room.

Despite the laudanum Dr. Miller gave me to lessen the pain of the examination I still felt the pressure and discomfort of his instruments. Luckily the headache was so strong, I didn't care. Mrs. Miller placed a cool damp cloth on my forehead.

"Ron's almost finished," she said.

I felt him remove the speculum and heard him set it in a pan of water. The look on his face was worse than the one he gave me the last time. He placed a hand on my shoulder.

"You have an infection. If it doesn't go away, I may need to operate."

While that news slowly sank into my drug-numbed mind, Mrs. Miller helped me put my clothes back on. I stretched out on the chaise until church let out. That's when my father helped Dr. Miller carry me to my room on a stretcher. Sheriff Koker followed and sat down in the rocking chair while I slept off the effects of the laudanum.

When Lucille fed Carol at one o'clock, I didn't do much more than open my eyes and smile at her. Finally around four o'clock my head cleared enough for me to sit up.

Koker still sat there. He looked a little pink in the cheeks. "I'm sorry I walked in on you earlier. If you don't mind me asking: What type of trouble are you having?"

"The female type," I said.

His cheeks turned a deep shade of red. I looked over at the door, hoping he'd get the hint I wanted him to leave.

He started to open his mouth, but someone knocked on the door. He stood up to answer it. One of his deputies stood outside and he left.

For a while I sat thinking about what Dr. Miller said. My heart ached as much as my head. Because of Cain, I lost my parents, Paul lost his brothers, and, whether with Paul or someone else, I lost any hope of ever having children.

I stood up and walked a couple of cautious laps around the room. I felt trapped and didn't like the idea of leaving my fate in the hands of others. This whole nightmare needed to end. If only I could remember what I took from Dad's office.

I thought about the events I remembered so far and wished I could look at my writings, which Sheriff Koker borrowed. I tried looking at the postcard of Nathaniel and me to trigger another memory, but all that accomplished was increasing the strength of my headache.

I took some medicine and sat down in the rocking chair while I watched out the window. Tears fell from my cheeks as I remembered my parents' funeral again.

Chapter 17

When I arrived at the restaurant on Monday, Lucille looked furious even though I assured her the fever was gone.

"Don't even think you're going to work the whole day!"

"You sound as bad as my father and Dr. Miller." I pointed out the back door to where the deputy stood. "Besides, I doubt my ringmaster will let me stay out of my cage that long."

Her face softened. "So you're still under arrest?"

I nodded. "There's nothing more frustrating than trying to prove your innocence when you can't even remember what you're accused of doing." I tied on an apron. "Even more frustrating is trying to figure out how I could shoot Sorensen near Grand Island at the same time someone saw Muskie alive and following me two states away in Illinois."

Deputy Frost entered the kitchen after checking the other two back doors of the building. He took a seat at the kitchen table and pulled a card deck out of his shirt pocket.

"Does seem a bit far-fetched," she said. "Unless some gal was pretendin' to be you."

"Only some gal with a death wish would do something that stupid."

I grabbed a mixing bowl and stirred up flapjack batter while Chen Sue arranged the prep counter. Lucille grabbed the laundry and we started another busy day.

Around eleven, a Cavalry troop from Fort McPherson stopped in for lunch. After three weeks of eating nothing but beans and hardtack, they enjoyed what they referred to as real homespun cooking. Each of them, including the two officers, insisted on kissing me on either the hand or cheek to show gratitude for receiving a taste of what they'd missed since leaving home.

Chen Sue laughed and washed a smear of chocolate icing off my cheek. "That last one needs to trim his mustache. He shared his cake with you."

"Just as long as that's all he shared with me," I said. "Can you and Lucille handle the dishes while I take a break and eat?"

Chen Sue smiled. "Sure. After you eat, you go take nap."

"Maybe," I said. Actually, for the first time since starting this job, I felt fine. Not once during the morning did I feel any cramps or sharp pains in my abdomen.

Deputy Frost followed me into the dining room with a plate of food. As I set my plate on a table, a man sitting near the front window took one look at me and rushed out without paying.

I ran after him.

Outside, I grabbed the reins to the sorrel horse he mounted. "Get back in there and pay for your meal."

He looked puzzled, as he turned his eyes from me to Deputy Frost. The moment he saw Frost's badge, his hand reached for his Smith and Wesson.

A double click of a Colt came from behind me. "You heard the lady," Frost said.

The man's eyes shifted back to me. For a moment, I thought he wanted to say something, but then he reached for the reins. He tried to tug them from my grip.

The tug-of-war lasted until I grabbed his arm. With a swift jerk, I yanked him out of the saddle. He hit the ground and rolled. He reached for his gun in the process.

I kicked it out of his hand.

He crawled toward the gun.

I booted him in the ass. That was a mistake because the surge forward put him closer to the revolver.

His hand wrapped around the gun butt as he rolled over to face me. I was coming at him and reaching for his shirt when the gun fired. The bullet tugged at my shirtsleeve before hitting his horse in the shoulder.

All hell broke loose as the horse started bucking. People either ran or gathered in a circle to watch the show.

I grabbed the man's wrist and stomped down on his shoulder. We were wrestling for the gun until that horse butted me from behind. I went flying.

I landed, rolled, and came up shaking my head, but in possession of the gun. I aimed it toward the man, but he was too busy avoiding the sorrel's hooves.

Deputy Frost grabbed the Smith and Wesson away from me. "Get inside. I'll take care of this fella once that hoss gets done with him."

Instead of doing what he said, I watched. The horse came down on the man's left leg with a bone-shattering crunch. The man screamed.

I reached down and grabbed his collar and pulled him away from further danger.

"Thanks, Jo," he said. "Tell Nate, I'm sorry. I only went along to try to keep your dad from getting…" His eyes closed and his body went limp.

That horse was still bucking in the middle of the street when I bent down and felt the man's pulse. He was still alive, but he was losing blood fast from where a jagged bone protruded from his leg. The ground soaked up the crimson fluid like a rain starved desert. It didn't take much to figure out the bone not only broke through the skin, it also cut the artery. Frost tied a bandana around the man's leg above the knee. I doubted the man would keep his leg or even his life if Dr. Miller didn't get here fast.

The horse finally stumbled and fell to the ground. The livery owner, Hap Nichols, approached the sorrel with extreme caution. "Easy boy. Just relax."

He bent down and stroked the horse's neck. His other hand felt along the injured shoulder. The horse didn't like that much and tried to rise, but Hap forced his head back down.

"How's he doing, Hap?" someone asked.

"Bullet missed the bone near as I can tell. Once he calms down a mite more, I'll take him over to my place and tend to it."

"Send his gear over to the Sheriff's Office," Frost said, as he tightened the tourniquet on the man's leg even further. "Miss Prairie, get inside and finish your lunch. I'll keep an eye on this fella until Doc gets here."

I looked down at the man who called me 'Jo' as if he knew me well. "He owes us a buck fifty." His face didn't open any doorways to my past, but he also called Nathaniel 'Nate.' He knew my brother and me, and from what he said, he was involved in the train robbery. "I need to know his name as soon as someone finds out who he is."

I walked back into the restaurant and sat down at the table my food sat on. Lucille brought out a pan of hot water and some clean white towels.

"Where should I put this for Doc Miller to use?" she asked.

"Just set it down until he gets here," I said. It was at that point I realized my left arm hurt. I tore open the sleeve and looked at the red mark. That bullet passed so close, it left a burn. "Get a cold cloth to tie on this. Will you?"

"Sure." She set down the pan and towels and disappeared into the kitchen. When she returned, she sat next to me and tied the damp cloth around my arm. "Why didn't you just let Deputy Frost take care of that feller?"

"Because she doesn't know better." Frost walked in and sat down at my table. "How is it that fella knows you?"

I shrugged my shoulders. "I haven't figured that out yet."

My head wasn't pounding, but I felt jittery. It wasn't the first time I came close to getting killed, but it was still unnerving. For that matter, it was downright frightening.

Halfway through my meal, Chen Sue came through the door with my father.

"Doc Miller outside," she said. "He say he need restaurant for surgery. Buford say no."

I stood up and walked outside. "Take him on in there, Doc."

"Now see here," Buford said. "I'm running a restaurant, not a hospital."

"Take him into the saloon then," I said. "The bar is a good height for a surgery table."

Buford started to take a swing at me, but I grabbed his arm, yanked him over, and kneed him in the chest. "He goes in the saloon!"

All the air left his lungs and he simply nodded. After I let go of him, he leaned against the hitching rail while he sucked air back into his lungs. One of the saloon girls brought him a glass of whiskey, but he shoved it away.

At Deputy Frost's insistence, I walked back inside.

"You should get rid of her," I heard the saloon girl say.

Buford's voice was a bit hoarse. "Don't worry, Dolly. She

won't be around too much longer. I need her to close a business…"

I couldn't hear anymore because Frost pulled me back into the restaurant. "Finish your lunch," he said. "Then we're going back to your room."

My father nodded. "I'm starting to think it would be safer if you'd just stay there. There's no telling when you'll run into one of those fellows." He took hold of my left arm and pointed at the cloth tied on it. "Next time they might not miss."

Chapter 18

After the bank closed on Tuesday, Neil came to visit me. He was so excited about his promotion to head teller he bounced when he sat on the bed.

I sat in the rocking chair watching out the window. The activity in the streets outside Mrs. Chalk's was twice the norm for that time of day. People kept stopping and pointing at the boarding house. I made it a game to see how fast they would scurry away when I stared directly at them.

"Did you really kill a man?" Neil asked.

I turned my head toward him. "Where'd you hear that?"

"Hollings printed an article in a special edition paper about you this morning. Koker's pretty riled about it because Hollings used the information from those writings you made as his source." He gave me a curious look. "What's it like having amnesia?"

Hollings' article explained why I was the target of everyone's curiosity and why Sheriff Koker refused to let me go outside for any reason, not even to visit the outhouse.

Watching out the window again, I saw nine geese fly over the town on their journey south. That inner voice of flight told me I should head someplace else before Cain read that article and discovered where to find me. But then, I was also sure Buford already had told him.

"It's like stumbling around in a heavy fog," I said. "Never knowing where you're going or where you've been."

"That's why you couldn't remember reading the Bible the first night you came?"

"Yes."

He fidgeted before he looked right at me. "Miss Angela, getting that promotion means I'll get paid more. Not that money is important, but…well…there's something I want to ask you."

My heart pounded faster. "What's that?"

He stood up and reached into his pocket. What came out was a small velvet pouch. "I want to give this to you. It belonged to my mother." He pulled an emerald ring out of the pouch and knelt down in front of me. "What I mean to say is: I want you to consider becoming my wife."

A sense of dread washed over me. The last thing I wanted to do was break his heart.

"You should save it for a different girl," I said. "You're going to be an important banker someday and the last thing you need is a wife with a sketchy past to drag you into the coals." I heard the floorboards creak as the new deputy shifted his weight from one leg to the other. Koker just hired the man the day before and as yet, I didn't know his name. I glanced at the door. "Besides, if I can't figure out what I'm accused of stealing, I'll be in prison soon."

He took my hands in his and looked directly into my eyes. "I don't care. You're the one I want to marry and have children with."

The sincerity in his voice made it difficult to say 'no.' He was nice, ambitious, and even good looking, but my heart wasn't searching for him. I really didn't have the courage to tell him that his best friend already asked me and did have what my heart wanted.

"I'm not the girl you want then."

"Why not?"

I took a deep breath. "Because I can't have children."

The ring fell to the floor as he started to rise with a dazed look on his face.

The window broke an instant before I heard a rifle report. Neil fell to the floor with blood soaking through the back of his suit.

"Deputy, get the doctor!" I crouched to the floor beside Neil just as another bullet hit the back of the rocking chair. His eyes were open and I felt a pulse.

"I'm so sorry, Neil. I never should've accepted your company. After that fellow showed up yesterday, I should've known there'd be more."

He coughed up blood and passed out.

A second later, my father rushed into the room. "Is he dead?"

"Not...yet." I choked back a sob. "He...took a bullet in the lung."

"You're bleeding!"

"Where?"

He reached under the collar of my shirt. When he pulled his hand out, his fingers were covered with blood. "You've got a crease on your right shoulder."

That was twice in two days someone shot at me. The bullets were getting closer. At this rate, Cain and his men would succeed in killing me before I even knew why.

"What is...going on?" Jarvis asked as he came into the room.

"Take Angela out into the hallway away from the windows," my father said.

"What's wrong...with Neil?"

"He was shot by someone trying to kill me," I said.

Jarvis helped me up off the floor. "No one...should kill you...Miss Angela."

I walked with him out into the hallway. Dr. Miller and the deputy came up the stairs with a stretcher and I pointed inside my room.

Mr. Peabody came out of his room wearing an old cap and ball Colt Dragoon belted around his waist. For the first time since I met him, he seemed alert and aware of everything going on. "I'll protect you, Miss Prairie. You just follow me down to the basement where they can't take any more shots at you."

Mr. Peabody and Jarvis led me down the stairs, into the kitchen, and down the cellar steps. Past the shelves of preserves and bushel baskets filled with fruits and vegetables there were three rooms finished off with brick outer walls and wood framed interiors. The first was used for storing trunks belonging to the tenants, the second looked like a workshop, and the third was a bedroom.

They led me into the bedroom. Jarvis lit a lamp on the bureau. There were no windows, just paintings of landscapes hanging on the walls.

"Whose room is this?" I asked.

"It's my room...for when...the storms...scare me," Jarvis said. "Or if...I get sleepy...while working...on my carvings." He pointed to some wooden statues on the bureau. "I make animals."

He picked up a white horse and a brown goat. They were so lifelike. "This is Ruth... and Margie's goat." His cheeks turned red. "I found...a billy goat...and she's...really happy...to have...a friend."

I smiled. "I bet she is."

I sat down on the bed. It felt comfortable.

Jarvis opened a drawer and pulled out a stack of white handkerchiefs. He turned and looked at me nervously. "I should bandage...your shoulder...it's bleeding...really bad."

Mr. Peabody stood guard in the hallway while I unbuttoned my shirt and pulled my arm out of the sleeve. Even with the camisole covering my breasts, Jarvis looked like he wanted to faint. To put him a little more at ease, I buttoned my shirt over my chest as far as I could with my right arm sticking out of the neck.

I carefully felt the wound. The graze was across the muscle that curves up toward my neck. I couldn't see it, but the front of my camisole was soaked with blood, as was my shirt.

"You've never seen a girl undressed before, have you Jarvis?" I asked.

He shook his even redder-cheeked head.

His mother stepped into the room carrying a water pitcher. "Go on, Jarvis," she said. "This is women's work."

He stumbled out of the room as though he were still in shock from seeing a partially unclothed woman.

"I'm sorry," I said. "I should've waited for you."

She smiled. "I expect he'll never know what it feels like to have a woman beside him. Most girls either laugh at him or walk a wide path around him." She talked while she cleaned the blood off my shoulder. "I moved here after Geoff died, hoping it would be different in a small town like this. The only good thing is that there are fewer folks to laugh at him."

She placed a folded handkerchief over the wound and then pulled a sheet out of the bottom drawer of the bureau. She tore a strip of cloth from the sheet and wrapped it over my right shoulder and under my left armpit a couple of times before tying the bandage off in front.

"That should hold you until Doc returns," she said. "I'll bring you some dinner later."

"Do you know if they found out the other fellow's name? The

one I tangled with yesterday?"

"Matt Smith," she said. "But the sheriff figures it's a fake name."

Smith might be, but Matt wasn't. That name did bring forth a memory. Mrs. Chalk left the room and I laid down on the bed thinking about a boy who used to hang around with my brother when we were children. I was five and Nathaniel and Matthew Pace were eleven. They often went fishing together and my mother would yell at them when they tracked mud into the farmhouse.

Dad used to say Matt would never amount to much and would wind up like his lazy, drunken father. Matt was taken to an orphan's home after his father was found dead from alcohol poisoning. We never saw him again.

The room was pitch black when I woke up. "Mr. Peabody, are you still out there?"

The door opened and light from the lantern in the hallway came in as the deputy looked inside. He walked in and lit the lantern on the bureau.

"I'll go tell Mrs. Chalk you're awake and ready for dinner," he said.

"What time is it?"

"Nearly nine o'clock."

"Did they catch the man who shot through my window?"

"As far as I know, the posse is still chasing him."

I placed a hand over the bullet burn on my left arm. "Is Matt Smith conscious?"

He shook his head. "Didn't they tell you?"

"Tell me what?"

"After Doc amputated his leg, we took him over to the jail. Around one this morning, someone stood on a barrel and shot him with an arrow through the cell window. Homer yelled for help, but by the time Frost got in there, it was too late."

"Did anyone chase after the shooter?"

"Frost and McDermott trailed out after him this morning, but they lost the tracks along the South Loop River."

After the deputy left, Jarvis came back into the room. He sat down on top of a trunk against the far wall. His cheeks were still red.

"How old are you Jarvis?"

He shrugged. "Twenty...um...six."

"Do you have relatives to stay with if something ever happens to your mother?"

"No one...wants me." He stared at a painting with rolling hills and mountains in the background. "Mommy told me...I would be sent...to a sand-eh-tare-re-um...when she dies."

"I won't let that happen to you, Jarvis." I pointed to the statues on the bureau. "For now, you should try making money by selling your carvings. You also sing well enough you could play piano for tips. Then, even if I don't stay in Welcome, I'll write letters to let you know where I am and if you ever need a home, just send me a letter or telegram."

"Even if you...marry Paul...or Neil?"

"Yes. That is if you don't mind being kind of like a brother to me."

Mrs. Chalk walked in with a tray and looked at Jarvis. He left the room smiling.

"You shouldn't encourage him so," she said as she set the tray down across my lap.

"All I said is that if he ever needed a home, he could live with me like a brother."

Her eyes lit up. "You would do that for him?"

"Yes."

She smiled. "You're going to fill you life with strays and orphans."

"It's the only way I'll ever have children."

She sat on the trunk while I ate.

"Kimberly Talbourne painted these pictures for him," she said after a long silence. "Until Sara Hauser came, she was the only girl in this town who never teased him. It excited him a bit when Kimberly came into town this afternoon and filed papers for a divorce on grounds that Homer was already married when they eloped. James Talbourne took her back into his house, but then she came and asked if I had a room available." A tear trailed down her cheek. "I told her I didn't know yet."

I fought against a lump in my throat at the idea that Neil might not make it. "Did she go back home?"

"The last time I saw her, she was carrying her carpetbag toward Buford's place."

Buford's was no place for a seventeen-year-old girl.

"Let her use my room while I'm down here," I said.

It was three o'clock in the morning when Dr. Miller finally came into the basement room. I stared at one of the paintings while he trimmed up the rough edges of the wound on my shoulder and sewed it up. Every time the pain felt bad, I took a deep breath and held it.

"Is Neil still alive?" I asked once the wound was bandaged.

He nodded. "That bullet shattered a rib and splayed out as if the tip had been notched. His right lung was so shredded, there wasn't much I could do except remove half of it. His chances aren't good, but so far he's hanging on. Kimberly's up there watching him."

After he left, I changed into a gown Mrs. Chalk left while I was napping. I felt restless and walked around the room. Too many people were getting hurt and killed. Locked inside my head was the answer as to why, but the key to unlocking everything still eluded me.

Chapter 19

When Jarvis came to visit Wednesday afternoon, he laughed because I wore my green bathrobe over my flannel shirt and jeans. The basement was cold and I didn't have a coat or even a shawl. If only Koker would let me take a trip to the general store, I could buy a nice fleece lined coat and gloves. Paula was making me a cape, but she didn't expect to finish it until later in the week.

I was cold now.

Even so, my frustration with confinement to Mrs. Chalk's house didn't compare to the sad look Jarvis gave me when he stopped laughing and sat down on the trunk.

"What's wrong?" I asked.

"Judge Hayes came…a day early…and gave Kimberly…her divorce," he said. "Then he…married her…to Neil." The anger I felt toward Buford didn't compare with the ire I now felt toward Kimberly. "I thought…Neil wanted…to marry you."

With the deputy following me, I raced up to Neil's room. The curtains were drawn shut, leaving the room dark except for the lamp on the nightstand. Neil barely stirred as I sat on the edge of the bed. When I took hold of his hand, he opened his eyes further.

"What happened?" I asked.

"I don't know." Neil's voice came out in a dry whisper. "She found Ma's ring on the floor of your room and when I asked her give it back, she said she wanted to keep it." He picked up the marriage license lying on the bed beside him. "I told her I would only give it to my wife. The next thing I know, the judge is marrying us." He took a shallow breath. "I don't even remember saying 'I do' or signing this."

"You haven't consummated the marriage yet, have you?"

"Uh…no," Neil said. "At least not, unless she did it while I was asleep."

I examined the signatures on the license. Neil's looked more like a scribble. The odd thing was that Buford witnessed it.

I looked up at the deputy. "I'm going to sit here with him a spell. Go get the judge to get this marriage annulled and James Talbourne to get the ring back from Kimberly."

"Yes, Miss Prairie."

Before long, Neil fell asleep. His breathing came in labored gasps and every time he coughed the color of his skin faded to a lighter shade of pale. I freshened the damp cloth on his forehead and put my ear to his chest. It didn't sound like what was left of his right lung even worked, and his left lung struggled to do twice its workload. As my fingers lightly stroked across his chest, I felt the empty space where Dr. Miller removed the shattered rib.

That bullet was meant for me and whoever shot it didn't want me to survive if the bullet missed my heart. That didn't make sense. If Cain wanted whatever I took returned, then why try to kill me? The second bullet only grazed my shoulder, but would have splayed out just like the one Neil took in the lung if it had entered my body. The shards would have perforated my clavicle artery, the top of my right lung, and maybe even my heart and breast.

My head started to throb, so I grabbed a blanket from the footboard of Neil's bed and sat in a high-backed chair. With my feet propped on a stool, I puzzled over Kimberly's motive for marrying Neil to keep my mind off the murder attempt. No matter how pretty the ring, taking advantage of an injured, half-conscious man sounded as bad as Homer marrying Kimberly while still married to Margie. Neil was poor with nothing to leave her if he dies, so what would she gain other than the ring?

When Dr. Miller came to check on Neil, I stood up and walked around the room. The green bathrobe I wore caught Neil's attention and he followed me with his eyes.

"Ma, is that you?" he asked.

I turned and faced him. "What is it, Neil?"

"My chest hurts. I feel so…so tired…and cold."

I placed the quilt over his legs. "Is that better?"

"Some." He licked his lips. "I found Pa. I don't think he knows who I am." He took a couple of breaths. "I'm sorry."

I looked at Dr. Miller and he nodded, so I continued to respond as if I were Neil's mother. "About what?"

"You told me Pa was no good. I should've listened and not run away to find him."

A sense of empathy soaked into my emotions. We were both running away and found our fathers in this town. Mine was good and his was apparently so bad he never mentioned anything about his father until now.

"It's all right, Neil. I understand how much a young man wants to know his father. You shouldn't worry yourself about it."

An emotionally pained look filled his eyes. "But I should've been with you. I should've been by your side when you died."

I looked directly into his eyes. "It's all right, Neil. You're by my side now." The door opened and the judge arrived with Talbourne and Kimberly. "Did you want to marry Kimberly?"

The change of subject threw Neil a bit and he didn't respond immediately. The uncertainty on his face mirrored how I feel when someone asks me a question to which the amnesia prevents me from having a ready answer.

"Who's Kimberly?" He asked finally. "I want to marry Angela. She's a really nice girl, Ma. You'd like her." He coughed and his eyes searched around the room until they came to rest on Kimberly. "Is that her, Ma?"

"Yes," I said.

"Honest, Ma. I don't remember marrying her. She wanted your ring, but I wanted to give it to Angela." His hand lifted up the marriage license. "I'm sorry, Ma. It's the only thing you left me and I...I...Oh, God, Ma, I'm dying."

His eyes closed and the marriage license fell to the bed. I stared at the slight rise and fall of his chest and fought to keep my own chest from heaving.

Judge Hayes picked up the marriage license and tore it apart. "This marriage never happened." He held his hand out and Kimberly reluctantly handed over the ring.

I glared at Kimberly. "I want you out of my room. And there better not be anything missing."

"I didn't take anything," she said. "I just wanted the ring. Homer never gave me one."

When Judge Hayes placed the ring in Neil's hand, Neil opened his eyes again. He stared at it with tears in his eyes. "Thank you."

"My apologies, Mr. Jones. If I'd known, I never would've let this happen."

Talbourne dragged his daughter out into the hallway.

"I owe you another apology," Judge Hayes said. "I thought it was odd you kept calling her Angela, but she told me that was her middle name and you seemed so alert earlier."

I don't think Neil heard what Judge Hayes said. His eyes were focused on the ring and the emotional pain he went through over losing his mother without saying goodbye. He coughed and closed his eyes against the physical pain in his chest.

For a moment, I thought he wouldn't open his eyes again, but he did. "Ma, are you still there?"

I stepped closer to the bed. "Yes, Neil."

I wiped a tear from my cheek. There was a gray tint to his skin and Dr. Miller shook his head to confirm what I already knew.

"I want to marry Angela, Ma. Is that all right?"

I couldn't say anything. The knot in my throat held onto the words until Dr. Miller put his hand on my shoulder. I nodded my head. "Yes, Neil."

Judge Hayes performed a very brief ceremony and made out a handwritten declaration that the ceremony was performed with Dr. Miller as witness. This time Neil's signature was plainly written whereas mine was shaky and barely readable.

"I suggest we keep this quiet between us until this matter with Homer Drummond and Kimberly is settled," Judge Hayes said. "I'll file this the next time I come through town."

I nodded and then looked into Dr. Miller's eyes when he placed his hand on my shoulder. "Be gentle with him," he said.

Again, I nodded.

I sat on the edge of the bed, leaned over, and kissed Neil on the lips. His lips responded to mine with so much passion I felt the muscles between my legs throb as if my body anticipated more than either Neil or I could handle. Every ounce of energy left within his body went into the oral consummation of our marriage.

For a few minutes I forgot about his boy-like charm or that two men were watching. Neil was a man with a mature love for me. I felt it through his lips, the rub of his tongue against mine, and the gasp of air that left his lungs when he slipped the ring on my left hand. In his last breath he said, "I love you, Angela."

I couldn't sleep. I spent hours crying on my father's shoulder and somehow, without telling him, he knew what went on in Neil's room. His thumb brushed over the ring, as he nodded his approval.

"The judge doesn't want anyone to know until after he comes back for his next visit," I said. "I'm sorry you weren't there."

"I know, but given the circumstances, I think it was better this way." He kissed my forehead. "Now get some sleep. You've got a big day tomorrow and need your rest."

He tucked me in and left.

As hard as I tried, sleep didn't come. I knew then, without a doubt, that I didn't leave a beau behind with my other forgotten memories. My first real kiss would be forever poignant in my heart because it was shared with a dying man.

Chapter 20

I joined the others at breakfast the next morning wearing the gray dress. My eyes were bloodshot and swollen, and sitting next to Neil's empty chair did nothing to ease my sorrow.

Jarvis stared at the ring.

Everyone stared at the ring.

After a few minutes, I hid my hand in my lap the way Paul slid his into his pocket. I understood Paul now more than ever. For Jenny's last living moments, Paul pretended to be Wyatt. In a way, he married her and filled her last minutes of life with love and passion. He was now twice widowed.

Just like Paul, I pretended to be Neil's mother until the last few minutes when I gave him his heart's desire. Now I was a widow and, like Paul, wore a ring as a testament to the courage it took to make Neil's last moments in life full.

Finding courage through my feelings for Paul, I brought my hand back up to the top of the table. Neither Paul nor I needed to feel ashamed. I prayed to have a chance to tell him how proud I am of what he did for Jenny. I also prayed he would understand that I did the same thing he did for Neil.

Paula reached over and took my hand. "Is there anything we can do?"

"Neil told me he grew up with five sisters. If someone can find their addresses, I'll write and let them know what happened."

"He grew up…in Omaha," Jarvis said. "Maybe they…still…live there?"

"Paula and I are going to inventory and pack up his belongings for Judge Hayes to probate the next time he's in town," Mrs. Chalk said. "I'm sure we'll run across some letters or an address book. If not, we'll check with the Newman brothers or Paul Garrett." She turned to my father. "When is the funeral?"

"Tomorrow morning at ten," he said.

"Tell the undertaker to get him a new suit," I said. "I'll pay for it. Make sure it's a suit fit for a respectable banker. I also want him to have the best casket available and a polished marble headstone. Even if it has to be shipped in, the stone should be green." I took a deep breath to steady my nerves. I looked down at the ring and realized his mother left it to him because it was his birthstone. "His favorite color was green because he was born in May."

"I'll make sure he has the best of everything," my father said. "You just concentrate on the trial today and let me take care of tomorrow."

The deputy showed up with three other men to escort me to the courthouse. Mr. Peabody joined the parade wearing his Dragoon. Homer stared at me with that stupid grin on his face. I now doubted whether he ever loved Margie.

While searching for relatives who should know about her death, my father learned that throughout Homer and Margie's marriage, they moved to one scrub farm after another. That knowledge made me wonder how many other women he slept with along the way. By her own admission, Mrs. Chalk slept with him. Deep inside I wondered if the reason the Drummonds moved so frequently was because Homer outstayed his welcome from one town to the next.

I kept my eyes on Homer while Kimberly gave her testimony. Under my gaze, he squirmed in his seat and the grin faded to a worried frown.

A preacher from Kearney testified that he married Homer and Kimberly in February. I didn't notice when the preacher stepped down.

My head throbbed so I forced myself to stop looking at Homer.

"Miss Prairie," the prosecutor said. "Please take the stand."

I looked up. Everyone was staring at me. "Of course." I stood up and walked toward the judge's bench. My eyes caught sight of a marriage certificate lying on the corner of the prosecutor's table. The fancy scrollwork around the corners made it look like a stock certificate.

Then it hit me. My mind brought forth the image of an office. I was there late in the evening to pick up a file I needed for some work I planned to finish at home. A light shone from Dad's office. The door hung partway open. I tiptoed to my desk, so that I wouldn't disturb him. Then I heard voices.

"Why didn't you go to the authorities?" Dad asked.

"There's a lawman already involved in Cain's network," a man said. "They hired me to make the counterfeit certificates Muskie sold through your office. But this...this goes beyond bilking innocent people for a few dollars per share on worthless stocks."

There was silence for a moment. Papers shuffled. Something heavy was set on the desk.

"So this is your handiwork?" Dad asked.

I peeked through the crack between the hinge side of the office door and the doorframe. A man in a brown suit stood in front of the desk. I couldn't see what was on the desk.

"Yes. They paid me quite well to do the engravings, but I can't go through with it. I'm supposed to deliver these to the warehouse tomorrow, but I intend to be halfway across the lake to Canada before they realize I don't intend to show up."

"I don't like being dragged into this," Dad said. "I have a family to watch out for and if Cain is as ruthless as you say, I could put them in jeopardy by giving the information you've shown me to the authorities." The safe door squeaked as it was pulled open. "I'm leaving for St. Louis tomorrow, so I'll have to keep these here until I get back." The safe door clunked and snapped as it closed and latched. "I suggest you go out the back door and through the alley." He slid some papers into an envelope. "As for these, I'll drop them off at the Pinkerton agency on my way out of town. Maybe they can take care of this without Cain finding out I'm the one who turned over the evidence."

The man slipped out the back door to Dad's office. A moment later the lamp went out. I grabbed the folder I was after and waited in the dark until Dad left. Then I headed home.

"Miss Prairie, we're waiting," Judge Hayes said.

His impatience brought me back to the present. "Just a few minutes," I said. "I need to write something down real quick."

I sat at the prosecutor's table. After I wrote out everything I remembered about the man in the brown suit and drew his picture,

I handed the sheets to James Talbourne. He read what I wrote while I told the court about how I found Margie abandoned on the homestead. I showed them Margie's Bible with Homer's name in it as her husband. The prosecutor showed me a marriage license from the State of Ohio.

"Yes, I found it inside of a metal box in Margie's cedar chest along with their birth certificates and the deed to the farm," I said.

The prosecutor picked up another piece of paper. "And this is the will Mrs. Drummond wrote before she died?"

I nodded. "Yes."

He picked up the other marriage certificate. "Your honor, please note that the marriage between Homer Drummond and Kimberly Talbourne took place February 26 of this year. The will of Margaret Drummond is dated September 10."

The judge looked at the dates, as did the jury before the prosecutor asked his next questions. "When did Mrs. Drummond die?"

"Three days after she wrote the will," I said. "September 13."

"No further questions, your honor."

The defense attorney stood up. "Is it true that Angela Prairie isn't your real name and that you're actually wanted for theft and aiding and abetting an escaped criminal in the State of Illinois under the name of Josephine McDonald?"

"Yes."

"What proof do we have that Carol isn't *your* child? Or that Margie didn't die before Homer came to town last February or that you wrote the will yourself?"

"I object," the prosecutor said. "Miss Prairie isn't on trial here. She's a witness in fact that Margaret Drummond was abandoned by her husband and left to starve to death while carrying his child."

"I object," the defense attorney said. "There is no evidence that Mrs. Drummond couldn't have left the farm long before she was too weak to travel."

"So you're admitting that she was alive and abandoned?" the prosecutor asked.

"I said no such thing."

Judge Hayes pounded his gavel. "Both of you settle down before I fine you for contempt." He looked at me. "Is there evidence that Carol isn't your child?"

"Yes, your honor," I said. "Dr. Miller can attest to the fact that I'm a virgin and have never borne a child."

The room mumbled about my answer and Judge Hayes pounded his gavel. "From what you saw of the farm," he said, "was there any way that Mrs. Drummond could've left on her own before she succumbed to such poor health?"

"She was only left with the chickens, a milk cow, and a goat," I said. "After butchering the chickens and the cow to survive, the goat was the only animal left when I arrived. The only way for her to travel anywhere would've been on foot. On horseback, it took me six days to reach town. On foot and pregnant, I don't think she could've walked the ninety miles, especially if she was carrying provisions with her."

He looked at the jury. "Miss Prairie's background is immaterial to this case. We are only concerned with what happened to Mrs. Drummond, and Miss Prairie's testimony is to be taken at face value without regard to her past." He looked at the defense attorney. "Do you have any further questions?"

"Uh, no, your honor."

"You may step down," Hayes said.

I sat beside my father.

He took my hand in his.

I was tired, sad, and my head hurt. I laid my head on his shoulder and fell asleep while other citizens of Welcome testified that Homer never mentioned he was married when he came into town. The next to last witness was a farmer who testified that Margie used to quilt with his wife before she died. The farmer said Homer told him Margie also died last winter and that's why he never thought about checking on her while Homer was in town. The last witness was the teamster Paul Garrett sent to the Drummond farm to get the furnishings. He testified that the grave was freshly dug and the headstone newly engraved when he saw it.

While the jury deliberated, I was escorted to Mrs. Chalk's where I slept until suppertime. My father brought my dinner and sat on the trunk.

"Homer was sentenced to ten years in prison," he said. "He signed the homestead over to Carol, and the farmer who testified that he was their neighbor has offered to purchase it."

"Find out what the going rate per acre is for me."

"The land agent is already sending an appraiser out there." He leaned forward with his elbows on his knees. "I think you should know, Judge Hayes granted temporary custody of Carol to Ron and Catherine. He said he can't let a single woman in your circumstances adopt her. He'll review the situation again the next time he comes to town."

"Well, at least she's close by. Will I be allowed to see her?"

"One visit per day," he said. "Do you think Buford is involved with Cain and the counterfeiter you saw in Ely's office?"

"Paul did say he saw Buford with Cain and Conrad in Kearney. Whatever I stole must be the evidence that man left with Dad."

I pointed to another stack of pages on the nightstand. "I also remember overhearing some talk about Cain wanting to get Indians moved off of some land somewhere. But I don't remember where I was, who was doing the talking, or whether it came before or after overhearing the conversation in Dad's office."

He paced around the room while he read what I wrote. I used the time to eat my dinner.

"I think you're getting close to figuring this out," he said as he sat down on the edge of the bed. "This could have something to do with why Buford disappeared again."

"He has some big business deal going on and I'm guessing it's with Cain. But I don't know if he's part of the scheme or getting taken by Cain. However, I did hear him tell Dolly that he only needed me around long enough to finish a business deal."

He patted me on the knee as he leaned over and kissed me on the forehead. "You get some rest. Paula has a real nice dress for you upstairs for the funeral tomorrow. She'll help you with it in the morning."

Chapter 21

The dress Paula altered to fit me was made of dark green and black gingham wool with a black velvet yoke and cuffs. I expected her to bring the black taffeta, but she knew I didn't like wearing black or taffeta. When I told her I would suffer through wearing the black taffeta for Neil's funeral, she smiled and shook her head.

"I doubt Neil would want you wearing a widow's weeds for him," she said. "This dress is black enough and will be serviceable for a variety of occasions." She touched the ridge in my skull. "Besides, your days have already been dark enough without clouding them more by wearing something you don't like."

After I bathed and dressed, she coiled my brown hair into a bun. She placed a black beaded hat on my head with a black lace veil. Sara, Mrs. Chalk, and Paula each wore the same type of hat and we all wore dark gray capes as we exited the house with my escort of deputies.

With all of us dressed alike, the assassin would have to think twice about which one to aim at since we were roughly the same height except for Mrs. Chalk. We rode to the cemetery in a black coach provided by the undertaker. Upon exiting the coach I saw that Mrs. Talbourne, Catherine Miller, Lucille, Chen Sue, and Agnes also wore similar hats and capes.

The undertaker lifted the lid on the black walnut coffin. The plush interior of the coffin was lined in green satin with black velvet trim. Neil wore a black broadcloth suit, white ruffled silk shirt, and bowtie. Even his hair was neatly trimmed in a style that made him look prosperous and distinguished.

He looked so peaceful and much too young to die.

A photographer took a picture of him for his sisters before the lid was closed.

The Newman brothers took turns eulogizing Neil's dedicated service at the bank and how on Tuesday morning they promoted him to head teller. They praised his heroism for taking a bullet for the girl he loved and wanted to marry. Everyone looked at me as they mentioned how the two of us could've shared a bright future together.

Sweat trickled down my back when the Newman brothers stopped talking and turned the service over to me to say a few words. I felt weak in the knees as I tried to think of something meaningful to say. After a prayerful moment of silence, I lifted my head.

"I was quite flattered to receive Neil's attention when I arrived in town. He was a gentleman with a very caring personality. He was a man with ambition and the determination to succeed in his career. When I took ill, it was a great comfort to have him visit me. He read poetry and talked about his dreams. On Tuesday, he was quite excited about his new position and nervous as he knelt down to propose to me. I told him how proud I was of him and how I believed he would have a great future in the banking business." I reached up with a handkerchief to wipe my cheeks. "It took a lot of courage for him to stand up in front of the bullet that crashed through the window and then pull me to the floor with him just as the second bullet came. I owe him my life and he'll forever be in my heart."

The guilt of knowing I belonged in that coffin flooded over me and I fought hard to keep from wanting to sink to my knees. I sobbed against Paula's shoulder.

Through the tears, I heard my father read passages of scripture. When he stopped, everything became quiet. I looked up and four men were lowering the casket into the ground. I walked back to the coach with Paula, unable to endure the sight of dirt being tossed on top of Neil.

The deputy held the coach door open. When I stepped up, I lost my balance and slid back down to the ground just as a bullet whizzed over my head. The other women pushed me inside and climbed in behind me while the deputy mounted his horse to chase the shooter.

The undertaker's assistant raced the coach to the back door of Mrs. Chalk's and we rushed into the kitchen. While several armed men surrounded the house, I was sequestered into the basement again with Mr. Peabody standing outside with his Dragoon.

Jarvis came in and sat on the trunk. He looked handsome in his suit. "Are you…all right…Miss Angela?"

I patted my chest and struggled to calm my breathing. "Yes. Just a little frightened. My heart…is still racing like a horse."

He put a hand over his chest. "So…is mine." He paced around for a few minutes before he sat on the bed beside me. He pointed to the emerald ring. "You and Neil…were married…after Judge Hayes…tore up Kimberly's…marriage license…weren't you?"

"How did you know?"

His cheeks turned red. "After Kimberly…and Mr. Talbourne left …I listened…at the door." The redness deepened. "Then I looked …through the keyhole…and saw you…kiss Neil."

I patted him on the shoulder. "Then you know the marriage is a secret until the judge comes back to town?"

He smiled. "Yes. I think…Neil liked…being married…to you …and dying…in…your arms." His smile faded. "My daddy died …in Mommy's arms."

"That's part of marriage," I said. "Reverend Alms said my parents were holding each other when they were murdered. After coming so close to dying out in the wilderness, I know how sad it would be to die alone. That's why I'm glad I was with Margie when she died."

He nodded. "I don't…want to die…alone…either." He rubbed his chin and looked at me with a very serious expression on his face. "Do you think…Miss Kimberly…would marry me…if I …asked her?"

"I can't believe you'd want her after the way she tricked Neil into marrying her."

He looked down. "I know…I shouldn't…like her…anymore …but she's nice…to me…like you." His eyes roamed over the paintings. "She paints…pictures for me…and sings…with me… and reads…to me."

"Sara reads to you and teaches you how to write."

"Do you think…she would sing…with me?"

"You don't know until you ask her."

He bounced out of the room. Two hours later he came back to tell me Sara agreed to court him. I talked with him about how he shouldn't do more than hold hands. Once she gave him permission, he could kiss her *gently* on the lips. If the relationship went further, anything else would have to wait until they married. He promised to be patient and ask my father for advice anytime he wasn't sure what he should do next as the courtship progressed.

Not long after he left, my father and Mrs. Chalk visited my basement room. Both of them looked like they wanted to turn me over their knees and tan my hide.

"Who would you rather have him court, Sara or Kimberly?" I asked before either one of them found the words to scorn me.

My father threw up his hands. "I can't argue with her when she's right. You're just like your mother."

"Jarvis can't marry," Mrs. Chalk said. "He doesn't understand the responsibilities. He has no means to support a wife."

"He's a man with passions like any other man." I pointed to the carved statues. "He has talent both with carving and the piano. Sara is a teacher. They'll be fine. Besides, I already promised to keep an eye on him if anything ever happened to you."

She looked at my father. "You're right. She's impossible to argue with."

My father stepped out into the hall when Dr. Miller arrived to check whether I tore any stitches loose in my shoulder during my harried escape from the cemetery. Mrs. Chalk stayed to assist with taking off the dress and then, after the doctor left, she helped me put on a gown.

"I do wish I had more children," she said. "I've always worried about what will happen to Jarvis when I'm gone. But you're right. Even men like him need someone to love." She put her arm around my shoulder. "You've gone through a tough time, dear. I hope Paul makes it back safe and the two of you have a good life together."

I laced my fingers together and put my hands in my lap. "I haven't given him an answer. Whatever I'm tangled up in is getting too many innocent people killed. I'm afraid to put Paul or anyone else in danger the way I did Neil until it's all over." I bowed my head. "Oh, Lord, I pray no one else gets hurt."

"Me too, dear. Me too." She patted my back. "But you must remember you're not to blame. You're just another victim of an evil man."

Chapter 22

I spent the day Saturday watching Jarvis carve a statue and the evening sitting in the parlor with the drapes drawn shut. The deputy returned around eight. He tracked the shooter for a day and a half before losing the trail and racing back to Welcome. I watched him pace around the house, peeping out the drapes.

"I wish Koker would get back," he said. "I hate having the town guarded by only three deputies, especially with that gold shipment coming through on Monday."

"Gold shipment?" Mrs. Chalk asked.

"The Black Hills Mining Company is hauling it through here with a decoy going toward North Platte. The actual gold will be loaded on the train at the station north of here." He looked right at me. "Does any of that sound familiar to you, Miss Prairie?"

Everyone stared at me. I didn't even remember ever hearing of the Black Hills Mining Company.

"I thought the Black Hills were off limits to white folks," Mr. Peabody said.

"They are," the deputy said. "Unfortunately, some prospectors found gold up there and now there's trouble brewing. Supposedly, the Black Hills Mining Company wrangled a deal with the Sioux for special permission to mine one shaft providing they shared the gold with the Sioux so the Indians could use it to purchase food and supplies."

Even for someone with amnesia that deal sounded a bit made up, especially with what I remembered about how Cain wanted to get some Indians moved off their land.

"Which gold exchange are they using to sell the ore?" I asked.

The deputy shrugged. "Someplace back east."

"Must be headed for the Pennsylvania mint," I said. "Although, with Denver so close, you'd think they'd take it there."

"Either way, I don't like having Koker out of town right now," the deputy said.

"If Sheriff Koker is still chasing that shooter, he must be following a fake trail," I said. "That is, if the fellow who shot Neil is the same man you chased yesterday." I leaned back in the chair and closed my eyes. "There were nine men who held up the train. If we count Mayor Cain, Conrad, Muskie, Sorensen, Marshal Becker, Matt Pace, and the other two I saw on the road near the cow pasture, that's eight. Muskie, Sorensen, and Pace are dead, which leaves six. Becker's the one who telegraphed Sheriff Koker and sent my picture and that newspaper, so he's still in Illinois. But then there was the man who turned some sort of evidence over to Dad before the train robbery. I'm pretty sure Buford's tied up in this somehow because Paul saw him with Cain and Conrad in Kearney in September." I glanced over at the deputy. "Near as I can figure it, there's at least five men still involved."

The deputy's eyebrows rose. "That's counting Buford?"

"Yep and not counting the man who gave Dad the evidence."

"How'd that assassin find out you're here?" Mrs. Chalk asked.

"My guess is he read that newspaper article Hollings printed after typesetting those pages Angela wrote," my father said. He tossed the toothpick he was using into the fireplace. "Either that or Becker sent him." He looked at me. "Buford returned this afternoon. I'll go over and pick up your pay. Maybe I can shake out of him where he's been the past couple of days."

It was midnight before my father came down to the basement with my pay envelope. Buford even included a copy of the accounting for the week.

"What did you do to get him to give this to you?" I asked.

He grinned. "Hung around quoting scripture and singing hymns to him and his patrons until he gave in and paid you."

"Did you find out where he went?"

He shook his head. "But he did have an Omaha newspaper on his desk."

"What's important about that?"

"It was Wednesday's paper. We usually don't see an Omaha paper around here until they're at least two weeks old. He either made it to Omaha and back in two days or picked it up at one of the more active train stations within traveling distance."

"Maybe he caught the supply train and went somewhere to meet with Cain again," I suggested.

"I think that's most likely." He walked toward the door. "I'd best go get some sleep. I have work to do in the morning."

"I wish I could go in the morning. I still haven't heard one of your sermons."

"In that case, I'll give you a command performance tomorrow when I return."

After he left, I was alone in my 'cell,' which is what I started thinking of the basement room as. I turned the wick on the lamp down low and crawled into bed. My whole night was spent listening to hoof beats thundering in my mind. There were no people, just Ruth's white legs running mile after mile. She ran fast and steady with a lot of endurance until she jumped a fallen tree and we both tumbled down a hill.

The hill gave way to a cliff and I flew through the air. As I fell, I looked up at Ruth. She limped along the cliff edge, bleeding. I continued to fall. Twenty feet, thirty feet, on down I went until pine branches bent and broke beneath me. My descent slowed. My head hit a rock when I landed. I rolled down another slope and landed in a stream. I managed to stand on my feet, climbed the bank, staggered a few feet until everything went black.

My body felt numb when I woke up in the basement room. The numbness I felt was like the time I fell flat on my back after falling off the corral fence one summer. I breathed in short, shallow breaths that gradually filled my lungs with oxygen.

As my mind cleared, I realized I dreamt about the accident. I slid out of bed, lit the lamp, and wrote down what I saw in the dream. I described the terrain the best I could, but it went by so fast, all I remembered were Ruth's legs running and the fall from the cliff.

At dawn, my father brought my breakfast and I handed him the pages. After he read them, we both knew that if the pine branches hadn't slowed my fall, I'd be dead. He held me in his arms for a long time, thanking God for sparing my life.

Before leaving, he left a list of Bible scriptures for me to read.

"Have those memorized by the time I get back," he said with a wink.

*****

Early Monday morning, I left my basement room. Deputy Frost stood in the hall instead of the new deputy, who never did tell me his name. Then again, I never asked.

"Did the sheriff return yet?" I asked.

He shook his head. "William is meeting with the town council about getting temporary authority as acting sheriff and to hire more deputies."

"So, he's been around here longer than I thought?"

"Only a week," Frost said.

"For a newcomer, he sure knew a lot about the gold shipment."

"With hostilities brewing in the Black Hills, he was sent here by the governor to make sure everything went okay with loading that gold on the train. When it comes down to it, he's the one who told me about the shipment."

"What's his whole name?"

"William Pinkerton."

"Pinkerton? As in The Pinkerton National Detective Agency?"

He grinned. "Figured you'd recognize the name, coming from Chicago like you do. This job's so important his father sent his oldest son to oversee that it gets done right."

I gulped and thought about how Dad mentioned Pinkerton during the conversation in his office with the man who gave him the evidence. "I need some air."

"I could maybe let you go upstairs, but William doesn't want you going outside no matter what happens today. He says you're a key witness to a conspiracy to steal the gold. He's investigating the Black Hills Mining Company and the truth behind whether the gold has been taken with or without the Sioux's permission for over six months. He said something about your stepfather being the one who first contacted him after receiving evidence from a man who decided he didn't want anything to do with it."

"That's what I remembered Thursday. But why would Koker hold me under arrest if he knew I was a witness?"

"He doesn't know that part yet," Frost said. "William didn't tell me about it until this morning. Since Koker is still missing, William sent a couple of fellows out to track him down yesterday. We haven't heard back from them yet."

We walked upstairs to the kitchen where I sat in a dark corner while he drew the curtains and drapes closed in the rest of the downstairs.

"You can go sit in the parlor now," he said when he returned to the kitchen. "I even stoked up a nice cozy fire for you."

We both looked up as the sound of footsteps upstairs indicated Mrs. Chalk and the other residents were stirring around for the day. While everyone took turns in the washroom, I sat in the parlor and flipped through a women's fashion magazine Paula received in the mail. Sara came downstairs first and sat on the couch. She looked exceptionally shy this morning. She kept her eyes on her lap.

"Are you all right?" I asked.

Her cheeks reddened. "Last night, I told Jarvis I'd marry him."

Shocked, I looked at her with wide eyes. "That courtship sure went fast."

Her eyes met mine. "I fell in love with him soon after I came here. He's so sweet and gentle." She looked down again. "He's smarter than most folks believe. Granted, his intelligence isn't much more than that of a fifth grader, but fifth graders can be quite smart. I think it's an age when children make the bridge between childhood and starting to explore adulthood. They want to go forward in maturity without giving up the freedom to play."

"I'm sure you'll be happy together."

She looked at me again and smiled. "Thank you for telling Jarvis it was all right to court me. I would've been quite heartbroken if he asked Kimberly to marry him. He said he was always afraid to have feelings for me because I live in his mother's house and he's not supposed to be more than friends with any of us." She lowered her voice into a whisper. "I heard Kimberly went to work at Buford's Wednesday night and hasn't been home since. I saw her yesterday and she has a bruise on her cheek. I think one of the men at the saloon slapped her around."

"That's too bad. I was hoping she would make up with her folks and start over."

She leaned forward a bit. "Well, apparently, Homer wasn't the only man she slept with. I heard one of my students tell the other boys that she slept with his older brother."

There were footsteps on the stairs and she quieted again. Still, it amazed me how talkative she was for those brief minutes. Jarvis reached the bottom of the stairs and smiled.

"Do you want…to help me…milk…the cow?" he asked.

Sara stood up. "I'd love to."

They held hands and Jarvis' cheeks turned red before they disappeared down the hallway.

I was alone again until Mrs. Chalk came downstairs and invited me to join her in the kitchen while she made breakfast. I helped her make two coffee cakes with brown sugar on top. Next, I started making bread dough for supper. It felt good to work in the kitchen, and when Lucille came by to let me visit with Carol, I told her to bring the ingredients for the pies and cakes needed at the restaurant. After all, with a perfectly good stove and oven at my disposal, there was no reason I couldn't earn my daily wages right there in Mrs. Chalk's kitchen.

I spent the whole day baking and making egg noodles. Every time Lucille finished nursing Carol at the Millers' house, she brought a cart with more supplies, which she unloaded and then filled with the baked goods.

Chapter 23

At four o'clock the town turned eerily quiet. I peeked out the window, but only glimpsed some men on horseback riding past the intersection along Main Street. Deputy Frost was on the front porch and waved for me to get away from the window.

I went upstairs to the attic and peered out a small window to see what was happening. Off in the distance, I saw the cemetery.

A man knelt beside Neil's grave with his hand resting on the temporary wooden marker. Although curious about who the man was, the activity on the street drew my attention away. From my vantage point, I saw a procession of wagons move slowly through the intersection of Garrett and First Street. There were ten wagons and thirty-six armed guards on horseback.

Another movement caught my attention and I saw William Pinkerton crouched on the roof of the general store.

I slid over to one of the dormer windows, which gave me a view of the hotel tents. A tent flap flipped open and three men stepped out. Even from that distance, I recognized two of them.

I rushed downstairs as fast as I could and out onto the front porch. Deputy Frost dragged me back inside. "Are you trying to get yourself killed?"

"No," I said. "But I was looking out the attic window. Cain, Conrad, and another man are in the second tent behind the hotel."

"Are you sure?"

"Yes. I may have amnesia, but my eyesight is very good. I saw them quite plainly."

He handed me his rifle. "You stay here. I'll go tell William."

With Frost gone, I realized I was alone in the house. I rushed through each room and locked all of the doors and windows. I just finished when I heard muted voices outside.

"Are you sure you saw the deputy leave?"

"Yeah. And then I saw someone reaching through the drapes locking windows."

My muscles tensed. I considered hiding in the basement room, but that would leave me trapped with no way to escape.

A window broke in the kitchen. I levered a bullet into the rifle chamber before tiptoeing up the stairs.

Someone fumbled with the lock on the back door. The hinges squeaked as it opened.

I kept the rifle aimed at the angled gap between the staircase and the floor to Mrs. Chalk's room.

The floorboards in the downstairs hallway creaked and soon a man stepped into view. I waited.

I recognized the man from the cow pasture as the one who didn't have any qualms about killing girls. The other man, I didn't recognize. They continued creeping toward the parlor.

"She's not down here," the cow pasture man said.

"Let's try upstairs."

They turned toward the staircase and the unfamiliar man spotted me. He raised his Colt.

I fired and levered another bullet into the chamber as he fell backward into Mr. Cow-Pasture, who pushed him aside and fired three wild shots at me. The bullets shattered the plaster in the hallway wall outside the washroom.

I fired back. The bullet hit his empty holster as he ran for the front door.

He fumbled with the lock.

I shot him in the leg and started down the stairs.

He turned with his gun pointed up at me.

I fired and he fell to the floor with a bloodstain over his heart.

I collected their guns and waited.

Jarvis was the first person to jump onto the front porch and pound on the door when he found it locked.

"Miss Angela!" he yelled. "Are you...all right?"

I unlocked the door.

Jarvis stumbled in and stared at the two dead men on the floor. He shook his head and grinned at me. "Men really...ought to... know better...than to fight...with you."

A smile played upon my lips at his gentle teasing.

He dragged the two men out onto the front porch before he mopped the blood up off the floor. He just finished cleaning up the foyer when Deputy Frost returned.

I handed Frost the rifle as he came through the door. "Thanks for the loan. I couldn't get you to give me back my Colt and rifle from Koker's gun locker, could I?"

"I'll ask William about it when he gets back."

"Where'd he go this time?"

"Chasing Cain and Conrad." He took a whiff of the air. "Is something burning?"

I rushed to the kitchen and pulled the bread out of the oven. The top crust was black, but at least it didn't smoke up the house.

"I'll make biscuits for supper's bread," I said. "About all I can do with this is cut the crusts off and make bread pudding."

My father rushed into the kitchen. His arms went around me. I felt his body quiver. "Are you all right?"

"Yes, but I burnt the bread while those two yahoos tried to sneak up on me."

He laughed and kissed the top of my head.

"Careful there, Rev," Frost said. "Paul Garrett's liable to get jealous."

"He already knows," I said.

"Knows what?"

"Reverend Alms is my real father."

Frost shook his head. "Lord, this tale of yours has more twists and turns than a mountain road in New Hampshire."

"Is that where you're from?"

"Yep. Came out here where I couldn't get snowed in on a mountain top ten months out of the year." He started to walk down the hall. "Now I just get snowed in on these prairies instead."

By the time my father let go of me, Mrs. Chalk arrived and shooed us both out of her kitchen. While the undertaker tended to the bodies, I sat in the parlor and wrote out a detailed report about what happened in the house, from when I saw Cain and the others in the hotel tent to when Deputy Frost returned. Frost took the report and carried it to the sheriff's office where he retrieved my guns even though William Pinkerton was still chasing Cain.

It didn't surprise me to find out Buford had disappeared, again.

Chapter 24

"They put the gold in Paul Garrett's warehouse until the train comes," Mr. Peabody said while we sat in the parlor that evening. "I haven't seen this much excitement since I helped capture Santa Ana back in thirty-six." He looked over at me. "Did I ever tell you about that pretty little Mexican gal I met in San Jacinto? Prettiest brown eyes and red lips you ever saw. Oh my, how she could make a weary soldier happy just by smiling. Emilita was her name and she knew just how to spread her legs—"

My father cleared his throat rather loudly. "Randall, I think that's more of a story to tell the boys at the saloon, not these gentle ladies here."

"Oh, dear, yes. My apologies, ladies," Peabody said.

Jarvis threw another nervous glance at his mother. He sat on the floor, a respectable distance from Sara's feet, sanding a deer he carved earlier in the day. Every so often, he smiled at Sara. She smiled back and his cheeks turned red.

Mrs. Chalk sat in her rocking chair, tatting a lace tablecloth. In a chair next to her, Paula sewed a hem in a dress she made for Mrs. Miller.

I picked up a ball of green yarn and a crochet hook from a basket beside the chair I sat in and started chaining.

Several minutes went by when Sara asked, "What are you making?"

I looked across the room at her. "Huh?"

She pointed at the six-foot long chain coiled in my lap. "At first I thought you were making a winter blanket for Carol, but that's much too long for a baby blanket."

I looked down at my handiwork. "I think I'll make a scarf. It's getting so cold and I don't have a winter coat, scarf, or gloves. But you're right; I should make some things for Carol too."

My heart ached to hold Carol.

"I'll bring you some scraps tomorrow," Paula said. "I keep them for the ladies who quilt. They pay me fifty cents a pound."

"That sounds like a good price. Do you have patterns for baby clothes?" Realizing I asked a dumb question of a seamstress, my cheeks turned warm.

Paula laughed. "I'll bring you those, too."

"How is your shoulder doing?" Sara asked.

"It's healing all right," I said. "Dr. Miller's going to take the stitches out tomorrow. He wasn't too pleased that I worked in the kitchen today or that I shot those two men." I looked at Mrs. Chalk. "Just let me know what the repairs cost and I'll pay for the damage to your walls."

She gave me a forced smile. "I laid the bill for last week's broken window on the bed downstairs. At this rate, I'm going to get a new house one bullet hole at a time."

My eyes filled with tears. "I should move out before someone else gets hurt." I looked over at Deputy Frost who leaned against the wall next to the front door. "Maybe I should let you take me back to the jailhouse."

"Heavens no!" Mrs. Chalk said. "I have no intention of asking you to leave."

"I never should've come here." I sniffled and wiped my eyes with a handkerchief I pulled from my pocket. "Even before I started remembering things, I felt like my life was in danger. I've killed three men and it's my fault Neil is dead. I should be in that grave, not him."

"Nonsense!" Mr. Peabody said. "It isn't your time yet. Besides, you have a baby to raise and no child should be orphaned twice while so young.

"You listen here, missy, Neil was a fine young man, but he just wasn't meant to live long. Lots of boys who come out here don't live long. It's just the chance we all take in life, especially when we go out seeking adventure."

My father stood up and walked over to my chair. "Come. Let's go downstairs and talk. I really should've spent more time with you about this sooner."

I picked up the ball of yarn and followed him down to the

basement room where I cried out my guilt on his shoulder. Guilt for losing my memory and not knowing the information William Pinkerton needed to catch Cain. Guilt for not knowing what I did with the evidence I removed from Dad's safe. Guilt that Wyatt died trying to save me from being whipped. Guilt that Neil took a bullet aimed at me.

I also cried because I couldn't hold Carol. She was the only good and innocent thing in my life right now. In fact, she was the only reason I could think of to keep living.

When I ran out of guilt to confess, my father handed me a package that lay on the trunk. I didn't remember it lying there when I changed for dinner. He must've brought it down while I helped clear the table.

"I know this isn't the happiest birthday you ever had, but I bought this for you just the same," he said. "I thought maybe you could use this journal to record your memories in."

"Today's my birthday?"

He pulled his watch out of his vest pocket. "You turned twenty-three about seven minutes ago." A tear escaped his eye. "I just wish I could've shared your other twenty-two years with you."

I kissed him on the cheek before I peeled the brown paper wrapping off the journal. I ran my fingers over the soft, brown leather. The journal held four hundred pages and I started by copying all the writings and drawings I already made into it. Then I remembered more about the train robbery.

Nathaniel and I received an anonymous note about the robbery and raced to stop the train. It was held up between Chicago and Wilmington. We arrived too late to stop the robbery. The gang spotted us as they mounted their horses to make their escape. Nathaniel thought that if we split up, they would chase after him. For the most part, he was right. All but two followed him. Cain and Conrad followed me, but I lost them. That's when I headed back to Chicago and took the satchel from Dad's safe.

I was exiting the back door to the stockbrokerage when I spotted Cain at the south end of the alley. He was alone, but Marshal Becker was coming up the other end of the alley. I grabbed Ruth's reins and stepped back inside the brokerage, leading her with me. After I locked the door, I led her through to the front door. We stepped out onto the sidewalk and after I locked the door, I rode her fast through the Chicago streets and out into the country.

On horseback and playing hide and seek with Cain's men, it took four days to reach Wilmington. A herd of cattle was in the pasture when I found it necessary to hide. After that danger was over, I went to meet Nathaniel at the barn. Again, all I remembered was Conrad stepping out of the shadows and grabbing me.

As I wrote, my father sat beside me, reading over my shoulder.

Each memory brought me closer to putting the puzzle of what happened together. I knew Nathaniel could fill in some of the gaps once we found each other. For now, these random remembrances were all we had to try and catch Cain at whatever he was up to.

According to Frost, the gold was scheduled to ship out of here in three days when a special train car arrived at the station north of town. If I could only remember by then what I knew about Cain's plan, maybe William Pinkerton could put an end to this whole nightmare that started back in March.

When I ran out of memories, my father spent an hour praying for the Lord to take the burden of my guilt away. The sadness inside of me ran deep. It didn't matter how much others told me I was wrong to feel guilty, I still felt responsible.

Cain and his gang were killers and needed to be stopped. Until that happened everyone I cared about was in danger.

The room was dark when I woke up with my head resting on my father's shoulder. He slept with his head and back against the wall. We were on the bed and the springs made noise as I stood up.

"Where are you going?" he asked.

"I have to leave. I don't want anyone else to get killed because of me."

He cursed and grabbed my elbow. "You can't go anywhere."

"I must go. I'm the one Cain wants. As long as I'm here, other people will get hurt."

"Even if I need to have Frost handcuff you to this bed, you're going to stay in this house and let Pinkerton deal with Cain and the gold."

As if summoned by my father mentioning his name, Frost knocked and entered the room. Light flooded in from the hallway lamp. "Is everything all right in here?" he asked.

"Angela has it in her head she wants to leave," my father said.

Frost shook his head. "The only place she's going is over to Paul Garrett's house. He just rode in with a bullet in his leg. His nephew came here after leaving Doc's place and said Paul is asking for you, Miss Prairie."

Chapter 25

The two-bedroom house Paul lived in stood about a hundred feet behind the feed and seed warehouse. The house used to be the stage depot Jared and Wyatt ran. After Wyatt married Jenny, they built the building that now served as the stage depot and platted out the town. To serve the growing number of farmers in the area, they claimed six sites for the feed and seed. It wasn't until two years after Paul joined them that Lynn Coolidge purchased a site to build a general store. Until then, the three brothers sold merchandise from the warehouse. The Garrett brothers sold Coolidge their inventory to help him get started while he waited for his first merchandise orders to arrive from a wholesaler in Omaha.

When I arrived at the house, Ruth stood tied to the rail fence, which penned in the dormant rose bushes. From the looks of things, no one had tended the roses or other flowering plants since Jenny died. Taking a rotary push mower to the grass was about the only work Paul and Lance did to keep the yard somewhat under control.

The interior of the house wasn't in any better condition than the outside. Thick layers of dust covered anything that wasn't used regularly. Clouds of gray and white cat fur floated across the hardwood floor as I followed Lance into Paul's bedroom. Beneath the goatee and over a week's growth of beard, Paul's face appeared pale and damp with fever.

Dr. Miller looked up when my father and I entered the room. His hands were covered in blood from probing into Paul's left leg for the bullet. After wiping his sleeve across his forehead, he returned to his search.

Spidery red lines surrounded the wound, which was two inches above Paul's knee. Paul suffered from blood poisoning. The deeper

Dr. Miller probed, the more Paul's body twisted from the pain. My father and Deputy Frost stepped in to hold him down.

Lance took his father's hand. "Pa, Miss Angela is here."

Paul's eyes fluttered open. He turned his fevered head to look at me. Those eyes were filled with pain, fear, and love. He pulled Lance's hand close to his heart and then reached up with one hand to touch the boy's cheek. My heart knew the fear in his eyes came from knowing Lance almost became or still could become an orphan. The love was directed at both his son and me. Lance hugged his father and kissed him.

"Son, I really need you to step back for a moment, please," Dr. Miller said.

Lance stood against the wall. I stepped in beside him and put my arm around his shoulders.

Paul looked at us both with a pleased look on his face. "I found the spot," he said in a raspy voice, "but someone else got there first. On my way back, I ran into one of those fellows you drew from the cow pasture. He's dead, so there's one less for you to worry about."

Dr. Miller let out a sigh of relief and dropped the bloody bullet into a bowl. "If that infection doesn't look any better by noon, I'll have to take your leg off." He cleansed the wound thoroughly and then bandaged it. "I'll have to let it heal from the inside out, which means Paul will have to be careful not to do anything to make it bleed again."

My heart raced and Lance's body tense up. I gave him a hug and then knelt down on the floor to pray. My father joined me. After a minute, Lance sank down to his knees. For six hours we knelt there, praying for God's healing grace to touch Paul. I prayed so fervently, I was only partially aware of Dr. Miller coming and going throughout the morning.

Around eleven o'clock I felt as though someone watched me. I opened my eyes and saw Paul staring at the emerald ring. Tears escaped the corners of his eyes. I rose to my feet and sat down on the edge of the bed as I took his hands in mine. "Neil gave it to me just before he died."

"Neil's dead?" The pain in his eyes showed emotional loss.

I brushed the tears from his eyes and told him what happened. "Please don't be jealous that I married Neil and that he was the first man I ever kissed." My eyes went to Wyatt's ring. "I know I won't be the first girl you've ever kissed, or taken to your bed for that matter."

He reached up and touched my cheek. "Does that mean you'll marry me?"

"I'll court you," I said. "But I'm not tying myself to marriage until this whole thing with Cain is settled." I told him about the memories I recovered while he was gone. I tried to smile as I told him the next part. "You'll be pleased to know I don't have a beau waiting for me back in Chicago, which means you won't have to worry about a jealous lover coming after you with a shotgun."

He tried to laugh, but he passed out while holding my hand. I cooled off the wet cloth on his forehead and bathed his chest with cold water. His fever continued to climb, so I sent Lance to the icehouse to bring back a bucket full of ice. I dumped the ice into a pillowcase, wrapped it with towels to absorb the moisture, and set it on top of Paul's chest.

At noon, Dr. Miller removed the bandages. The red lines were more of a pink and not near as long and spidery.

"Thank God," I said.

"He's not out of the woods yet," Miller said. "This only buys him some more time for keeping this leg. If that fever doesn't break or the infection doesn't continue to recede, I'll still have to amputate before the blood poison has a chance to reach his heart or his brain."

After lunch, Dr. Miller forced me to go into Lance's room to take a nap. When I woke up at three, he removed my stitches and told me to stay in bed longer. Lance walked into the room a little after four and sat down on the foot of the bed. His cheeks were streaked with tears.

"Your father…?"

"He's fine," he said. "Doc just said he'll keep his leg." He wiped his eyes. "Are you really going to court Pa?"

"Yes."

"We could use a woman around here again. It just hasn't been the same without Aunt Jenny." He wiped his eyes again. "Not that Pa can't cook, but things always seem happier in a house when there's a woman around."

He walked out of the room. A few minutes later, I saw him

moving through the parlor with a dust rag and then a broom. I was glad to see that he knew how to clean, if not how often. Then it struck me as to why the house and yard were in such a state. Paul and Lance were now responsible for all the duties they once shared with Jared, Wyatt, and Jenny for running the businesses they own.

Guilt once again grabbed hold of me. I better deserved Paul's wrath than his love.

With Deputy Frost or another deputy always on guard at Paul's house, I moved into Lance's room and Lance slept with his father. I baked breads and pies for the restaurant, prepared our meals, cleaned the house, and nursed Paul back to health.

Each evening after the feed store closed, Lance brought the ledgers, cash box, and receipts to the house. I balanced the books and made out the deposit slip for Lance to take to the bank on his way to school the next morning.

Paul's warehouse foreman visited at lunchtime each day to update Paul on how business was going and discuss orders and contracts. It was while listening to their conversations I learned Paul owned the hotel. It didn't burn down until *after* Paul refused to sell it to Buford. After weeks of searching through the hotel's remains, Sheriff Koker couldn't find any evidence to support Paul's accusation that arson caused the fire. Thankfully, no one was hurt.

On the third day, we watched out the window as the gold was loaded back onto the wagons and hauled north to the tracks. William Pinkerton returned to town in time to oversee the exodus and then came to visit Paul. He handed Paul an envelope of money and received a receipt for the storage of the gold.

"Has Koker shown up yet?" Paul asked.

"No," William said. "I've sent telegrams to every town within a hundred miles, but no one has seen him." He pointed to Paul's injured leg. "I'm hoping he didn't wind up on the wrong end of a gunfight like you did."

Paul looked at me. "I've been doing some thinking about that. I wonder what the odds are that Koker met up with Nathaniel. There were two sets of tracks around the place Angela hid the evidence, and one of the boot heels in those marks was notched like the crack in the bottom of Koker's right boot."

My mind took a soaring leap as I remembered mailing a copy of the map to Nathaniel. I grabbed the journal and wrote down that I was in Grand Island when I mailed it to him in care of my grandmother. Coming out of the Post Office, I spotted two of the men from the train robbery and ran toward Ruth. They chased me westward until it became dark. I turned to the southwest and kept going until the terrain became too treacherous to navigate without sunlight. The next day, after spotting the two men kicking up dust, I continued riding hard and fast. I crossed the Platte River several times while trying to lose them, and each night I altered my course of travel. Finally, there was one night when they continued to chase me after dark. That was the night I fell over the cliff.

"Where was the hiding place?" I asked when I finished writing down what I remembered.

"About thirty miles east of Grand Island," Paul said. "After leaving there, I tried to figure out where you were hurt. Not knowing where to start, I headed for Homer's farm. I thought if I backtracked along the creek, I might find where you camped. On the way to Homer's, I ran into the fellow who shot me. Just before he died, he pointed at Ruth and apologized for thinking I was Nathaniel. I decided to come back home to see Doc Miller instead of heading to Kearney. That decision nearly cost me my leg or possibly my life."

William nodded. "You were closer to Kearney?"

"Yep," Paul said. "I should've gone there and then hopped a ride on the supply train when it came up this way on Saturday."

"Even if Koker is with Nathaniel, I wish he'd contact me," William said.

I shook my head. "I wish I could remember what was in that case the counterfeiter gave Dad. It had to be more than phony stock certificates for it to be so important."

Lance pointed in the direction of the train tracks. "Has anyone ever opened those crates to see if there's actually gold inside of them?" he asked. He stood leaning against the doorframe to Paul's room with his schoolbooks hugged against his chest. No one heard him come in. "Maybe we had the decoy and the real load already went to North Platte."

William Pinkerton left the house in a hurry and didn't return until after dark. He held two telegrams in his hand. The expression on his face and in his eyes looked as though he was both bemused and angry at the same time. He sat down at the dinner table with my father and me. "Both loads were fake," he said. "The Black Hills Mining Company swears they sent the real shipment here and is threatening to sue the Agency even though their own people were the ones guarding the shipments. I'm going to head up to their office in Chadron and start an investigation from that end. Angela, if you remember anything else, send me a telegram." He gave me the address of the head office in Chicago. "My father will forward the information to me."

"Do you think Koker and Nathaniel might've found out from the evidence that both loads were fake and went up there also?" I asked.

William nodded. "It's possible." He showed me another telegram. "Nathaniel was deputized as a federal marshal after he received his pardon. If he knows what you knew, then he may be several steps ahead of us. I just wish he would've coordinated his investigation with mine so we wouldn't be chasing Cain from opposite ends."

"Have you heard anything about the charges against Angela?" my father asked.

"The governor of Illinois ordered that they be dropped and a warrant was issued against all the men she's identified as being involved. When they went to arrest Becker, he was gone."

"I bet Becker's the one who shot at me," I said.

"Why?" William asked.

"He always won the ribbons for marksmanship at the county and state fairs."

William Pinkerton appeared to digest that information for a moment.

"If he mailed the photo and paper to Koker," my father said, "then he must've taken the train right afterwards to have arrived here when Neil was killed."

Nodding his head, William agreed. "He might've even been the courier who delivered the packet to Koker. I'll contact my father and have him find out if Becker bought any train tickets."

He left again and I cleaned up before going into Paul's room to let him know what we talked about. As I talked to him, I noticed that the wedding ring was gone.

"You lost enough weight while you've been ill to get that loose," I said.

Paul looked down at his hand. "Actually, it fell off. I think it's lost in the sheets."

The next morning Dr. Miller came with a pair of crutches for Paul. While the doctor taught Paul how to maneuver on the crutches in the living room, I stripped the sheets and swept under the bed. I didn't find the ring, just lots and lots of cat hair.

In the four days since I moved in to Paul's house, I never did see a cat, just the never-ending hair that floated around no matter how often I swept.

Chapter 26

Friday afternoon, I sat on Paul's couch, sewing a dress for Carol. As with cooking, I found the motion of sewing familiar. Using the patterns and scraps Paula sold to me, I made dresses, sleepers, bonnets, and booties. The dress I currently worked on was made of dark green velvet with ivory satin sleeves. I wanted Carol to wear it for Thanksgiving and Christmas, so I left plenty of growing room in it.

Paul sat in an armchair with his leg propped up on a footstool. He held the newspaper in his lap, as his eyes skimmed each page and lingered over articles that caught his interest.

He looked different without the goatee. He shaved it off earlier in the day when he gave up trying to correct the poor job I did at barbering him while he was sick. He looked five years younger without it, but still very distinguished.

Lance walked in from the kitchen with a pile of papers. "I'm done with my homework, Pa. Can I go over to Jeremy's house now?"

Paul folded the newspaper and placed it in his lap before holding out his hand. Lance handed him the homework. I learned earlier in the week that Jeremy Tate was the boy Lance stayed with while Paul was away. The two ten-year-olds were virtually inseparable and even though they saw each other at school not more than an hour ago, Lance was anxious to see Jeremy again in a less academic setting. The way Lance fidgeted while Paul read through the pages made me want to laugh.

"Go correct problems six and thirteen on your math," Paul said. "Then bring it back."

Lance took the math page and stomped off to the kitchen. He returned ten minutes later and received permission to visit his friend.

"Was your father that strict with you?" I asked.

"Worse," Paul said. "I not only had to do the assigned homework, I had to do every problem on the page before I could go anywhere."

"Except for the math, my mother is the one who checked my work," I said. "After I finished my homework, I practiced the piano for half an hour and then if my chores were done and it wasn't too late, I could go visiting."

"Who checked your math?"

"Dad. He was the stockbroker after all." I laid the baby dress down in my lap as a perfect image of Dad came into my mind. He was sitting behind his desk, reviewing my math. "I knew how to balance debits and credits by the time I was ten."

Several images of growing up flowed through my mind. Weekends and summers at the farm, Christmases in New York, and the 1871 Chicago fire when Dad and Nathaniel came home covered in soot after saving Dad's files and ledgers from the office. Without any effort, my mind opened up and gave me back everything except the missing pages from the last ten months.

I spent the remainder of the evening writing in the journal. By the time I finished, my wrist ached.

Before going to bed, I handed the journal to Paul. It felt good to know who I was before the amnesia and that my accident didn't completely wipe out my past. What amazed me more was how the memories returned without a headache.

It was almost eleven o'clock when Paul knocked on the bedroom door. When I opened the door, he stood there, leaning on the crutches, with the journal pressed between his elbow and the right crutch. I took the journal from him and smiled.

"You're a beautiful woman, Angela."

He leaned over and kissed me. A spontaneous sensation gave me goose bumps. In a confused state of emotion, I felt nervous and scared, yet anxious and wanting. I curled one hand around his neck. His hands took hold of my waist and the belt to my robe came undone. I started to move in closer…then the kitchen door opened and closed.

"Paul, it's Deputy Frost. Jeremy Tate and your boy are both missing."

Paul almost fell as he released his hold on my lips and turned on the crutches in his rush toward the kitchen. I tied my robe and followed.

Frost and my father sat at the kitchen table studying a map.

The deputy pointed to an area five miles south of town. "There's an old Indian camp here where the schoolboys like to hunt for arrowheads and other trinkets left behind by the Pawnee. We should ride down there tonight to see if that's where they went. If they aren't there, we'll have to try to pick up their trail first thing in the morning."

Paul sat down at the table. "What happened?"

"George Tate says the boys went out to the barn after supper to check on the animals," Frost said. "When they didn't come back right away, he thought they climbed up in the loft to play on the hay bales. He went out there around nine to call them in and send Lance home, but they were gone. So were two of his horses."

"We checked with all the other boys in town and no one's seen them," my father said. "We're hoping that with it being a Friday night, they might've decided to see if that old Indian story about the white buffalo that roams the plains on a full moon is true."

Paul shook his head. "Lance would never take off like that without telling me, and Jeremy never goes out of calling distance of his house without his big brother along."

My father stood up. "Even so, we'll go check that campground before the moon goes down. You stay here in case Lance comes home."

"Let Deputy McDermott know if the boys show up," Frost said as he and my father walked out the back door.

Paul refused to sleep until he knew Lance was safe, so I put a pot of coffee on to boil. My every instinct told me something bad had happened to those boys. My biggest fear came that their disappearance was connected to the gold, the evidence, and me.

Paul hobbled from one window to another while we waited. At midnight, he left the house and searched through his warehouse. Another cloud of cat hair blew across the floor when he returned. I watched the hair float around until it settled into a corner.

"Paul, where's the cat?"

He laughed as he sat down in the armchair and propped his leg up. His face was pale and his leg was swollen beneath his trousers.

"Haven't seen that fur ball since Jenny died. She's around here somewhere though. I found a nest of kittens in the warehouse loft." He pulled the wedding ring out of his pocket. "This was there with them. She must've picked it up and carried it off the other night."

He lifted the lid to a wooden box on the end table and placed the ring inside.

"What are you going to do with it?"

He shook his head. "Wyatt and Jenny never had any kids to give it to." He closed the lid and looked at me. "If you'll marry me, I could have it remade into a ring for you."

"I'd like that." I gave him a teasing smile. "That is *if* I decide to marry you."

We sat in silence for over an hour while he read the Bible. When he started to fidget like he wanted to start roaming the house again, I shoved him back into the chair.

"Sit. I'll go get you some coffee."

It was well after two o'clock when two horses approached the house. I opened the door when my father knocked. He and Deputy Frost entered and sat down by the fire to thaw out.

"They weren't there," Frost said. "We did find Crow Chaser and he's agreed to come in the morning to track those horses."

The paternal pain in Paul's eyes showed how much he wanted to go with them. I felt the same way. But like him, I was trapped inside the house. If it wasn't for Lucille coming each day to let me play with Carol and to bring the hotel, restaurant, and saloon receipts as well as the supplies I needed to bake food for the restaurant, I'd go crazy.

I knelt beside Paul's chair and took his hand in mine. His eyes looked into mine with love and acknowledgement that I understood how helpless he felt.

My father looked from Paul to me. "I probably ought to go get a few things and stay here tonight, seeing as how you don't have Lance around to chaperone you two. Lord knows there's enough rumors floating around about you two living together without adding a night of being completely alone to the gossip."

Paul's eyes shot toward my father. "Is it really that bad?"

My father nodded. "If it wasn't for Lance's presence, folks knowing that you're convalescing, and the guards standing outside, I'd probably have to shotgun you two into matrimony to keep things from getting completely out of hand."

My lips tingled in memory of the kiss Paul and I shared earlier and how tempted I was to let him go further than touching my lips. Although neither of us was in the right physical condition to handle complete intimacy, the exploration of mouth and body with hands might have dispelled the rumor that I hate men.

"I can assure you, sir, that I haven't done more than kiss her," Paul said.

My father gave us a thoughtful look. "Keep that up and you'll be having a double wedding with Jarvis and Sara."

"So he told Mrs. Chalk about their engagement?" I asked.

"Yes. You'd be amazed at how confident he's become since starting his relationship with Sara. He's worked a deal with Coolidge at the general store to sell his carvings on consignment and he's playing piano at the restaurant."

"There isn't a piano in the restaurant," I said.

"He rolls the saloon piano in and plays during dinner," my father said. "The patrons give him tips and when the dinner crowd is gone, he rolls the piano back into the saloon." He wrapped his arm around me. "Both Emma and I appreciate what you've done for Jarvis. You definitely inherited Melinda's compassion and talent for helping others."

I gave Paul and my father each a kiss on the cheek before I then went to bed. I heard the men talking for a long time.

Hearing that Jarvis was making his own way in the world warmed my heart. It felt good to know I helped encourage him.

Before falling asleep, I prayed for Lance and Jeremy's safety. I prayed for Paul. His life was filled with so much tragedy with losing his wife, two brothers, Jenny, and now his friend, Neil. The last thing he needed was to lose his son.

Chapter 27

I stayed busy on Saturday with baking and sewing. Paul left the house to take care of his customers and to watch for the posse's return. After lunch, he tried to climb up onto a horse without much success. Thankfully, Dr. Miller was close at hand when he fell. The deputy on duty helped Dr. Miller drag Paul back into the house.

Doctor Miller sent me to the kitchen for a pan of hot water. He must have expected the task to take longer than it did because when I walked into the bedroom, my eyes caught a clear view of Paul's manhood before Doc covered Paul's midsection with a towel. My pulse quickened and my cheeks felt as red as the blood seeping from Paul's wound. I set the wash pan on the nightstand and scurried from the room.

A few minutes later, Dr. Miller came out of Paul's bedroom and pointed to the dining room. "I need you to clear the table off so that I can examine you. I brought my instruments for that with me. Of course, we'll have to trust Paul to stay in his room while you're indisposed."

No such luck with keeping Paul in bed. He hobbled in on the crutches while I lay covered by a sheet with my feet resting on the backs of two chairs and my knees spread open. He sat next to my shoulder and held my hand during the exam. It didn't hurt near as much as it did the previous two times, but it was still plenty uncomfortable.

"You're improving," Miller said as he pressed on my abdomen. "I hate to admit it, but I think the lighter work you've been doing since being under confinement is actually helping you."

"How long before it will be safe to marry her and consummate the vows?" Paul asked.

Dr. Miller removed the speculum, placed it in a pan of water, and leaned back in the chair. "Given that she's allowed you to be here during this exam, I suspect she's contemplating that herself."

I nodded. "It's been on my mind most of the day." I lowered my legs. My eyes focused on the emerald ring. "I wish I could get over the guilt that I'm involved in what caused the death of your brothers and Neil. He said you were his best friend."

Paul reached over and stroked my cheek. "Actually, you might say he was sort of my brother-in-law. Rose was his twin sister. He came here in June for Jenny's funeral. When he decided to stay in Welcome, I helped him get that job at the bank."

"Did he ever tell you who his father was?" I asked.

"No." Paul rubbed his thumb across the emerald ring. "He never even mentioned to me that he was in love with you."

Dr. Miller finished cleaning his instruments and dried them. "In answer to your question, she needs to wait at least until after Christmas. When you do get married you'll have to take it slow with her, one step at a time."

"Lucille said I would need a man who's willing to just use his hands," I said.

Miller looked at me with a mixed expression of shock and agreement on his face. "That would be a first step. Although I'll deny I ever suggested such a thing, you two might consider doing a little of that between now and the first of the year." He put the instruments in his bag. "Just remember, if you want to get custody of Carol, you better make sure no one finds out."

Paul shook his head and stood up. He grabbed the crutches. "I already got anxious once in my life and wound up in trouble. Even if it means taking things slow and easy after getting married, I'm going to do things right this time." He looked down into my eyes. "I love you, Angela, and I don't want to take a chance that we'll lose Carol." He placed the backs of his fingers against my temple. "As for that guilt you're carrying around, I already said I don't blame you. Cain is the one responsible for their deaths, not you."

Paul followed Dr. Miller into the kitchen and shut the door so I could get dressed in private. I dropped the sheet to the floor and put my hands over my abdomen. I did want to marry Paul, but I also wanted to give him children.

One I could do, the other I couldn't.

There are stories in the Bible about how women let their husbands have children through their handmaidens. Would I have the courage to let another woman carry a child for Paul? The idea of letting Paul sleep with another woman was out of the question, but maybe, just maybe, there was another way. After I finished dressing, I went into the kitchen and sat down at the table with Paul and Dr. Miller. I took Paul's hand in mine.

"I do want to marry you," I said. "But first we have to find Lance." I looked at Dr. Miller and wondered how he would react to my suggestion. "Then after a couple of years, I would like you to help us have a child or two."

Both men stared at me.

"How would he do that?" Paul asked.

"The same way ranchers artificially inseminate their cattle," I said. "We'd have to find a woman willing to allow Doc to inject your seed inside her womb and carry the child for us."

Dr. Miller pointed a finger at me. "You, young lady, are going to get yourself in real trouble one of these days." He stood up and grabbed his bag and hat. "But I guess you could always blame it on that head wound of yours. There's not a person in town who doesn't think you aren't right in the head, and doing a stunt like that would surely prove it."

Paul and I were alone after he left. We kissed and kept our hands in all the proper places although we both wanted more.

When we stopped kissing to catch our breaths, he placed a hand over my stomach. "If you can't carry my children, then I'm satisfied with what I have."

A tear escaped and slid down my cheek. "Then we'll pray that I'll at least give you one."

He bent over and dried my tears with his lips. His fingers parted the hair away from the scar on my head and he placed several kisses along its length. The kisses trailed across my ear, the thin scar along my jaw, and finally met up with my lips again.

My body heat rose as I reached out to unbutton his shirt...

A knock on the front door separated the kiss. I went to answer it, but felt a sudden rush of anxiety as I reached for the knob. My hand stopped. I stood to one side.

"Who's there?" I asked.

"Deputy McDermott, there's a letter here for you."

I opened the door and allowed the deputy inside. He handed me the envelope, which didn't have anything written on the outside except my birth name.

"Where'd this come from?"

"I found it on the desk at the sheriff's office when I went to pick up a rifle for standing guard duty this evening."

Paul limped to the door without his crutches and took the envelope from my hands. He ripped it open and his face turned pale as he read the letter. "Cain has Lance and Jeremy. If you don't ride out to the location on the map he's enclosed and turn yourself over to him, he's going to kill them both."

I looked at McDermott. "Go saddle Ruth for me."

"You can't go!" Paul protested.

I peered deep into his eyes. "Enough people have died because of me. Maybe if I meet Cain face to face, I'll remember the rest of what I forgot."

"He'll kill you...and the boys," Paul said.

McDermott nodded. "He's right. If you go, nothing will keep him from killing those boys. I'll send Whitney to track down the posse and show Frost this letter. Don't try going anywhere until we can sit down and hash this out somehow that will keep anyone else from getting hurt."

Paul strapped on his gun and put on his hat.

"Where are you going?" I asked.

"To the telegraph office to send a message to Pinkerton. I'll be back in a few minutes. Stay away from the doors and windows until I return."

I went to the kitchen and brought him the crutches. He only took one for his left side.

He was gone more than a few minutes. During his absence, I fretted that he might try to meet up with Cain himself. I fixed dinner to occupy my mind and just when I figured he was gone long enough for my fears to be right, Paul returned.

We ate in silence, unsure of what to say. Lance was kidnapped because of me, his brothers and Neil were dead because of me, and he almost died because of me. More than ever I felt the need to leave, but there were too many people involved now. Given Cain's determination, my leaving might get just as many people hurt as my staying.

Paula arrived a little before eight o'clock with a carpetbag in hand. "I'm your chaperone tonight. Emma decided we should take turns since your father's out with the posse. I do hope he gets back in time to give his sermon tomorrow. Sundays just wouldn't be the same if he wasn't here to preach God's word."

I smiled. "I have yet to hear one of his sermons."

She placed a hand on my arm. "He really is wonderful. The Lord speaks through him like no other preacher I've ever heard."

"And to think I was scare of him when I first came."

She laughed. "So was I when he arrived, but once I heard him preach, I knew he loved the Lord because all his gruffness melts away when he talks about faith and following God's word."

It felt comforting to have Paula sleep beside me that night, not that I slept much. Even with the sleep he lost the night before, I heard Paul limping around the house.

At the sound of my father's voice, I picked up the clock on the nightstand. Holding it at just the right angle to the moonlight, I made out that the hands read 3:43. I slid out of bed and put my robe on.

My father was standing in front of the fireplace thawing out when I stepped into the parlor. Silhouetted by the firelight, I noticed how much Nathaniel looked like him in profile.

"Did you find anything?" I asked.

"Crow Catcher is watching their camp. The boys are still alive and don't appear to be harmed in any way. After everyone gets some sleep, we're going to meet at the Sheriff's Office and work out a plan to get them back."

"I'll go with you," I said.

"You'll stay here," Paul said.

"I'm the one they want, the one they're going to be looking for. If they're watching me ride toward them, the posse might be able to sneak up behind and grab the boys."

My father shook his head. "It's too dangerous for you and the boys."

"Maybe, but it's the only way. I have to go and do what Cain says."

Chapter 28

On Sunday, November 8, while the church bell rang, Paul picked up the reins and drove a covered wagon north out of town. I sat next to him, wearing an oversized coat, which hid the Peacemaker tucked behind my belt. Beneath Paul's coat, in a shoulder holster, he also carried a gun. Two rifles were strapped to the underside of the wagon seat and several boxes of shells were hidden in the toolbox under our feet.

The only part of Cain's instructions that we obeyed was the route and destination.

It was our hope Cain would accept that, as Lance's father, Paul refused to stay home and because of the leg wound, we needed to take a wagon instead of horses.

The back of the wagon was loaded with blankets, cooking equipment, bandages, clothes, and enough food to last three weeks. Everyone agreed Cain planned to play games by making us travel to a more distant location. He intended to get us out in the open to make sure no one followed. Once convinced, he would leave instructions for the next trek of our journey.

Paul left the crutches behind, but did accept bringing a cane Mr. Peabody loaned to him. The cane was actually a .44-40 single shot rifle. The thick oak shaft concealed the barrel while the silver plated handle shaped like a horse's head provided the chamber, trigger, and hammer. When twisted to the left, the chamber opened from under the horse's mane. The empty cartridge ejected, so that a new load could be put in into the chamber. Twisting the head fully to the right dropped a hidden trigger. Like the Colt, the rifle was a double action mechanism. With one pull of the trigger, it cocked the hammer, which was disguised as the ears, and let it fall onto the firing pin. To keep the barrel free of debris, a leather cover, which the bullet could easily pass through when fired, was held onto the bottom of the shaft by a brass ring.

It took six practice shots using blanks inside the warehouse for Paul to master using the cane rifle left-handed and only two shots to shoot the cane gun with his right hand.

After church let out, my father planned to join the posse at the McGregor farm west of town. Deputy Frost already waited there with twelve men whom he led out of town at four in the morning. They planned to travel a parallel route to ours and once they knew where the boys were located, the posse would split up to surround Cain and his men.

Ruth was already taking a parallel route to ours with Michael Drake who, dressed like a Kiowa brave, took her out of town before sunup. In reality, Michael's father was a Kiowa warrior whose tribe lived in northern Texas. His mother, a mulatto slave who ran away from New Orleans, was captured by his father while crossing the Red River. Two Black Horses married his captive and took her home to his village where Michael was born a year later. When Michael was seven, his father was killed in a battle against the Apache, which wiped out most of the village. Those who weren't taken captive left the village to join other Kiowa bands. Without a husband to provide for her and her son, his mother headed north toward Canada, where she could live free without the fear of capture by runaway slave catchers.

While crossing Nebraska Territory she met Christopher Drake, a white man, who was abandoned by his wagon train because he took ill. She nursed Christopher back to health and after getting married, they homesteaded in Nebraska in what was then a fairly unsettled region.

Because part of Michael's mission was to keep Ruth close at hand, but out of sight, he rubbed her fur with dye made from walnut oil. The dye gave most of her fur a rich brown color. The coarser hair of her mane and tail turned caramel in color. Whenever he could do so without Cain's men spotting him, Michael kept us in sight. At the very least, he planned to stay close enough to hear gun shots. If the need for his assistance came about, his sudden appearance would give us an edge in a fight.

Although I didn't expect to be able to see Ruth, my eyes still searched for her as we traveled. Paul smiled at me.

"She's out there keeping an eye on you like always."

I laughed. "She is more of a mother hen than a horse."

He touched his leg. "I know. I never would've made it back home without her."

I laid my head on his shoulder. "Do you have any idea who we could convince to carry a child for us?"

Paul choked on the air he breathed. "You're serious about that, aren't you?"

I nodded. "You deserve to have children, Paul."

"Like I said before, we'll have Lance and Carol."

My eyes felt watery, so I dropped the idea for the moment. Maybe he was right. I should forget about my maternal instincts to provide him with children and be satisfied that I was giving him an adopted daughter.

"Carol will need to attend a school for the deaf," I said.

"I know." He sounded relieved that I changed the subject. "I mailed some letters to inquire which schools are the best and what the fees are. I also ordered a sign language book, so that we can start learning how to teach her to speak with her hands."

The water in my eyes escaped as I straightened up and looked into his eyes. "When did you do that?"

"The day after Doc found out she was deaf." He reached up and wiped the tears from my cheeks. "I love you, Angela. I was certain of that the day we met. Loving you is all I need to love Carol as my own."

I leaned in toward him again and laid my head back on his shoulder. "I love you, too."

His arm reached around my back. "In that case, once we get Lance back, let's get married and be content as a happy family of four."

We crossed the railroad tracks and headed out across the prairie. We passed farms and small ranches until we entered unsettled land. The road ended and by dark we made our camp where Cain's instructions told me to wait.

After dinner, I changed the bandages on Paul's leg while he laid on his bedroll with his pants and underwear lowered below his knees and a towel pulled over his waist. My heart thudded when I saw how much the wound bled from his climbing in and out of the wagon.

"You need to be more careful."

He breathed deeply as I rinsed the raw opening with warm water and alcohol. "Is torture another one of those hidden talents you keep discovering?" he asked.

"Just Amazonian instinct, I think."

"Huh?"

"Neil thought I might be descended from the Amazon women he read about in a book."

Paul laid back with his hands behind his head. "I'll miss Neil. He always managed to find some of the most interesting books to read. Lance always liked listening to him read out loud." He rose up on his elbows. "Did Lance go to the funeral?"

I fought a guilty twinge while I finished bandaging his leg. An image of Lance dressed in his best Sunday suit standing with the Tates went through my mind. "Yes. He looked very handsome." I blinked to keep from crying. "I'm not sure because the cemetery was so far away, but I thought I saw Buford kneeling next to Neil's grave Monday while I was in the attic watching the wagons."

He shook his head. "That's just about as odd as him witnessing the marriage between Neil and Kimberly. I'd sure like to know what the connection is and whether it has anything to do with what Cain and Buford are up to with that gold."

I wiped my eyes. "I don't think Neil had anything to do with the gold."

"Neither do I."

He spoke so softly, I turned my attention away from his leg. "You're not upset that I married him, are you?"

He sat up completely and put his hands around my face. "I know better than anyone why you did it, and knowing that you had the courage to make Neil's last moments on earth happy makes me love you all the more."

He gave me a quick, yet emotionally charged kiss that made my skin tingle and my breath catch. When he released me, I almost tipped over from light-headedness.

He grabbed my arm to steady me. "Are you all right?"

I nodded. "Yeah. I'd best fix dinner before I pass out from starvation."

While I cooked, Paul pulled his long underwear and pants back up while keeping the blanket pulled over him. I laughed at how he tried to preserve as much modesty as possible considering how we had both already seen more of each other than what was proper. My cheeks didn't even warm up this time. I loved him and needed to take care of him, that's all there was to it. There was nothing to get embarrassed about, especially not here in the middle of nowhere with who knows how many men watching us from Cain's gang and the posse.

After Paul fell asleep, I climbed up in an elm tree to keep watch. Far off to the north, I spotted a campfire. My best guess put it at eight miles away. We traveled about twelve miles before making camp, which meant Cain moved his camp farther out than where it was last night. With any luck, Crow Catcher was still watching the boys or at least close enough to rescue them should their lives become further endangered.

Just before dawn, an arrow sailed into camp with a note and two locks of hair tied to it. The dark brown tuft of hair belonged to Lance and the strawberry blond to Jeremy. Paul untied the note while I climbed back into the tree and tried to spot the archer. It was still too dark to see anything, but I heard hoof beats heading to the north.

The archer was most likely the same one who shot Matt Pace in his cell. The arrow was too straight, too perfect to be handmade. The metal tip also confirmed that it was machine made. The man certainly wasn't an Indian. Even a city girl like me knew that.

I climbed down and joined Paul.

"They want us to head northwest from here toward Box Butte, which is on the way to Chadron near the Niobrara River."

I rubbed my head while I looked it up on the map. "That's over a hundred miles away."

He pointed to the limbs and sticks lying on the ground under the tree. "Best collect what firewood we can. There's going to be stretches where there won't be any trees or water."

I wrapped my arms around his waist and placed my head against his chest. "I'm so sorry. This is all my fault."

He placed his hands on both sides of my head and tilted my face upward. "I wish you would get it through that thick, cracked skull of yours that you are not to blame for any of this."

"But I never should've come to Welcome. If I had just stayed away from people—"

"Carol would be dead and most likely, you would be too. That man who shot me was looking for either you or Nathaniel. Sooner or later he would've come across your trail and ambushed you the way he did me." I wanted to say that I should be dead, but he placed his fingers over my lips. "Maybe they won't make us go that far. Maybe they're just trying to make sure we're not being followed and that we didn't bring weapons. We'll have to make our own bows and arrows, so that they won't see or hear us using the guns to catch game."

After breakfast, I climbed up the tree again. I scanned the area. Nothing moved out on the prairie except a herd of deer and Ruth, which meant Michael was close by. She stood by a creek without bridle or saddle. To all appearances she was a stray or wild horse.

I climbed down and gathered the firewood while Paul limped down to the creek to fish up our lunch for later and fill the canteens. He also left a copy of our instructions hidden beneath a rock for Michael or the posse to find once they felt it was safe to approach.

By the time Paul returned with a string of six trout, I was finished loading every scrap of loose wood I could find into the wagon. He drove while I cleaned and gutted the fish. To keep from having to make a noon camp, I made a small fire inside one of the Dutch ovens we packed. I fried up two fish and smoked the rest by setting another Dutch oven upside down and slightly askew over the top of the one I made the fire in.

On the third day, I tried and failed to shoot a rabbit with the bow Paul made. I ran to retrieve the arrow and on the way back to the wagon, I almost stepped on a rattlesnake hiding in the grass. I jabbed the arrow down its throat when it lunged and then bashed its head with a rock.

Hearing a thud followed by a cursed oath, I ran back to the wagon because Paul fell while trying to get down fast enough to come rescue me. Blood soaked through his trousers, so while the snake cooked I tended to his wound.

Midway through the fifth afternoon, Paul made a rather uncomfortable looking bed on the woodpile in the back of the wagon and fell asleep while I drove. He kept denying it, but I knew his leg bothered him. The low-grade fever he fought didn't help. Before sundown, I scraped a supply of willow bark from a tree and boiled some fever-reducing tea.

What I saw when I changed his bandages didn't look good. The wound was infected and it looked like gangrene had started to set in. I rolled over a rotted log by the creek bank and found a nest of maggots. I picked up three of them and placed them on top of the wound. They automatically began eating away at the dead gangrenous looking tissue around the opening.

Showing a great deal of trust in me, Paul did his best not to squirm. "Where'd you learn that from?" he asked.

"Mom served as a nurse in an Army hospital during the war. I remembered her telling Granma how the doctors used maggots to clean out decaying wounds."

He bit at his lower lip. "Just as long as that's all they do. I don't want them deciding to take up permanent residence inside my leg."

While Paul watched the maggots squirm in and out of his wound, I boiled all of his clothes to kill off anything that could infect the wound further. I also washed out an empty bean can and collected a supply of maggots, rotted wood, and dirt to keep just in case I needed to put Paul through another night or more of having his leg eaten upon.

In the morning, I placed the maggots from his leg in the can and flushed out the wound with alcohol before wrapping it with a double layer of bandages. His clothes were still damp, so I strung some rope between the ribs of the covered wagon to hang his laundry from while we traveled.

He used the time I spent inside the wagon to belt a towel between his legs like a loincloth and wrap a blanket around his waist. When I climbed down from the wagon, I did my best not to laugh at his attire. From his expression, I felt sure my eyes betrayed my mirth as well as my admiration of his chest and shoulder muscles. Paul Garrett was one well-proportioned man with contours that attested to his strength, which came from years of lifting heavy grain sacks.

"I sure hope no one's watching this through a pair of field glasses," he said, pointing at my jeans and then his blanket skirt. "Something's a bit backwards in our attire here."

At least he kept a sense of humor about it.

"It will be our secret," I said before kissing him. "Ours, Cain's men, and the posse's."

He didn't exactly laugh, but he did react when I traced the contours of his muscles with my fingers. I kissed a bruise he received when he fell. The scent of his skin spoke to my feminine senses and desires.

"Easy there," he said, pushing me gently to arm's length. "Don't forget your father's riding with that posse. I have every intention of keeping my word about doing things right with you."

The breath I took was long and deep. "Grandpa always said it was dangerous around the farm when the mares were in heat. I think I'm starting to understand why."

"Providing your father doesn't get any ideas of turning me into a gelding, we might be able to find out what goes on between mares and stallions someday, but not now."

While he drove the wagon, I walked a parallel path and scouted for game. Shortly before noon, I shot a rabbit with the bow and arrow. As soon as it was cooked and Paul changed into dry clothes, we left our noon camp and ate while we traveled.

Our next camp was chosen for us. A half-hour before sundown, we found two arrows sticking out of the ground in a crisscross pattern. The notes attached were written by the boys.

The first one read: *"Dear Pa – You're supposed to stay with the wagon. – Lance"*

The second said: *"Dear Mr. Garrett – Miss Prairie is to walk north from here. – Jeremy"*

Chapter 29

The wind turned bitterly cold that night. There were no trees to climb, which made it impossible to spot Cain's camp. After dark, I walked to the highest point available. During the climb, the wind cut into my face and blurred my eyes. It didn't matter which direction I looked, I couldn't spot the yellow glow of a campfire. Not even that of the posse.

As I walked back toward camp, I saw Ruth about a half mile away in a buffalo wallow. She was chewing on the tall grass. Occasionally, she lifted her head, looked around, and then went back to eating.

"Did you see anything?" Paul asked when I returned.

He sat by our fire, cleaning his wound with hot water and alcohol.

"Nothing."

I climbed into the wagon and grabbed the gun belt Paul normally wore around his waist.

"What are you doing?" he asked.

"It's going to be more difficult to keep my Colt hidden without the wagon to hide in when I change clothes, so I'm going to strap this to Ruth's neck. Michael will remove it during the day and put it back on her at night."

He shook his head. "I'm not letting you go."

I took a deep breath. "I have to. They'll kill the boys for sure if I don't." I slid the belt under my coat. "Keep an eye out for anyone spying on us until I return."

He wanted to protest, but he knew the dangers of crossing Cain as well as I did, so he kept quiet and returned his focus to tending his wound. Thinking more about that wound made my stomach quiver. The hole was three times as big as it was before the gangrene. That made Paul more attentive with taking care of it better. He not only wanted to keep his leg, but he also didn't want to go through the jitters of having the maggots eat on him again.

Finding those maggots was just pure luck. Luck that until today, the warm weather held. Luck that there was a nest of them under the log. Luck that I even knew how they would eat the rotting flesh in Paul's leg without touching the healthy tissue.

I prayed he could keep the wound infection-free until he returned home where Dr. Miller would treat it properly. Even without medical training, I knew Paul needed to have skin grafted from someplace on his body like his butt cheek to cover the hole.

Ruth walked toward me when I entered the buffalo wallow. I gave her a hug and strapped the belt on her before sliding my Peacemaker into the holster and pulling the loop up over the hammer.

"What's going on?"

I spun around as my father showed himself from behind a boulder. "I'm to walk north and Paul's supposed to stay with the wagon." I began collecting buffalo chips for our campfire, so that Paul could conserve the remaining wood. "I couldn't spot their camp, but they've been keeping a camp about eight miles north of us each night."

"I'll tell Frost," he said. "Maybe it's time we split up the posse and send a few men to travel around toward the east and then north."

I looked up at the clouds gathering in the last purple light of evening and nodded. "Looks like there's a storm brewing, which means Cain's men will want to stay under cover. That means they won't likely see any movement."

My father pointed toward the camp and as he talked I heard the struggle between the minister and the father within him. "I've been watching you tend to that wound of his and I saw the way you were groping him the other day when he was dressed in nothing but a blanket. Is there anything else going on between you two that I should know about?"

"No, Poppa. Paul's determined to wait until we get married."

He squatted down behind the boulder. "Even so, I should marry you two as soon as possible. Even with the posse keeping an eye on you, I doubt too many folks will believe nothing unseemly is going on between you two."

"I guess it's a good thing we've been sleeping out in the open so you can put your own mind at rest."

"That only helps when I'm not watching him lie there half naked in front of you. Or when I see you sharing the same blankets on cold nights."

"Well, at least you know I'm incapable of—"

He made a downward slashing motion with his arm. "Ah, get back to camp before I learn more about you than I already do. Lord knows I've already learned that you aren't the sweet innocent angel Melinda always claimed you were."

"One does what one must to survive."

I heard him suck in a deep breath as I bent down for another buffalo chip, then I heard him crying. "What's wrong?"

"My father said that same thing after he failed to rob a bank when I was twelve." His voice was so soft, I strained to hear him. "He asked me to wait with the horses while he went inside to withdraw some money. A few minutes later I heard gunfire from inside the bank. I ran inside and he died in my arms after saying the exact same words you just did. He'd been out of work for seven months and Mom was ill. Even though I didn't know he was going to rob the bank, I spent a year in a correctional home for boys for holding the horses. Mom died while I was there. When I came out, I went to live with my aunt in Wilmington. That's when I met Melinda. Loving her gave me a reason to overcome what happened to my parents." He was quiet for a moment and I almost walked over to him. "You'd best get back. They'll wonder why you've been gone so long if you don't return soon."

I carried six buffalo chips back to camp and set them beside the fire. Paul was dressed and standing by the wagon, staring off towards the north. He held another note in his hand.

"What's that?"

"I had a visitor while you were gone. They want me to chase the horses off in the morning. I'll be stranded with the wagon."

"Chase them south. Poppa and the posse will find them and keep them for you."

"Was he down there?"

"Yes." I stirred the rabbit stew he started while I was gone. "They'll send half the posse north tonight to search for Cain's camp. I'm sure Michael will keep watch on me, which means once you join up with the posse, you can concentrate on circling around and finding the boys while Cain's watchdogs keep me in sight."

His only response was to point up at the clouds. "It'll rain tonight. We should make our bed in the wagon."

"So much for waiting to get married until January," I said with a smile.

"What do you mean by that?"

While we ate I told him about my conversation with my father. "I guess getting in trouble with the law kind of runs in my family whether we're actually committing a crime or not," I said.

Paul gave me a sarcastic grin. "Well, at least your father still speaks to you. Mine hasn't even written since he kicked me out. I can only imagine what he'll say when he finds out Jared and Wyatt died because of the same trouble that brought you into my life."

I took a deep breath and tried to ignore the returning stab of guilt. "Do you ever try to talk to him?"

"Every time I go to Omaha." His sad eyes stared into the fire. "He just slams the door in my face. I write my folks several times a year and send a new picture of Lance every time I get a chance to have one taken. The least he could do is acknowledge his only grandchild."

I wiped away a stray tear from his face. "What makes your father so stubborn?"

He made a fist and slammed it into the palm of his other hand. "He's a fire and brimstone preacher man." He reached for his cup and downed the coffee in three gulps. "Be thankful your father teaches the forgiveness of Christ and not the condemnation of sinners like mine does."

I looked up at the clouds gathering. "He sure won't be happy about our sleeping arrangements tonight, but I don't think he'll throw any stones."

I spent the night listening to the rain hit the wagon tarp. Paul's arms stayed wrapped around my waist as we shared the blankets and each other's body heat. I knew from the heavy sighs he made every so often that he was awake, most likely doing what I was doing, thinking about tomorrow.

"If I free the boys and they return without me," I said, "take them on home to safety."

He remained silent, but pulled me closer. So close that I felt his want and desire through the backside of my pants. An anticipatory throbbing started between my legs and I considered telling him that it was all right to touch me. But then his hand slid down inside my pants and pressed against my abdomen. I gasped at the pain the pressure caused and prayed that the infection wasn't back again.

"You're not ready yet." He pulled his hand out. "We'll wait."

I rolled around to face him. "You read my mind?"

"Just thinking the same thing you were, I reckon." He kissed me. "Must come from us both being preacher's kids. Be careful out there, I want you back in one piece."

Our lips melded together until exhaustion allowed us to sleep.

Chapter 30

When daylight came, it made strange patterns on the wagon top. I slid out the back and almost lost my footing on the ice-covered ground. The prairie was an endless sea of crystal-covered grass. My eyes scanned the glassy fragility surrounding our camp. Every so often the sunlight hit the ice just right to create tiny rainbows, which bridged out from one blade of grass to another. It looked beautiful in the sunlight.

But as beautiful as it was to behold, it was cold and slippery. My breath came out in wispy clouds, and I tucked the ends of the green scarf I made down into the collar of my coat and slid on my new leather gloves that were still stiff and clumsy.

I walked to the south side of the wagon where the horses took shelter and peeled ice off their backs. Once freed from their icy armor, they shook out their manes and tails, showering me with ice. Paul laughed as he brushed ice fragments off my hat.

"It's a good thing we still have a small supply of dry wood inside the wagon," he said. "I really should've asked you to collect more buffalo chips and put them under the wagon last night."

"I'll go get some now to dry out next to the fire."

I walked off, slipping and sliding as I headed toward the buffalo wallow. He watched for a moment, but when I looked over my shoulder he turned and pulled a shovel from the wagon. I watched for a few minutes as he broke up the ice around the campsite.

Not having much time, I returned to my task. All the way to the wallow, I listened to him tossing the ice to the camp's edge. Each shovel full landed with a crackling crash.

Ruth was gone from the wallow, but I found a note my father left.

Angela Josephine Prairie! I can only pray you two behaved yourselves last night in that wagon. Whether you did or not, you will most definitely be married as soon as we get the boys back safely. – Your Father.

I laughed and showed it to Paul when I returned with an armload of frozen, ice-caked buffalo chips.

"I hope that means we have his blessing," Paul said.

"I think it does." I stared at the buffalo wallow. "It must be rough being a father and a minister, especially having lived through the torments he went through when he was younger."

"Do you wish you'd known him sooner?"

My fingers instinctively reached into my hair and felt the ridge. "In many ways I'm getting to know my father and stepfather at the same time. The life I had before the accident doesn't feel any more real to me than a dream I've awakened from."

"What about all those memories you wrote down?"

I looked into his eyes. "I never should've left the journal at your house. What if I remember something more during this ordeal?"

He leaned over and kissed me. "You'll write it down when we get back."

I made three trips back and forth to the wallow while Paul cleared the ice from around the camp, cooked breakfast, and made me a pack of provisions to sling over my shoulder. After breakfast, I carried two more loads of buffalo chips while he chipped the ice off the ones I already carried into camp. It was my hope to leave him enough fuel to last until the ice in the grass melted and it was safer for him to walk over with his injured leg to get more.

It was eight o'clock when I finally picked up my pack and bedroll and faced northward to begin walking. Paul walked about fifty feet with me, but even with Mr. Peabody's cane rifle it was difficult for him on his bad leg.

"You'd best go back and chase off the horses," I said, pointing to where a man sat on a horse a mile away to the northwest. "They're going to watch you, so don't take any chances that'll give them ideas about coming over and shooting you."

For a minute his lips took possession of mine with such a branding heat I thought for sure the icy world around us would melt. But when he lifted his head and hugged me, the crystal sea was still there and so was the man on the hill.

"Be sure you follow your own advice." Torment filled his eyes.

"I'll be back," I said, only halfway believing it. "We have two kids to raise after all."

The wind blew crisp and caused my eyes to water as I walked northward. I turned around after a mile. Paul still stood there, watching me. After the second mile, I couldn't see him past the rise and fall of the land, but in my heart knew he still stood there. Watching. Hoping. Scared we would never see each other again. I knew because I felt the same way.

I looked to where the horseman still watched from the hill. The sunlight glinted off his field glass lenses and out of spite I stuck my tongue out at him.

For several miles I plodded through ice-covered grass, which crackled and crunched beneath my half-frozen feet. At noon, I stopped and ate jerky and crackers. To conserve water in my canteen, I sucked the ice off the blades of grass.

An hour before dark, I found a pile of dry wood marking the campsite Cain chose for me. I halfway expected to see an arrow sticking out of the ground, but there wasn't and in some ways that worried me. I don't know why, but it did.

Something else worried me. Looking around, I didn't see one bush, rock, or tumbleweed to hide behind to answer the call of nature. After walking all day without stopping for such needs, my insides were aching for relief. If I didn't do something soon, I would wet and mess my pants like I did those first few days after the accident. The last thing I wanted to do was to bare my rear end in front of Cain's men.

Thinking about that possibility, the image of Conrad's scarred face taunting me when Cain whipped me sprang into my head. In all likelihood, he was the one watching and waiting to get his joys through a pair of field glasses. The only solution I came up with as I prepared to settle into camp was to take the ground tarp from my bedroll and drape it around me while I squatted. Sure enough, while I took a position several feet downwind from camp, I saw the setting sun reflect off something on a hill a half-mile east of my location. I lifted a hand and waved, hoping Michael would see me and check out the trail of whoever was gawking at me.

While I ate a plate of beans, I dried out my boots and socks beside the fire. In addition to my feet being red and blistered, my left shoulder ached from carrying the pack all day. I was unable to use my right shoulder to distribute the weight because the graze wound still felt tender. Most irritating was that, even with the scarf pulled up over my chin and nose, my throat felt sore from breathing the crisp air. Basically, it came down to feeling down right miserable and not having anyone here to comfort me like Ruth did after my accident. I didn't like feeling lonely, especially after spending the last several days in such close company with Paul. I missed him and Carol and Lance and my father and…

Not long after I started out in the morning, I used an arrow Paul packed to stab a fish in a creek. I think the fish was already half frozen to death anyway because it didn't even swish its tail to get away when I bent down to aim at it through the thin crust of ice on the water's surface. I carried that fish a good distance before I found a tree with broken branches lying on the ground around it that I could burn to make my lunch camp. I stayed in that camp long enough to eat, change to a dry pair of socks, and climb the tree to see if I could spot anyone moving about. The only movement was a coyote chasing down a rabbit.

Once again, I found a campsite prepared for me that night. This time a note attached to the arrow told me to start walking west. My hike followed a river, which allowed me to have a ready supply of water. That was a good thing because the ice on the grass was gone and the water in my canteen didn't usually thaw out until it sat by my campfire for at least half an hour.

I started coughing on the fourth day. My body ached from the cold and I didn't like the sight of my feet. They were so covered with sores from broken blisters I wasn't even sure they resembled feet. Out of four pairs of socks, I wore two and washed two each day. I didn't wear two pairs at once, but rather changed socks halfway through the day when I stopped for lunch. So far the sores were free from infection, but it was on this fourth day of walking that I ran out of the bandages Paul packed for me.

Around four o'clock, I felt my forehead. It was warm, so I stopped at a willow tree and skinned some bark off of it. The hot tea felt good and I stayed by that tree for two days until the fever went away.

When I woke up on the third morning after finding the willow tree, Conrad sat in my camp. The boys were tied up and sitting on either side of him. Their faces were bruised and they shivered because they weren't wearing coats.

"You should've kept going," he said. "You would've been at the cabin by now."

"I'm sick. I needed the willow bark to break the fever."

Not one fragment of concern showed on his scarred face. He rubbed his crooked nose. What my father said about Nathaniel beating him half to death that night in the barn came to mind. From the looks of things, Nathaniel used more than just his fists to defend my honor.

"Where are the plates?" he asked.

"I don't know what you're talking about." I sat up. My head hurt and I still felt achy. "I can't even remember why you're chasing me."

"Yes, well, amnesia can be a strange ailment." He leaned forward and put another branch on the fire. "What *do* you remember?"

I reached for a pair of clean, dry socks hanging beside the fire.

"You read the Welcome Gazette, didn't you?"

"Yes, but that was four weeks ago. I was hoping you'd remember more by now."

I shrugged and pulled on my socks and boots. "Only stuff that happened before this nightmare started." Jeremy sneezed. Snot ran down his lip and onto the bandana that gagged his mouth. "It's November, why haven't you given the boys coats to wear?"

"They won't be needing them where they're going." The sound of a horse's hooves echoing through the morning caught his attention. "That should be Lietz getting back from taking care of your lover."

A sick, angry feeling filled my chest as I sprang to my feet and kicked the fire into his face. His arms went up to shield his eyes from the embers and I pounced on him. The boys rolled to either side as I wrestled with Conrad. I scratched three parallel stripes down his face and grabbed for his gun.

His hand clamped around my wrist so hard, I thought my bones would break. His other hand balled up into a fist and punched me in the stomach.

I gasped at the breath-stealing pain. My fingers tried to ball into a fist, but they were entangled with his hand and the gun. The result was that the gun went off.

He screamed as the bullet went into his knee.

I freed my hands. As I tried to stand up, I fought against the sharp pain that still raged in my abdomen. Air slowly returned to my lungs and I made another attempt to grab his gun.

He let go of his knee and drew the weapon.

I dove to the right as he fired.

His arm swung in my direction and I rolled the other way. The bullet he fired whizzed past my ear.

That's when Ruth ran out of the brush and charged at Conrad. His attempt to change his aim toward her stopped in a scream as her hooves knocked against his skull and crushed his ribs. I heard bones break and when Ruth turned around to make another pass, I held my hand up to stop her.

Conrad's body lay twisted with his neck at an odd angle.

"He's dead, girl," I said as I rose to my feet. I staggered toward her. "Easy, girl."

She came to me and I stroked her neck while I listened to the early morning sounds. The dye in her hair was growing out and the white fur was a half-inch long beneath the brown. Over all, between the brown and white hair and her winter coat thickening, she looked like a very scruffy horse.

After listening for a full minute, I felt confident no one heard the gunshots or Conrad's scream. Even so, I transferred the gun belt from Ruth's neck to my waist.

I untied the boys and removed their gags. "Where's their camp?"

"About twenty miles west," Lance said. "There's a cabin with a bunch of beer kegs stored in it."

Something clicked in my memory. "Blue Mountain kegs?"

"Yeah. How'd you know?"

"I saw it on some invoices in Buford's office."

The boys shivered, so I stripped Conrad's clothes off of him. Lance put on the coat and Jeremy pulled the flannel shirt, vest, and pants on over his own clothing. Lance strapped on Conrad's gun belt and picked his gun up off the ground. I found Conrad's horse and Jeremy dug out two more shirts from the bedroll to put on. He also wrapped the blanket around his shoulders.

We ate a quick breakfast of hardtack and jerky. After putting out the campfire, I lifted the boys up onto Ruth's back before I mounted Conrad's buckskin. Worried about Paul, I headed back toward the last campsite we shared together by traveling in a diagonal path from the one I walked.

Once during the day, we hid behind some boulders from three men searching for us. My heart nearly stopped when Jeremy choked on a stifled sneeze. The sound startled a rabbit, but luckily Cain's men didn't take notice.

I pulled Conrad's Winchester from the scabbard and handed it to Jeremy. "Do you know how to use this?"

He nodded. "Pa and I go hunting one weekend a month."

"Good. If we have to separate, you two keep heading southeast and go home. Most likely, these men will chase me. But if they do chase you, shoot to kill."

"How will we find our way home?" Jeremy asked.

"Don't worry about getting lost. Ruth will get you there."

"She's a pretty smart horse, isn't she?" Lance asked.

"Yes. She was trained by a Blackfoot who owns a farm next to my grandmother's place."

Lance put his hand on Conrad's gun. "Do you think that Lietz fellow killed Pa?"

I tried not to let the sick feeling in my chest say 'yes.' "Your pa has two rifles, a six-gun, a cane gun, and plenty of ammunition. If Lietz attacked him, he would've put up a good fight."

He smiled. "Pa's good with a gun. Never saw him miss more than one shot out of six."

I gave him a hug and helped him back up onto Ruth. We traveled until dark and burned some buffalo chips. The boys curled up together in Conrad's bedroll while I kept watch. Climbing to the top of a hill, I looked for signs of other camps. I spotted two. One was a good distance to the southeast and another a mile to the northeast. The one to the southeast was probably the posse. The one northeast would be Cain's men and they were just a bit too close for comfort.

Chapter 31

I spent most of the night watching the campfires and praying for Paul. I also wondered where Michael Drake went after sending Ruth into my camp. Was he still out there keeping an eye on the boys and me? Or did he go join up with the posse? Two of my biggest questions were: Who was Lietz? And did he attack Paul like Conrad said?

Not knowing what went on outside the immediate world around me bothered my sense of security. The important thing was the boys were safe. And so, keeping us safe and finding our way back to Welcome was the extent of my immediate world.

I didn't know what day it was or how far I traveled. On a clear night like this, I roughly told time by the position of the Big Dipper and during the day by the sun. The Blackfoot who trained Ruth taught me those things. Only he called it the Big Bear. His name was John Six-Toes.

It was four in the morning when I woke the boys. I showed them where to find the camp I thought belonged to the posse. "Head straight that way, but stay to the lowlands and hide anytime you see or hear anyone coming."

"What are you going to do?" Lance asked.

Jeremy sneezed as I helped him up on Ruth's back.

"I'm going to ambush that camp to the north. I'll run off their horses and then catch up with you." Jeremy sneezed again. "I'll also try to grab another coat for Jeremy."

He smiled. "I'd like that."

I left our campfire burning and walked ahead of the buckskin as I made my way toward the camp. The moon was gone from the sky, but even in the dark, I spotted the silhouette of a man. He paced just out of the firelight. I ground hitched the buckskin twenty yards out and snuck up on the camp just the way John Six-Toes taught me.

With the arrow Paul packed for me held in my hand, I approached the guard from behind. His spurs jingled and his soft whistling of a lively saloon tune overpowered the swishing sound my legs made brushing against the tall, dry grass. I was three feet behind him when he turned.

As his hand reached for his gun, I surged forward and stabbed the arrow through his throat, choking off his cry for help. Blood squirted over my coat sleeve from his severed jugular vein. With my other hand, I grabbed his gun and stuffed it in my coat pocket. He was dead before he hit the ground.

Unfortunately, I didn't get a chance to take his coat because two other men were in the camp. They stirred and reached for their guns. I pulled mine and shot it as I ran toward their horses. When it emptied, I holstered it and pulled the guard's gun. During my trek toward the horses, I approached an empty bedroll. I dove into a somersault, rolled, and came to my feet holding the blanket, which I tossed over my shoulder.

One man was bleeding from his shoulder; the other rushed at me with his gun drawn. I fired at him and he rolled to the ground.

I reached the horses and pulled their ground hitching pins. One horse was hobbled, so I pulled the strap out away from its leg and shot through the leather close to its hoof. That started the horse to prancing. The man with the wounded shoulder shot at me. His bullet missed, but nicked the ear of the horse I just freed. The horse reared up with a wild scream and led the other two in an all-out run to the southeast.

My mission was accomplished, so I ran for the buckskin. As I rode away, I headed southeast, herding the other three horses ahead of me. When daylight came, I stopped and tied the horses together with Conrad's rope. It was noon before I caught up with the boys. They each chose a horse, and Jeremy made a poncho out of the blanket I grabbed. I also gave him the spare Colt I took from the guard and put the Winchester back in the scabbard.

The boys kept staring at the blood on my coat, so I washed it out the best I could when we came upon a small trickle of a stream.

"Did you have to kill many of them?" Jeremy asked.

"One," I said. "Another one is wounded. I'm not sure about the third. He rolled after I shot at him, but I didn't stick around long enough to know whether I hit him."

"I don't think I would've stayed either," Lance said.

Jeremy shot a rabbit midway through the afternoon and we stopped long enough to cook it. After eating a late lunch, we continued on until dark.

The boys curled up together. Jeremy only sneezed once during the night and so far he didn't have a fever. I still worried about him getting sick. The night was cold and a freezing mist greeted us the next morning until the sun came out. For breakfast, we ate what was left of the rabbit and shared one piece of hardtack that I found in Conrad's saddlebags.

I took a few minutes to search through those saddlebags. All I found were a coffee pot, a set of dishes, a box of ammunition, a map, a couple of towels, and Conrad's shaving gear. While none of us needed to shave, we did use the shaving soap to wash with and the razor made a good knife.

Throughout most of the morning, I let the boys keep an eye on where we were going while I studied the map. I located the position of the cabin and from there, made a good guess at our current position, which was roughly seventy-five miles from Welcome if you didn't count having to skirt around hills and find water crossings. There were lines drawn on the map showing the paths the fake loads of gold traveled and a third path that went through the cabin.

"How many kegs were in the cabin?" I asked.

Lance squinted and cocked his head in a thoughtful manner. "About four dozen five-gallon and two dozen ten-gallon ones. Outside, there were twelve wagons and twenty-four teams. Cain also had thirty-seven men camping out in the barn plus the horses to go with them."

"Do you think he has the gold?"

"That's my guess. Several men were guarding a shack behind the barn. A few of the men looked familiar from when the fake load came through town. I figured they must've gone to the cabin after the shipment was found to be fake."

"That's pretty good guessing. My guess is Cain's going to haul it out in the beer kegs." I looked at the map again. "Looks like he plans to take it to Grand Island and load it on a train."

"What plates is Cain wanting you to give back?" Jeremy asked.

Plates? I forgot about Conrad asking about the plates. If they were trying to steal gold from the Black Hills, it didn't make sense for Cain to have counterfeiting plates.

"Did you see any of the gold?" I asked.

Lance shook his head. "No, but they kept arguing about needing die plates before they could process the ore and ship it. Some of the men kept saying they should just load the gold and get out of there before either the Pinkertons or the Sioux caught up with them."

"Maybe what I stole were the die plates for minting the gold into coins," I said.

"How would turning the gold into coins help them?" Jeremy asked.

"If the gold ore is minted, they can circulate the coins to purchase property or exchange for money." I folded the map and stuffed it in my coat pocket. "Plus, if they mix the gold with a cheaper metal, they can make gold eagles that aren't worth their face value. The plates won't do them much good though."

"Why not?" Lance asked.

"I sabotaged the engravings on the dies."

His eyes widened. "You remembered?"

"That part of it." I grinned at him. "The government needs the plates for evidence, but to make them useless, I carved them up a bit before I buried them."

Jeremy's head jerked downward as he sneezed and a bullet flew over his head. I looked over my shoulder just as the rifle report echoed. Seven men chased us.

"Let's run!"

I drew the Winchester and let the boys race ahead while I fired at the horsemen. A hat flew off one man's head and they separated. Our horses ran with Ruth leading the way. She seemed to know where she was going, so we followed.

Four miles went by before we reached a pond with a cluster of four boulders beside it. The coals left from a campfire were behind the boulders, so I figured Michael must have camped there with Ruth during the journey north. Seven cottonwoods grew near the pond and we were able to collect firewood and build barricades in a half circle behind the boulders by stacking up some of the larger pieces of deadfall.

Lance clubbed a hole in the ice on the pond and filled the coffee pot with water while I made a rope corral to hold the horses. Meanwhile, Jeremy continued to gather firewood. Our activities ceased when bullets started flying into camp.

"Keep an eye on our backside," I said as I settled in between a couple of boulders. "I'll hold them off with the rifle. Don't shoot unless you know you have a clear shot."

"Yes, Ma."

I jerked my head around to look at Lance. He smiled at me.

"Well, you will be my ma once we get Pa, you, and your pa together again."

It warmed my heart to know Lance wanted me for his mother as much as I wanted him for a son. My need to race back to Welcome increased with the anxiousness spurred on by knowing Paul, Lance, Carol, and I would be a family. I thought about Granma and whether she was still alive to come to the wedding and about Nathaniel. He should be there too.

A bullet ricocheted off the boulder to my left and I searched for the source. A man rode down a hill and I took aim at his chest. He fell from his horse an eye blink after I pulled the trigger. He rolled a couple of times, came to his feet, and dove behind a bush. I briefly saw a red stain on his shirt.

Scanning the area around our camp, I counted six men plus the one behind the bush. We were sorely outnumbered, but if we didn't waste any shots I figured we could hold our own. The question was whether we should stay here or try to escape after the sun went down.

A shadow fell across one of the boulders, so I turned and shot at a man trying to ride up on us from the west. After his body fell from the horse, Jeremy ran out and grabbed the reins. He made quick work of unsaddling the horse before putting it in the corral.

I glared at him after taking a shot at another gunman. "That was foolhardy! Your pa wants you back home alive, not shot full of holes."

He dragged the saddle into our stronghold. "Sorry. I thought he might have some grub."

He nestled into a protected spot and dug through the saddlebags. Sure enough, he came up with three cans of beans, two cans of peaches, a bag of jerky, coffee, and a tin full of crackers.

He handed us each a piece of jerky and a cracker before putting the coffee on to boil. We also now possessed three sets of dishes, a third bedroll, and two more boxes of ammunition.

Jeremy stood the saddle on end and stuffed it between two boulders to create a little more protection from stray bullets. At the age of ten, he had already developed the ability to come up with problem solving ideas and the ability to act on his instincts.

Throughout the afternoon, I kept the gunmen under cover while the boys continued to crawl on the ground to drag over wood to build up our defenses and add to our fuel supply. Jeremy dug a trough along one edge of the rope corral and lined it with rocks. He then made several trips back and forth from the pond with one of the coffee pots to fill the trough with water for the horses.

I watched as the man behind the bush started to crawl out. I fired and he ducked back behind it. Another man tried to use the distraction to move closer. I shot him in the leg.

One by one their horses edged up to the pond, looking for water. Lance caught one and put it in the corral. He stripped the saddle off and, after removing the bedroll and saddlebags, shoved it into another gap between the boulders.

The saddlebags yielded two more cans of beans, hardtack, and a bag of dried apple slices. Whoever owned the horse already pulled his ammunition supply out, but we now possessed another ground tarp and two blankets from the bedroll.

"We're going to need to watch carefully tonight," I said. "They'll try to sneak up on us in the dark. Be wary of what the horses do. They'll hear noises long before we do."

Jeremy pointed at the twigs scattered around under the trees. "We could toss a bunch of those around out there and we'd hear them snap when those fellers stepped on them."

I grinned at him. "You can just go ahead and keep up that smart thinking of yours, partner." I pointed to the frozen pond. "While you're at it, toss rocks on the ice to break it up. That way they can't sneak up on us by walking across the pond."

That idea started a contest between the boys to see who could break the biggest hole in the ice. Lance won when he heaved a rock the size of my head into the center and created a hole the size of a wagon wheel.

"Guess you win first watch tonight," I said. "Wake me up if

you hear anything. Jeremy should spell you at midnight and then wake me up at four."

"I don't have a watch," Lance said.

I pointed at the moon. "When it gets above the trees, it'll be midnight. When it gets to the horizon, it'll be four."

"What if it clouds over?" Jeremy asked.

"Just wake me if you get sleepy."

I snuggled down behind a pile of branches, which helped block the wind. My body warmed beneath the blankets and I soon fell asleep. It was a light sleep that allowed me to be aware of when the boys changed guard. Lance snuggled up to me and we shared three blankets while keeping each other warm. It wasn't quite the same warmth I received from snuggling up with Paul, but the mother and son closeness more than made up for the difference in sleeping partners.

Some time later my ears became alert to the horses milling around in the corral. I slid from the blankets just as a twig snapped northwest of the boulders. I grabbed the Winchester and tiptoed toward the last boulder. Jeremy was already there with his Colt aimed at a shadow. Hearing another movement, I looked over my shoulder. Lance was settling in behind the saddle wedged between the two boulders closest to the pond. I saw something move from the direction he watched. He fired.

"Oomph!" The man's shadow disappeared as he fell to the ground.

Jeremy fired and a string of curses erupted from his target.

I swung around the edge of the boulder and a man holding a hand to his rear end searched for something in the grass. He found his gun and started to raise it.

I fired. His hat went flying and he fell to the ground. I ran up beside his body and grabbed his gun and coat.

Lance fired again, so I rushed back into our stronghold, tossed the coat to Jeremy, and squatted down behind the boulder to Lance's left.

"What's out there?" I asked.

"Varmints." Lance pulled the trigger again and a man limped off toward the north.

I peered over the boulder. The first man he shot crawled in the same direction the other man went. That meant out of seven, there were three wounded and two dead. We were still outnumbered, but the odds had improved.

I ordered the boys back to their bedrolls while I kept watch. An hour before sunup, I sent them out to cut grass for the horses. Two more horses were close enough to catch, so they brought them into camp, stripped off the saddles, and put them in the corral. With the new ropes at our disposal, I enlarged the corral while Jeremy refilled the water trough.

Sunlight showed clouds moving in and by midmorning it started to snow. The large flakes covered the ground fast. I prayed it wouldn't turn into a blizzard. Just in case, Lance lassoed some tree branches and with all three of us tugging on the rope, we broke off enough limbs to make a tent-sized lean-to, which we covered with one of the ground tarps.

After lunch, Lance lassoed a tree limb stump. I climbed up the rope high enough to see what was moving around on the prairie. I located the gunmen's camp. They were hunkered down in some bushes a half-mile to the northeast.

I also spotted the body of the man I shot off the horse.

"Lance, Jeremy," I said, pointing to the body. "Go get that one's gun and ammo."

I kept an eye out while they approached the body slowly. They rolled the man over.

"Is he dead?" I asked.

"Yeah," Lance said.

They removed the man's gunbelt, coat, and hat. Lance unbuttoned the vest and removed a watch and wallet. I watched him open the watch. After staring at it for a minute or so, he wiped his eyes and then walked up to the tree I sat in.

"This is Uncle Jared's watch. That fellow must be the one who killed and robbed him."

I climbed down the tree and wrapped my arms around him. Paul wasn't the only one who suffered the loss of losing Jared, Wyatt, and Jenny. Lance's heart also broke.

His arms held tight around my waist as he cried with his head buried against my chest.

One by one the original nine train robbers were paying the penalty for killing five innocent people for one man's greed. I doubted we would catch all of Cain's current gang. That was

William Pinkerton's job with the help of Nathaniel, Sheriff Koker, and the posse. My job was to get these boys home safely.

"Go curl up and get some sleep," I said. "We're going to sneak out of here tonight. We'll leave the campfire burning and lead the horses out on foot until we're far enough away to ride without being heard. The snow will make it bright enough to see where we're going."

He nodded and crawled in under the lean-to with Jeremy.

Chapter 32

My plans for escaping suddenly altered when I climbed up the tree during the last light of day. From my vantage point, I saw three sets of men closing in on our position. To the west, I counted eight riders coming through the brush. Thirteen more were riding down the hill on the other side of the pond. Meanwhile, Cain and Becker were riding in from the north with six more men. One woman and two boys were no match for twenty-seven well-armed outlaws.

I climbed down so fast I almost fell before running to the lean-to. "Wake up, boys," I said. "We're in big trouble."

They scrambled out of their blankets beneath the lean-to and took positions behind the boulders while I started saddling horses.

"What are we going to do?" Jeremy asked.

I took a quick look to the south. No one was coming from that direction. It was a slim chance for escape, too slim. According to the map, there was a creek down that way that led to the Birdwood River. The trouble was that the terrain dropped a couple of times getting to it. If we got caught on the edge of a steep hill or cliff, we could get trapped.

I chased the thought of Cain shooting the boys in cold blood out of my mind. It was one thing for me to die. I already cheated death once. But the boys were too young to die like this.

"Roll up your bedrolls," I said. "Take the food in two saddlebags and then crawl over to the horses. When I start shooting, cut the south side of the corral and ride like hell."

"We can't leave you!" Lance's worried eyes spoke louder than his words.

"Go!"

I divided my attention between watching the boys and keeping an eye on Cain's army. Luckily the snow still fell and obscured their ability to see what we were doing.

The boys hopped onto the backs of two horses after tying on their saddlebags and bedrolls. I watched as Lance leaned against the neck of the buckskin with the razor in his hand.

Raising the rifle to my shoulder, I aimed dead on to Cain's chest. He must've seen me because he dove to the ground just as I pulled the trigger. I changed my aim to Becker. He took the bullet in his right arm. I searched for Cain again, but he was keeping his horse between us.

The sound of horse hooves thundered toward me. I kept firing until the Winchester was empty. I pulled my Colt. Men lay on the ground bleeding, but not enough for my satisfaction. My best target to end this madness was Cain, but he was nowhere in sight.

It wasn't until both of my guns were empty that I realized I was bleeding. Red drops dripped into the snow while I reloaded. Before I could figure out where I was injured, I was yanked to my feet, disarmed, and pushed against a boulder. I swallowed and felt blood trickle down the back of my throat. My nose was bleeding, most likely from breathing the frigid air.

Cain's left hand wrapped around my throat. "You killed my boy!"

"You murdered my parents!"

I tried to see if the boys got away, but there were too many men and horses in the way. His hand tightened. I couldn't breathe.

"Cain!" Becker yelled. "We need her alive if we're going to get those plates back."

Cain's grip loosened.

I sucked in a strangled breath of air. "I don't have them."

"Where are they?" Cain asked.

"I buried them."

His hand tightened again. "Where?"

The world started to turn black, but then his feet slid in the snow and we tumbled to the ground together. When he lost hold of my neck, I rolled away from him and sprang to my feet.

Surrounded by horses and men, there was nowhere to go, so I kicked Cain. My right boot caught him in the stomach. The left landed on his shoulder as he pushed himself to his feet. The men laughed at his feeble attempts to defend himself. He stumbled backward over the branch barrier and towards the pond. I followed, kicking again and again until we were at the pond's edge.

The holes the boys made in the surface of the ice the day before partially froze over during the night, so after throwing a well-aimed kick between Cain's legs, I ran across the ice. I stayed away from the holes that were hidden beneath three inches of snow and did my best to keep my weight over the balls of my feet to keep from slipping backward.

Bullets whizzed past me and I felt a couple tug at my coat. I reached the other side just in time to hear the ice crack.

Men yelled for help. I didn't look back.

I ran south with the sound of men and horses chasing me.

Before long, I found the tracks the boys made during their escape. There was blood in the snow and soon I came upon a dead horse with a bullet hole in his chest. Even after passing the carcass, I saw more blood in the snow. I kept going, but didn't see either of the boys or another horse lying on the ground. The blood must be coming from a non-fatal wound. I prayed the red stains in the snow came from another horse and that Lance or Jeremy weren't injured.

The trail swung to the left, but I jumped down a six-foot drop and slid on the seat of my pants to the bottom of a hill. Bullets hit the ground around me and when I began running again, I felt one hit my right boot heel.

My lungs ached from breathing the crisp air.

My nose continued to bleed.

Another hundred yards and I slid to a stop at the edge of a dry creek bed. It was a good twenty-foot drop to the rocks below. I liked the height of the opposite bank better. It was only five feet above the creek bed.

I glanced behind me. Cain and his men turned along the path the boys took toward the east. The ridge I jumped from angled downward in that direction until it met up with the plain I stood on. That meant they would catch me in a matter of minutes if I didn't go one direction or another.

East was definitely out of the question because that would lead me straight to Cain.

I looked to the west. The plain sloped upward back to where I came from. A quick scan of the countryside in all directions didn't reveal any sign of the boys, the posse, or Ruth. I was on my own with only one direction I really could go—straight down into that dry creek where I could hide among the rocks and boulders.

Despite how dark it was getting, I sat down on the ledge and turned over to face the ridge. My feet searched for toeholds and lips of rock strong enough to support my weight. My fingers slid into crevices, the edges of which cut into the leather of my gloves. As layers of shale crumbled beneath my feet, I scrambled to find better footing.

I was about ten feet down when the sound of horses and men roaming around above prompted me to look up. All I saw was the tall creek bank until one of the men stepped too close to the edge and fell. He yelled until he landed on the rocks below. He didn't move.

The sounds above disappeared. I contemplated the idea of climbing back up, but then I heard a horse snort and stomp its foot. One or more of them had stayed behind.

I continued to descend and when I reached the ground, I took the dead man's gun belt.

As I walked eastward, I kept close to the bank, which slowly decreased in height. The moon started its descent in the sky and still gave off enough light to see the first riders headed my way along the top of the opposite bank. I slid down behind a snarl of driftwood and waited for seven men to pass.

A half hour later, a campfire burned across the creek and above where the dead man lay.

I stood up slowly and continued to walk eastward. Although fatigued, I kept moving because stopping meant freezing to death, or being captured. My right heel hurt and my toes felt like someone was stabbing them with forks.

I kept walking.

The moon completely disappeared by the time I found where the ledge leveled out at the base of a hill. The snow and creek bed were churned up enough that I knew this was where the men back at that camp crossed. While it gave me a good place to get out of the creek bed, I also found trouble not more that thirty feet away.

Cain and Becker were camped near a cluster of cedars. Lance and Jeremy were with them. So was Ruth.

I crouched down behind a bush while I mulled over what to do. From what I remembered of the map, we were about thirty miles north of the North Platte River and forty miles from the town of North Platte. It wasn't home, but at least we could get protection, providing I rescued the boys from Cain and stayed away from his men.

Chapter 33

A half hour went by before Cain woke Becker to take over the guard. He wasted no time in hibernating into his bedroll.

Becker's wounded right arm hung at a strange angle in a bandana sling. He held a rifle awkwardly in his left hand as he sat on top of a fallen tree. This was the chance I needed.

I slithered in the snow and came up behind the tree. His head nodded, rose, and nodded again before I knocked him across the skull with the butt of the gun I took off the dead man. I caught his arm to keep him from falling too quickly and making noise. My Peacemaker fell out of his coat pocket, so I took it and put it back in the holster.

I gagged Becker with his own pants belt and tied him up with the ropes I untied from Lance's hands and legs. Jeremy sneezed while I was untying him, but Cain took no notice of the noise, which came so frequently from the boy.

I pointed toward the horses and the boys started saddling them.

Cain barely stirred when I tied his legs together. In a swift move, I pulled his bandana up between his teeth before tightening the knot. He grabbed at me, but I shoved him onto his stomach and put my knee in his back while I tied his hands together.

The boys and I loaded Cain and Becker on their horses, belly down. We left the campfire burning just in case someone was keeping a watch for it.

Once again I gave Ruth the duty of leading the way while I rode her bareback with a halter and reins made out of rope. Sometime during the early morning hours I fell asleep with my head resting against Ruth's neck.

"Ma, this is going to smart a bit," Lance said.

I opened my eyes to see Lance getting ready to shove the burning end of a stick up my nose. A persistent trickle of blood still slithered down the back of my throat, so I took a deep breath as he slid the stick in my left nostril to cauterize the bleeding.

Doing my best to lay still, my eyes stared straight up at the clear blue sky while my hands dug through the snow and grabbed hold of the grass beneath. Through watery eyes, I noticed the bare branches of cottonwoods, and to my left I heard the muffled movement of water. It seemed like an eternity before the blood stopped flowing and he removed the stick with the tip still sending up a wisp of smoke.

I breathed through my mouth in short gasping breaths before saying a very scratchy sounding, "Thah-anks." My sore throat made talking very painful.

"I think we're lost," Jeremy said.

I looked over toward him. He stood guard on Cain and Becker who were tied together back to back with so many rounds of rope they were probably losing blood circulation.

"Yah...sleep?" I asked through the soreness in my throat.

"Some," Lance said. "We took turns." He pulled his Uncle Jared's watch out of his pocket. "It's one-twelve." He pointed to my nose. "Sorry about having to stop that the way I did, but putting pressure on it and stuffing a bandana up it just wasn't doing any good."

I reached up and patted him on the arm. "Yah...ded...gud."

He helped me sit up and handed me a cup of hot coffee. The warmth felt good on my hands as well as my throat. That's when I noticed I was wearing a different pair of gloves. The ones I wore now were a couple sizes too big.

"Where'd these come from?"

Lance pointed at our prisoners. "They're Cain's. He donated them to you out of the not so goodness of his heart."

"We got company coming," Jeremy said.

I tried to stand up, but my head spun and I fell back down. I was too sore and too frozen to fight again. "Leave me here and get away," I said.

"Not this time, Ma. We're in this together, no matter what."

I twisted around and studied the thickness of the ice on the river behind us. It was too thin to walk on and the water was too deep to cross without chilling oneself to the bone. A brief look at the horses showed they were saddled and ready to go. Ruth even carried a saddle.

"Where'd that come from?" I asked, pointing toward her.

"We walloped another feller in the dark, early this morning," Jeremy said. "His horse was dead, so we took the saddle and left him tied up." He pointed to Cain and Becker. "The way we figure it, these are the two we really want. The others can be bounty hunter fodder."

I started to rise again, gasped at the pain in my feet, and fell again.

"You'd best stay put," Jeremy said.

"We need to ride."

"Too late for that, Ma," Lance said. "Besides, two of them have badges."

He pointed at a group of three riders. I squinted against the blinding sunlight, which bounced off the snow. I recognized Sheriff Koker and the man to his right looked familiar, but I wasn't quite sure from where. Then my eyes focused on the man riding to his left. Nathaniel!

I tried to stand up, but couldn't. The pain and stiffness in my body just wouldn't let me; neither would the dizzy feeling.

"You'd best sit down, Ma. You lost a lot of blood."

Lance guided me back down and my eyes spotted the redness in the snow and on the blankets from where my nose bled. The front of my coat was covered with dried blood. As sore as my throat felt before drinking the coffee, there was probably just as much blood that seeped down into my stomach. The amount of blood loss certainly explained why I felt so sick and lightheaded. In addition, my hands throbbed from the climb down the ledge. I looked at my aching feet and saw my right boot was missing. I twisted my leg around and looked at the torn up strips of shirt, which bandaged my foot.

"How bad?"

Lance waved a hand in a nonchalant manner. "Ah, it's just grazed a bit." His eyes told a different story about the condition of my foot.

"But it sure swelled up some," Jeremy said. "Had to cut the

stitching in your boot to get it off and even then you hollered something fierce."

I didn't remember what happened after rescuing the boys and capturing Cain and Becker.

The three riders stopped, and while Koker and the other man tied their horses to the hitching rope the boys strung among the trees, Nathaniel ran toward me. He slid into the snow on his knees and gathered me into his arms.

"Jo!" He kissed the top of my head. "My Jo."

He cried and I put my arms around his waist. It was a strange sensation. Reuniting with a brother I grew up with, yet in many ways, I was meeting for the very first time.

In the background, I heard Lance and Jeremy take turns telling Sheriff Koker about how they were kidnapped and how I rescued them. How they almost got away, but were captured again until I rescued them again. The story gushed out in ten-year-old enthusiasm and I imagined Koker standing there looking baffled.

"Well boys, this adventure's not over yet," Koker said. "We've got dead bodies scattered between here and the Dismal River. Most of them are up in those hills back there near a pond."

"We only killed two of them there, Sheriff," Jeremy said.

"I guess I can believe part of that," Koker said. "Looked like five of them froze to death. But there's still three more dead up there."

"Maybe Ma killed them last night when she was helping us escape."

"Ma?"

"I mean Miss Prairie, sir," Lance said. "Pa hasn't married her, yet."

Nathaniel opened the gap between us and looked down at me. "Who are you marrying, Jo?"

"Paul Garrett, providing Cain's men haven't killed him."

"When was the last time you saw him alive?" Koker asked.

"I can't remember how many days it's been since Cain made the boys write the notes telling me to go on foot without Paul." I looked at Koker. "Have you seen a covered wagon?"

"Nope."

"You didn't happen to bring my pack with you?" I asked. "It was by the pond."

"Sorry, Jo," Nathaniel said. "There wasn't anything left up there except the dead men."

"You need your headache medicine, don't you, Ma?" Lance asked.

I nodded and couldn't keep up with the multitude of expressions that showed on Nathaniel's face and in his eyes. I laid down and rubbed my temples to get the headache to go away. Nathaniel pulled my hands away and then pressed the back of his hand against my forehead. He shook his head.

"Koker told me about your cracked skull and amnesia," he said. "We never should've split up after Cain robbed the train." Tears dripped from his cheeks. "It's my fault. It's just that I thought they'd chase me and let you go because you're a girl. But you knew too much about their scheme from hearing Nutter tell Dad what Cain planned to do with those die plates."

"Are you the one who found them before Paul got to the hiding place?" I asked.

He nodded and wiped his cheeks. "Yeah. I was trying to find you when I ran into Koker. He'd lost Becker's trail and was heading back to Welcome. I showed him the map you sent me, so he helped me find the plates."

"I bet that fellow who shot Pa was trailing your brother," Lance said.

"Paul was shot?" Koker asked.

"Dang near lost his leg trying to get back home to Doc Miller," Jeremy said.

Koker jerked his thumb over his shoulder, pointing toward the wide expanse of prairie that surrounded us. "And he's out there in a wagon somewhere?"

"Yep," Jeremy said. "He was supposed to run the horses off after Miss Prairie started walking north. Conrad said that some feller named Lietz was supposed to kill him."

I looked over at Lance. He was staring at Cain with all the hate a ten-year-old could hold.

"Lance," I said. "The posse wasn't too far away from that camp. They would've seen or heard trouble. Besides, like I said, Paul had plenty of weapons and ammunition."

Cain laughed. "He never would've heard Lietz coming."

"Yeah," Becker said. "With that crossbow Lietz carries, Garrett would've been dead before he even knew he was in danger."

Lance kicked and punched at Cain and Becker. His foot connected with Becker's wounded arm and the man screamed out so loud the horses tried to break free. While Sheriff Koker grabbed Lance, the other man that came with him rushed over to settle the horses.

I forced myself up off the ground and Nathaniel helped me walk to where Koker held Lance. I wrapped my arms around the boy and he melted into my embrace.

"We have to have faith that your pa's alive," I said.

Out of the corner of my eye, I saw the other man start to draw his gun. My draw was quicker and he soon lay dead on the ground.

"Where'd you find him?" I asked.

"He said he was one of William Pinkerton's men," Koker said.

"He came through with the gold wagons, but he was actually part of Cain's gang." I scanned the snow-covered plains beyond the camp. Except for the scattered trees along the river, we were too out in the open. "Did you see William?"

"Yeah," Nathaniel said. "He's with Frost's posse. They have the rest of Cain's gang corralled at the cabin. They were getting ready to haul the gold to North Platte. Some fellow named Michael stayed with them to be a scout and told us to head this way to help you and the boys. He said we should run into an old Indian named Crow Catcher along the way."

Jeremy shook his head. "The night before we reached the cabin, Conrad beat up on us. Crow Catcher came out of nowhere and tried to save us, but Becker shot him in the back."

I ran through the math in my head. Lance said there were thirty-seven men at the cabin. Twenty-eight came after the boys and me at the pond, which left six at the cabin if I subtracted the three I stole the horses from. Near as I figured there were fourteen dead and at least ten wounded. That left fourteen plus any wounded who could still ride. Those men most likely didn't know that the gold was seized and were still looking for the boys and me in order to rescue Cain and Becker so they could still share their ill-gotten treasure.

I pulled the map out of my coat pocket. "Where are we?"

Koker took the map and studied it for a minute. "This here is the Birdwood River. If we follow it down to the North Platte River, we should make it to North Platte in two or three days providing we don't run into Cain's men and you can sit a saddle that long."

"I'll ride double with her," Nathaniel said.

Sheriff Koker and Nathaniel piled rocks on top of the dead man while the boys tightened up the cinches on the horses. I kept watch on Cain and Becker, not that they needed much watching with all that rope tied around them. It took less than five minutes after they were untied and handcuffed to their saddles for them to begin complaining about the pins and needles they suffered from the return of circulation.

Jeremy laughed. "Guess we overdid it a mite when we tied them up."

"Just a bit," Nathaniel said. "But I can't say I feel sorry for them."

I hugged Nathaniel tighter and he patted my right knee. I was riding on top of the bedroll tied to the saddle Ruth wore. My head leaned against Nathaniel's back and the steady rhythm of his heart beating calmed the throbbing in my head. The memories of all the good times we shared on the farm filled my mind as I fell asleep.

Chapter 34

Throughout the afternoon, Nathaniel and I switched between riding his horse and Ruth. Each hour we dismounted, switched horses, and traveled south again.

During one stop, Nathaniel changed the bandaging on my foot. He scowled at how raw the skin looked from all the walking and running I did through the ice and snow over the past several days.

He removed my other boot and tossed it away after seeing that my left foot was in bad shape as well. To replace the boots, he made me booties by cutting a blanket in half, folding it in thirds, and then using strands of hemp unwound from a rope to sew up the sides. Jeremy helped by sewing up the thick wool stocking that went on my left foot.

The next step in bundling up my feet against the elements involved emptying out a pair of saddlebags. Nathaniel cut off the connecting width of leather and the flaps and then sliced the stitching along one side of each pouch. Again Jeremy figured out what he was doing and helped by working on the left one. My feet were slid inside the pouches, the unstitched sidepiece became a shoe tongue, and then the front and back panels were wrapped around the sides of my ankles. Finally, they used rope to hold the saddlebag boots onto my feet.

The coverings felt thick and clumsy, but my feet were warm for the first time since I left Paul with the wagon.

"That should keep your feet nice and cozy," Nathaniel said as he lifted me up onto Ruth's back. "When we camp tonight, we need to figure out some way for you to soak these feet. If something's not done soon, the infection will get too bad for them to be saved. And you sure can't walk down a wedding aisle with your feet amputated."

Just before dark, we watched four columns of smoke rise into the sky from campfires about eight miles behind us. We were definitely being followed, so we continued on for three more miles. It was well after dark when we stopped.

Clouds filled the sky and the boys took bets on whether it would snow or rain. Either way, Nathaniel and Koker made a lean-to while Lance kept guard on Cain and Becker, who were simply handcuffed to each other left wrist to left wrist and left ankle to left ankle this time.

Jeremy corralled the horses and then busied himself with a project of his own. I watched as he banked up a ring of snow, hardened it by pouring cold water from the river over the snow, and then pressed flat stones around the bowl-like interior. He then used clay from the riverbank to mortar the space between the rocks. Next he took shirts out of the dead man's bedroll and lined the bowl. The final step involved pouring two coffee pots of hot water inside the basin he created before inviting me to sit down on a log beside it.

"You can soak your feet now," he said as he started untying my saddlebag boots. "Best do it quick before the hot water melts the snow."

"If I didn't know better," I said, "I'd swear you and Nathaniel share the same blood."

"Why do you say that?"

"You're both inventive in finding solutions to problems."

While I bathed my feet, Jeremy continually kept snow packed around the basin to keep it from collapsing. Meanwhile, Nathaniel refilled the coffee pots and took a look at Becker's arm.

"Hate to say it, Wayne, but this arm needs to come off," he said. "I can do it, but it's going to hurt like hell unless you want me to knock you out."

"Got nothing but a gallows waiting for me anyway," Becker mumbled. "Leave it be."

Nathaniel cleaned the wound thoroughly before coming over to tend to my feet. He boiled a strand of horsehair from Ruth's tail and then sewed the bullet graze on the bottom of my right heel closed. It wasn't the most enjoyable experience to live through, but by focusing on the similarities between him and our father, I was able to ignore the pain to a certain extent.

I thought about my father, wondering where he was. Nathaniel didn't say anything about him being with Frost at the cabin, which meant he was most likely with Paul and the wagon. I studied the map again and tried to figure out where the last camp Paul and I shared was located. Lance said that my willow tree camp was twenty miles from the cabin and I was able to find that approximate location on the map. We were now over forty miles south of the Dismal River, which made us roughly thirty miles west of where I think I last saw Paul.

"There, that should hold it together until we get to North Platte," Nathaniel said.

I looked at my heel. Boiling the hair lightened the walnut stain in the horsehair to where it almost looked white again. That is, except for where my blood turned it red. "Maybe you should've stayed in medical school."

He cocked his head to one side. "I thought you had amnesia?"

"It's getting better."

The cleanest thing Nathaniel found to bandage my feet with was a pale yellow, cotton plaid shirt from his bedroll. He cut it in two, slid the sleeves over my feet, tucked the cuffs in over my toes, and wrapped the rest around by feet and ankles.

"One thing's for sure," he said.

"What?"

"You won't be kicking fellows into a bloody pulp for at least a couple of weeks."

"Who'd I ever do that to?" I asked.

He laughed and pointed at Cain. "Him for one. Some fellow named Drummond, Koker told me about. And then there was…" He turned his eyes away. "I'd best wash out some more shirts to use as bandages before this basin melts."

I grabbed at his sleeve as he started to move away. "Who?"

"It doesn't matter now. Be thankful you can't remember it."

Koker squatted down and picked me up. "Bedtime," he said as he slid me in beside the boys under the lean-to. The back of his hand pressed against my warm forehead. "Remember that there're some things best left forgotten. There's no need to remember, just close your eyes and sleep."

Nathaniel obviously told him something I still couldn't remember. Despite my curiosity, my exhaustion forced me to do as

Koker said. I slept without dreaming or if I did dream, I didn't remember it. All I did remember was that sleet hit the tarp cover of the lean-to for a time. When we awoke, two inches of fresh snow covered the ground.

Nathaniel crawled out of his bedroll and filled one of the coffee pots. Next, he walked to where Cain and Becker lay sharing their bedrolls on the other side of the fire. He nudged the bottom of Cain's boot and the former mayor rubbed his eyes. When Nathaniel reached down to tap Becker on the shoulder, nothing happened. He tried again, but Becker was dead from blood poisoning. Cain scooted as far away from the body as he could.

"U-Un-c-cuff me from him!" He shouted in a frightened, tremor.

"Oh, I'll do that," Nathaniel said. "Then you're going to start piling rocks on top of him."

"Me!"

"Yeah, you."

Jeremy kept guard on Cain while Lance helped me strap on my saddlebag boots. I then limped over to the fire and fixed what I could for breakfast, two cans of peaches and coffee split six ways. That left one can of beans for dinner unless we caught a rabbit. I cooked up the peaches and sprinkled some coffee grounds over them like cinnamon.

"That sure was good, Ma," Lance said. "Kind of like eating peach cobbler with no crust."

"That was always my favorite part," I said. "That and Granma's cinnamon buns smothered in peach preserves."

Lance pulled out his uncle's watch. Inside was a picture of his grandparents. "I've never met my grandma or grandpa."

I leaned over and wrapped my arms around him. "We'll invite them to the wedding."

He nodded and snapped the watch shut. There was something in his expression that told me Paul's parents wouldn't come even if we hogtied them and dragged them here.

"I'd best help clean up camp so we can get going before those other fellows catch up with us," he said.

I let go, even though I wanted to hug all his emotional pain away.

Nathaniel squatted beside me. "He's Paul's son and not his

nephew, isn't he?"

I tapped the badge on his chest. "I guess being a lawman is your calling after all. Nothing gets by you."

"Actually, I was just taking a wild guess. Jenny was Koker's cousin. He told me what he knew about Paul and his brothers. He said it surprised him to find out about Lance when no one else in the family ever knew she was pregnant. But then, her father wasn't too pleased that Wyatt dragged her out into the middle of nowhere, so Koker figured she just never told anyone."

We reached the North Platte River and followed it until a half-hour before sundown. Lance climbed a tree and spotted three trails of smoke about six miles up river. Cain's gang was gaining on us and we were still a day away from North Platte.

"Jo, I want you and the boys to head out before first light tomorrow," Nathaniel said.

I looked up from where I sat bathing my feet in another one of Jeremy's washbasins. "We're not splitting up this time," I said.

He squatted down and pointed at the two smallest toes on my right foot. They were turning black from the frostbite that set in during my walking journey. "That bullet graze is also infected," he said. "You have to get to a doctor or you could lose your whole foot. The only way you're going to get to a doctor is if we hold those fellows off and let you ride on ahead."

Lance climbed down out of the tree and nodded his agreement to what Nathaniel said. "Sheriff," he said, pointing toward the east. "I saw a sod cabin over that way. Maybe we could hold out there and fight those men."

"How far away is it?" Koker asked.

"About a mile, I reckon."

Koker looked at me. "After you get those feet taken care of, I want you and the boys to head to that cabin. We'll camp out here until daybreak and then come join you."

I didn't like that plan much, but I didn't argue. After sharing the can of beans, the boys and I took Cain with us and left the two extra horses with Nathaniel and Koker just in case one of them lost a mount during their sprint for the cabin.

The moon was out by the time we reached the abandoned

soddy. The boys took the horses into the sod barn while I entered the cabin with Cain. Half the roof was caved in and I broke up the roof timbers by hacking at it with a sharp-edged rock. It was slow and tedious work, but I was able to make a fire in the middle of the floor. The boys found a hitching stone outside and dragged it into the cabin so we could handcuff Cain to the iron ring.

"The barn's not much better than this," Lance said. "But at least it's a windbreak for the horses. We also dug through the snow and cut grass for the horses to eat and gave them a tub full of snow." He rubbed his stomach. "Not sure what we're going to eat though."

"All I have is enough coffee to make half a pot," I said. "We'll figure something out in the morning."

Before stretching out for the night, the boys dragged some more timber from the barn into the cabin. All I could think about as I tried to fall asleep was Nathaniel and how there was something he wanted me to forget permanently.

I stared at Cain. In the firelight, I saw him looking back at me. He knew. "What is it I'm not supposed to remember?" I asked.

He laughed and rolled over. "The sheriff's right. You shouldn't try to remember so hard. Personally, I'd be happy if you'd forget everything you ever saw or heard this past year."

I closed my eyes to the night I snuck into the jailhouse. I waited until the deputy went to the outhouse and tied a rope around it. Finding the keys was easy. They were hanging on a hook outside the cellblock.

Nathaniel was beaten so badly he could barely walk. I half-carried him outside. When we reached the alley, Ruth knelt down long enough for me to mount with Nathaniel in front of me.

"You shouldn't have taken the blame," I said.

"He would've done it again," Nathaniel said through cut, swollen lips. "And then forced you to give Cain back the die plates." He grabbed hold of the saddle horn. "Jo, I'd rather heal up from a couple of broken ribs than see you hurt again."

We rode through the night to the home of John Six-Toes. His name came from having six toes on each foot. Although a reservation doctor removed the two extra toes, the name stuck. After Grampa Shepard died, we adopted Six-Toes as our surrogate grandfather. Not trusting Indians much, Dad didn't like it when we went hunting with the Blackfoot Indian, but he rarely found time between brokering stock deals to stop us.

I helped John carry Nathaniel down into his root cellar where he wrapped Nathaniel's ribs and smeared an herbal medicine over the cuts and bruises.

"You should go now," Nathaniel said. "Get as far away as you can. Go find Poppa. He wants us to come live with him. He might be able to help."

"Dad's dead."

"Not McDonald," he said. "Our real father is Joseph Alms. He's the preacher who came to the funeral yesterday. He's moving to a town called Welcome, Nebraska. He said its northwest of Kearney." He winced when he coughed. "Now go while there's still darkness to hide you. If you wait until morning, Cain's men will find you."

John Six-Toes pulled me by the arm and dragged me out of his cellar. "You go," he said. "Ride like the wind and don't stop until you find your father."

Ruth's mother paced the corral and stomped as if she also wanted to chase me off. I mounted Ruth and took the back roads toward Peoria. That's were I bought a copy of *The Prairie Traveler*. I was born and raised in and around Chicago and other than knowing how to hunt and farm, I didn't know anything about roughing it on the prairies. The store clerk said folks traveling with wagon trains usually carried a copy with them when heading for Oregon or California. It contained information on everything from building a fire to treating snake bites.

A week later, I stopped at a country church across the Mississippi River from Burlington, Iowa because I found out from another minister that Joseph Alms served as pastor there before heading to Nebraska. I wanted to find out if the new pastor could tell me anything about my real father. No one was home at the parsonage and when I stepped off the porch, I spotted Cain and Conrad. They were at the fence where I tied Ruth. I ran into the woods. They chased me, caught me, and strung me up by the hands to a tree limb…

Reliving the pain of the whipping woke me up. I was covered

in a cold sweat. I looked around, disoriented, unsure of how I wound up in the soddy.

"Are you all right, Ma?" Lance asked.

I looked down and it took a minute for my mind to bring me back to the present. I needed air.

"I'm going to go check on the horses," I said. "Keep an eye on him."

Lance switched places with Jeremy, who stood guard near the doorway with a rifle. I strapped on my saddlebag boots and belted on my gun.

"Be careful," Lance said. "The east support to the barn door isn't very sturdy. If you bump it, the whole wall might tumble down."

The boys were right when they said the barn wasn't much more than a windbreak for the horses. The roof of the barn was completely gone, and the boys used the timbers, poles from the old corral, and rope to create an extra large stall for the horses to share in one of the back corners. The wooden washtub they found and filled full of snow for the horses was full of holes that they plugged with rocks. Jeremy most likely thought of that.

Ruth walked over to me. As I stroked her neck, I remembered her real name was Florence Nightingale, another woman known for taking care of people. Her new name was shorter and easier to remember, so I decided to keep calling her Ruth.

I stood rejoicing in her loyalty and care-giving instincts until Ruth's ear pricked.

Chapter 35

A noise, ever so slight, moved through the early morning stillness. It was an hour before dawn and without taking a look, I knew Cain's men were out there and that we were surrounded.

I tiptoed to the barn door and looked over at the cabin. Lance wasn't in sight.

"Boys, are you all right?"

"Yeah, Ma. I saw them," came the soft reply.

I drew my Colt and checked the chambers. My cartridge loops were full, which meant I was good for thirty shots. After that, I was in trouble.

Gathering up wood from the fallen roof, I made a fire in the barn. There were three timbers the size of torches. I set one end of each timber into the flames. It was still dark enough that firelight could be seen and the crisp air was just right for the sound of gunfire to echo a good distance. I was counting on Cain's men to provide the gunfire.

Picking up the first torch, I stood back and tossed it as far into the air as I could. Sure enough, one of those men shot at it. The bullet splintered the torch into a half dozen flaming pieces, which fell to the ground.

I picked up the second torch and smiled when the same thing happened with two guns popping off shots. When I tossed the third one, six guns fired. Some of those men fanned their guns, emptying as many as six shots into a harmless piece of wood. The resulting noise echoed into the morning air like fireworks on the Fourth of July. If all went well, Nathaniel and Koker should arrive long before the boys and I ran out of ammunition.

I let the fire burn down while I stood guard by the doorway. A shadow moved around the north side of the cabin, so I watched it.

When I made out the width of the shoulders, I fired.

The man fell.

I spun away from the doorway as three bullets sailed my way. Two of the bullets hit the right side support post. The wood splintered and cracked. I heard the weaker left side complain as it took on more responsibility for holding the sod wall up.

The sod bricks were three feet long, two feet wide, and four inches thick. They could block the wind and stop bullets. They were also heavy. If that rickety doorframe gave way, those bricks would fall and most likely the whole wall would collapse like Lance predicted.

That may or may not be to my advantage, but I kept it in mind as I watched for more shadows. I didn't have to wait long. Someone scurried across the open space between the base of a rise west of the cabin and the front door. A shot came from inside the cabin. The man tumbled and grabbed hold of his arm. A large dark spot in the snow grew around him quickly. That bullet hit an artery and he was frantically trying to untie his bandana to use as a tourniquet. He didn't succeed. He passed out and a minute later all movement stopped.

The sky turned gray before the next sound came. Someone was trying to dig through the back wall of the barn. I moved into the shadows and waited.

All the horses except Ruth milled around in the stall. Ruth watched one spot just inside the ropes along the wall. Ten minutes later two arms appeared just before a head peeped through. The man pulled his shoulders through, got his hips stuck, and then Ruth reared up. Her front hooves came down in the middle of his back with a bone-crunching thud.

I rushed over and took the man's gun and the ammunition from his belt. "Thanks, Ruth."

She tossed her head and daintily pranced to the other end of the stall where she took a mouthful of what remained of the grass the boys piled up.

That was three down and a dozen or more to go. I walked back over to the doorway and peered out. Nothing stirred as the sky turned red. A rhyme about a red sky in the morning being a sailor's warning popped into my head. I wasn't a sailor, but I sure was paying attention to the danger that sky foretold.

A head appeared over the back of the soddy and I fired. The man's hat flew off and he grabbed his ear as he fell.

Two more bullets hit the doorframe and I heard that left doorframe post groan some more. The right side answered. That portal was definitely becoming unsafe.

Bullets flew from every direction when Cain's men spotted Koker and Nathaniel. They rode low in their saddles as they fired at the men surrounding the cabin. The two spare horses charged out in front and then took off to the east. Nathaniel followed while Koker swung around the other direction.

A big commotion started from the direction Nathaniel went, and men started yelling about a horse stampede. They were on foot and knew where they could find at least four horses. Nine men rushed the barn.

Lance and Jeremy fired from the house and I fired two guns at once. Two men fell. Another spun around, but stayed on his feet. More shots fired. Another man fell, but two more took his place.

They surged forward and I retreated until I was a safe distance from that doorway. I fired at the doorframe.

Koker and Nathaniel were also firing at those men, but they kept coming. Four of them reached the barn.

I aimed both guns at the base of the left side. The wood snapped under the weight and all four men looked up just as the heavy sod bricks fell. They tried to run, but only one cleared the doorway.

He fired at me and I felt a red hot sensation across the left side of my ribs. I dropped the left-hand gun and shot him in the chest with the Peacemaker.

When the dust from the falling bricks settled, the front end of the barn lay in a heap. The horse stall collapsed, but the horses remained in the back of the barn well away from the fallen wall.

A few straggling gunshots sounded outside the barn. Then the whole world went quiet, except for the horses.

My stomach rumbled and my mouth felt dry.

A V-shaped, fluttering shadow flew overhead and I looked up at the Canadian geese flying toward the river. I didn't think about whether I was still in danger of getting shot as I quickly reloaded three chambers. Out of three shots, I managed to shoot two geese. Jeremy shot a third one down before they flew too far away.

"That sure was good shooting, Ma," Lance said as he climbed over the rubble.

I was busy reloading again and caught a movement out of the corner of my eye from beneath the rubble. I looked up and saw an arm rise with a gun aimed at Lance.

"Get down!" I yelled.

At the same time, someone fired from the top of the hill behind the barn. The hand jerked and went limp.

Lance stumbled and fell.

I rushed over to where he lay on the ground. "Are you all right?"

He looked around and nodded. "Guess I should've stayed put in the soddy."

Sheriff Koker climbed up and over the pile of sod bricks. "Yes, you should have. Now get back in there before I arrest you for interfering with the legal duty of a lawman."

Lance stood up, but he wasn't able to put weight on his right ankle. "Did I break it?"

I took off his boot and felt it. "Sprained, I think. Go cut a two inch strip off a blanket and wrap it in a crisscross pattern around your foot and halfway up your leg. Then you can help Jeremy pluck those geese."

"Go with him," Koker said. "You're losing blood and need to wash that wound."

After he and Koker tied up the prisoners, Nathaniel used another boiled horsetail hair to sew up the graze along my ribs. When he finished, he handed me a plate with a drumstick on it.

"Happy Thanksgiving, Jo," he said. "After you eat your fill, I want you to ride on ahead and get to the doctor in North Platte. Take Jeremy and Lance with you."

I wanted to argue, but didn't. It would take the rest of the day for them to bury the dead because the only shovel available was a broken handled spade they found in a junk heap behind the barn.

Jeremy grinned. "You could always just lay the bodies out and pile those sod bricks on top of them," he said.

Koker rubbed his head. "Kid's got some smarts in his brain."

Jeremy and Nathaniel saddled six horses, so we could ride relay and hopefully get to town by mid-afternoon. In addition to getting medical attention, we were to send a posse out to help

Koker and Nathaniel bring in the prisoners.

We raced along the riverbank, switching horses every eight miles. As we rode, I kept looking over my shoulder and to the north. Some instinct told me we weren't out of danger yet. Maybe it came from knowing Buford was involved in Cain's plans.

A clock in a church steeple read two-twenty when we rode down the main street of North Platte. I halted Ruth outside a building with a sign that read "North Platte Medical Clinic" and tried to dismount. My feet hurt so much I fell to the ground.

Lance came to my side. "Are you all right, Ma?"

I nodded. "Yeah, I think so." I grabbed the stirrup to pull myself up, but I couldn't do it.

Jeremy ran inside. A short time later, a man in a white smock coat came outside and picked me up off the ground. Lance limped in right behind us while Jeremy held the door open. The doctor laid me on a table in the surgery and chased the boys back into the waiting room.

A woman in an apron stripped me down while the doctor removed my saddlebag boots. "What are the boys' names?" the woman asked.

"The dark haired one is Lance Garrett," I said. "He's my son."

"You're a bit young to be his mother."

"I'm engaged to his father." My eyes watered as she started cleaning the graze wound and removing the horsehair stitches. "The other boy is Jeremy Tate."

"What's your name?" the doctor asked.

"Angela Prairie." I looked at him. "Sheriff Koker and my brother, Nathaniel, need help bringing in the men who attacked us. They're at an abandoned sod cabin a day's ride west along the river."

"I'll inform the marshal as soon as we get done here," he said.

He shook his head when he finished unwrapping my feet. "I'm going to have to remove two of the toes on your right foot."

Before I could object, the woman placed a chloroform mask over my face. In a panic, I struggled and my pulse surged until the fumes drifted into my lungs. The tenseness in my body relaxed and my eyes closed.

Chapter 36

I blinked and swallowed dryly as I contemplated an urge to get up and run away. But my muscles wouldn't respond. They ached and so did my joints. The thought of moving, shifting, or even turning my head was foreshadowed by the knowledge such activity would bring excruciating pain.

As I tried to remember why I was in so much pain, images of riding in a wagon with Paul, hiking across the prairie alone, rescuing the boys, climbing trees, running across a pond and snow, and finally a shootout at an old sod homestead flipped through my mind. I couldn't remember how many days passed, but then I remembered Nathaniel thanking me for shooting down Thanksgiving dinner.

Paul and I left Welcome on the eighth and Thanksgiving was on the twenty-sixth. Was it really only eighteen days? It seemed much longer. I know it was longer, maybe Nathaniel meant that it was a belated Thanksgiving dinner. I studied the calendar on the wall across the room. The top read December. There were Xs through the first two days. Thanksgiving was a week ago.

My stomach gurgled and told me it was well past mealtime. The last thing I remembered eating was goose cooked over an open fire. That belated Thanksgiving goose that I shot down just before one of Cain's men tried to kill Lance.

Hearing a cough to my left, I forced myself to turn my head in that direction. Lance lay there with his right foot in a splint. It was elevated on a pile of pillows. I tried to rise.

Two hands shoved me back down. "Lay still," the woman said. "You'll rip your stitches."

I looked up into her smiling face. "How is he?"

"It's a bad sprain, but a boy like him will be up and running around again in no time."

"Where am I?"

"You don't remember?"

I heard a train whistle. "Oh, yeah, North Platte. How long have I been here?"

"Three days." I tried to rise again and she shoved me back down again. "I'm Mrs. Iola Bonedale. The doctor is my husband, Zeke."

I remembered a doctor telling me that he needed to remove my toes. I looked at my feet. They were elevated and wrapped in clean white bandages. From the shape of the bandages on my right foot, I knew the two smallest toes were indeed gone.

"Nathaniel! Is Nathaniel all right?"

"Yes. He'll be back after he finishes his dinner at the hotel." She put a cold cloth on my forehead. Yes, that cloth felt good, really good. "Do you feel like eating?"

I nodded. "Did anyone find Paul?"

"Doctor Miller telegraphed. Paul Garrett is recovering from an arrow wound. He said it wasn't serious, but bad enough to keep Mr. Garrett off his feet for a spell." She patted my shoulder. "I'll be right back with some soup."

After she left, I managed to sit up in bed without pulling the stitches. I looked over at Lance. He was asleep. On the nightstand was a bottle of laudanum. It was obviously a drug induced sleep to keep the pain from his ankle from bothering him. Beneath the splint and bandages, his right ankle looked swollen to twice the size of his left.

I viewed the rest of the room. There were six beds and four doors, one on each side of the room. When Mrs. Bonedale left, it was through the door to my right. It led into a room filled with benches, which I recalled seeing when the doctor carried me in through the waiting room. The door between the first and second bed across the room was painted with the word "Private." I decided that must be Dr. Bonedale's office. I leaned forward and read the word "Surgery" on the door beyond Lance's bed. The last door, I determined must be the back door because the words on it read, "Exit To Outhouse."

The movement of looking around tired me out, so I lay down. My heel throbbed and so did those missing toes. I felt my left side, but other than being a little sore to the touch, it felt fine. I pulled the sheet up over me, unbuttoned the gown I wore, and peeked underneath the bandages. Dr. Bonedale had replaced the horsehair stitches his wife took out with silk. Hearing the outer door open, I quickly buttoned the gown back up.

Nathaniel entered the patient ward and sat down in a chair between Lance and me. I watched him twirl his hat between his hands.

"William Pinkerton and I have arranged a private car to take us to Chicago. Another car is being reserved to carry Cain and the other prisoners." He focused his eyes directly on me. "The governor needs to know whether you'll be able to testify."

"I don't know." My fingers reached up and touched the ridge on my skull.

"What do you remember about what happened since last March?"

"I have remembered quite a bit. Most of it's written in my journal. I didn't remember the night I broke you out of jail until the night I slept in that soddy."

He stood up and paced the floor. "You have to remember exactly what you overheard about the die plates and the rest of the plans Cain made with Buford while you were hiding under his bed the night after the funeral." He leaned over the foot of my bed with his hands on the foot rail. The look on his face was that of a lawman, not my brother. "Do you remember that, Jo? Do you remember them making love above your head while they talked about the gold?"

"No." Actually, the thought that I may have witnessed two men making love sounded like something best left forgotten. "I haven't remembered anything between entering the barn and the funeral or from the funeral to when I broke you out of jail."

His face went pale. "You…you remembered entering the barn?"

"I can't remember all the details, but I entered the barn and saw your horse." I rubbed my eyes. "Conrad came out of the shadows. He grabbed me and laughed." The image went blank from there. "That's as far as it goes."

He straightened up as he let out the air held in his lungs. "Good. I don't want you to remember the rest of what happened the night we met at the barn."

"Why not?"

The door opened and Mrs. Bonedale entered carrying a tray.

"Get some rest, Jo," Nathaniel said. "I'll bring some paper in the morning so you can write down the things you remembered while trying to get the boys back." He paused a moment and looked at Lance. "Always figured I'd marry Kitty before you ever got your first kiss."

His body shook as if a chill went up his spine. Even without remembering it, I sensed that my first kiss wasn't pleasant because it came from Conrad. I stared into Nathaniel's face.

"You told Poppa that Conrad tried to rape me in the barn. That's what you don't want me to remember, isn't it? You're afraid I can't handle the truth of what happened that night." Iola Bonedale's hands shook and she set the tray down in a hurry. "I've dealt with far worse things in the last few months. I fell off a cliff, Nate. I cracked my head open, ruptured my uterus, and now I can't have children. I won't even be able to make love with Paul when we get married because I'm in too much pain for anyone to touch me down here." I placed my hand over my lower abdomen. "But you're wrong. The truth is I wasn't raped. Conrad may have tried, but he didn't succeed. Just ask Dr. Miller. He can tell you. No man has ever touched me." A tear trickled down the side of my face. "And unless the pain goes away, no man ever will."

"Mr. McDonald, you better leave." Mrs. Bonedale shooed him out and then sat down next to me. Her fingers wiped away the tears. "It's all right, Angela. You're safe here."

She reminded me of Mrs. Miller with the way she soothed and comforted me. The potato soup she brought was also comforting because it was something my grandmother used to make. Yet as comfortable as I felt with Mrs. Bonedale taking care of me that instinct to run still nagged at me, telling me the boys and I still weren't safe.

Chapter 37

The following morning, my father arrived by stagecoach. When he entered the clinic, he handed me my journal, Lance a letter from Paul, and Dr. Bonedale a letter from Dr. Miller. I immediately read through the journal before I wrote down everything that happened from when Paul and I left Welcome to the present. Then I wrote down the memories I recalled while I was out on the prairie.

After I set the pen down, Nathaniel skimmed through my writings. He seemed both worried and relieved when he finished. He held up the journal. "This case will be tried in front of a federal judge and jury. If you can't testify without relying on these writings, what you say might not hold up in court."

"Do they really need her testimony?" my father asked.

Nathaniel nodded. "Over in the jail, there's a trooper who's been locked up for desertion and waiting for the Army to come get him. He's made a deal to not be executed if he reports back everything Cain and his men say to each other. Part of the information he's heard so far includes deals for denying that Cain was ever involved with the train robbery, the murders, or stealing gold from Indian land. The trooper's willing to testify to everything he's heard in exchange for a light sentence."

His eyes focused on Lance who sat in bed, reading his father's letter. "As it is, Jeremy and Lance are the only two not involved with the gang who can testify that Cain was ever at that cabin where Pinkerton found the gold or that he and his men kidnapped them. Jo and I are the only ones left who can testify that Cain not only planned the train robbery, but also participated in it. Because he knows he's the only one alive out of the original nine, he's denying that he ever knew anything about the train robbery or the gold. He's claiming he's been out here the whole time on an extended buffalo hunting trip."

Nathaniel tapped on the journal. "If Jo can't remember everything, it leaves Lance, Jeremy, and me to disprove his alibi. As it is, we're keeping Jeremy under lock and key because two attempts have already been made on his life since we've been here. And this morning, someone took a shot at me, which means Cain must have some men still running around loose."

My father paced up and down the aisle between the beds. "This whole thing doesn't make sense. If Pinkerton has the gold, what does Cain have to bargain with for these men's loyalty? You'd think they'd want to do like that trooper and testify against him to get lighter sentences."

"Maybe William Pinkerton didn't get all of the gold," I said. "Maybe he and Buford already shipped some out before they kidnapped the boys. According to the invoices in Buford's office, he's been receiving kegs of Blue Mountain Beer since January. The shipments came in every three months during January, April, July, and October. So they might've already taken one or more loads of gold back east to Cain's canning factory, which shut down after the '71 fire. Maybe that's where they're going to mint the coins."

Nathaniel smiled. "Well, at least that's part of what you heard the night you hid out under Cain's bed." He headed for the door. "I'll send a request for a search and seizure order to be made on all of Cain and Buford's property. I'll also have the Blue Mountain Beer Company checked out. I've never seen that brand in any other saloon or pub, so maybe it's fake too."

My father sat down and told me about how Paul was shot with an arrow an hour after he chased off the horses. The arrow went through his left leg, just above the bullet wound. When Lietz and three other men rode into Paul's camp to finish him off, Paul grabbed the cane rifle and shot Lietz through the heart. Paul was able to get under the wagon and shoot it out with the other three men until Frost and the posse came to rescue him. After the posse rounded up the horses, my father took Paul back to Welcome for medical treatment.

"Pa says he had to let Doc Miller put those maggots on his leg again," Lance said, holding up the letter. "Sure wish I could've been there to see that."

"I think your father's glad you weren't," my father said. "Never saw a grown man look so petrified in all my life as he did while those maggots ate away the dead tissue. I saw it done during the war and it takes a strong stomach to put up with that happening to one's body."

I laughed until the doctor came in carrying a stretcher and asked my father to help him carry me into the surgery. Mrs. Bonedale was waiting there and took my hand once I was laid on the table. I recognized the instruments on the tray and knew they planned to take a look inside at my female parts to assess for themselves the amount of damage done by my fall.

"Is that really necessary?" I asked.

The doctor nodded. "Dr. Miller has asked me to check to make sure the infection you had before leaving Welcome didn't reappear while you were out stomping around in the wilderness."

I groaned as they gave me more chloroform.

"I don't understand," my father said. "Why would you lie to me?"

"I didn't want to," Nathaniel said. "Becker was listening in when you visited me at the jail. I had to tell you I was the one who beat Conrad, or Cain would've found out it was Jo and hunted her down with an even stronger vengeance. He only waited until after the funeral to beat me half to death because he knew if I showed up with bruises, folks would ask too many questions. The only reason I'm not dead now is because he was late for a meeting with Buford."

The muffled conversation came from behind Dr. Bonedale's closed office door. I sat up and strained my ears to hear more.

"How much of the attack did you see?" my father asked.

A long pause preceded Nathaniel's answer. "All of it. He was on top of her, Poppa, and I was helpless do anything to stop it."

My head throbbed as horrifying images flashed through my mind. I entered the barn and Conrad dragged me into a stall where Nathaniel lay tied and gagged. I knelt down to see if he was alive. He flinched and opened his eyes when I touched his cheek. I tried to remove the gag, but Conrad yanked me away and forced me to the ground.

I struggled as Conrad ripped away my blouse and riding skirt. He tore away my underclothes and unbuttoned his pants.

I slapped and scratched at him, pulled his hair and broke free long enough to crawl three feet.

He grabbed my waist, rolled me over, and used his hands and legs to hold me down while his mouth seared my breasts with hot lips. He moved on top of me as he searched for the right place between my legs and kept missing.

I spit in his face.

He let go of my right wrist to wipe his cheek.

I reached up, grabbed his ear, and yanked hard.

Conrad yelled. He pushed himself up a bit and punched me in the mouth.

My right leg came free. I used it to knee him between the legs.

He gasped in pain.

I freed myself from him and rose to my feet. When he came at me again, my feet went flying. With a pair of brand new riding boots, I landed one kick after another until he lay bleeding and unconscious on the ground.

I grabbed a sledgehammer and was about to bring it down between Conrad's legs when Nathaniel stopped me.

Somehow he managed to get free. He held me in his arms for a long time while we both heaved deep breaths until the fierce desperation in our blood cooled.

"Are you all right?" he asked.

I nodded and shivered at how close Conrad came to…

Ruth let out a loud whinny, as the echo of horses pounded through the night air.

"Hurry, go inside the house," Nathaniel said. "Hide out in the attic until it's safe."

Through the round slatted attic vent, I watched Marshal Becker handcuff Nathaniel.

"I'm telling you, Jo's here somewhere." Conrad stumbled out of the barn.

"Her horse isn't here, she's gone again," Becker said. "But as long as we have him, she won't go far. If nothing else, we'll catch her after the funeral. What's important now is to get you to a doctor." Becker shook his head. "He sure did a number on you."

Conrad faced off in front of Nathaniel. "That's right. You're the one who jumped me, Nate. But I'm telling you, I'll sure enjoy making Jo pay for every scar *you* left on my face."

"Leave her alone!" Nathaniel leapt at Conrad, but Becker pounded him in the chest with the butt of his rifle.

Conrad laughed. "She sure tasted sweet while it lasted."

"I should've let her go at you with the sledgehammer!"

I waited a half hour before climbing down from the attic and taking the hottest bath I could tolerate. Thankfully, Granma was staying in town with friends that night. When I went outside, Ruth walked out of the trees behind the barn. Knowing I couldn't stay at the farm, I rode to John Six-Toes' place where I hid out until the funeral.

My father and Nathaniel came out of the office while I was writing down what I remembered about the barn. It wasn't easy to write, but I did it with every detail.

"He didn't get a chance to do more than slobber on me, Nate," I said when I handed the journal to him. "I got myself free before he could do what he really wanted."

Nathaniel read what I wrote and then passed the journal to Poppa. "But Bonedale said your…uh…" He looked away. "I saw Conrad lower himself down on you. He broke your—"

"Dr. Miller did that when he examined me." I glanced over at Lance. He looked puzzled and curious about what we were talking about. I looked back at Nathaniel. "Have you read the whole journal?"

"No," he said. "Just the parts that talk about Cain and Buford."

My father put his hand on Nathaniel's shoulder. "Read the whole thing, son. She's right, Conrad may have tried, but he didn't succeed. Granted, it was a horrible ordeal, but she fought well and was able to keep him from taking her."

While Nathaniel sat down and read the entire journal, Dr. Bonedale came and examined Lance's ankle. He took the splint off and nodded.

"How's he doing?" my father asked.

"The swelling's down." Bonedale tied the splint back on. "He'll need to stay off of it for several weeks."

Lance frowned. "I was hoping to go sledding when I get home."

"You won't be doing anything like that until at least February," the doctor said.

"Oh, man! That means I won't be able to help Pa at the warehouse, either."

"I'm afraid not, son. But from what I hear, your pa's off his feet, too, for a spell."

Lance nodded and picked up the letter. "Yeah. It figures that fellow would shoot him in the same leg. He sure did good with that cane rifle though. Shot that Lietz fellow dead on." He grinned and looked over at me. "Ma's really good with a gun, too. You should've seen her out there, Reverend Alms. She shoots better than most men."

My father cleared his throat. "That's not something worth boasting about, son. Even if it's to save one's life, killing another man is never anything to take pride in."

The grin on Lance's face turned into a frown. "I know. I'm kind of sick about the ones I killed too. But I guess it's kind of like David going up against Goliath. It had to be done so we could get back and make sure Cain gets convicted for what he did to my uncles and Ma's folks. I know I shouldn't say it, but I hope he hangs."

My father shook his head. "I hate to admit it, but so do I."

Doctor Bonedale finished with Lance's ankle and walked over to change the bandages on my feet. I didn't like the looks of those feet. They were pink and red and covered with scabs that were white and slimy from being warm and moist beneath the bandages. Just seeing where the two missing toes were was enough to churn my stomach. I turned my eyes toward Lance while the doctor cleaned my feet.

"I'm going to wrap these loosely so the air can dry out the wounds," Bonedale said. "Try not to shift around so much that they become uncovered."

He just finished tying the bandages on when a deputy marshal entered the room with Jeremy. The boy looked pale, and a bit green in the cheeks.

"Kid says he's got a stomach ache, Doc," the deputy said. "Mind taking a look at him?"

Bonedale took Jeremy with him into the surgery. A few minutes later, I heard the sound of Jeremy retching over and over again.

Jeremy's moans and screams alerted my maternal instincts. I wanted to run in and comfort him, but my father kept his hands on my shoulders. I looked over at Lance and saw that he was also going through the same heart-wrenching experience with Nathaniel keeping him from trying to rush in and get in the way.

An hour went by before the doctor and deputy brought Jeremy into the patient room on a stretcher. They laid him in the bed across the aisle from Lance. He was unconscious and if it wasn't for the shallow breathing, I would've thought he was dead.

"What's wrong with him?" I asked.

"His food was poisoned," Dr. Bonedale said. "I've purged him the best I can for now and gave him charcoal to absorb any remaining poison." He started to leave the room. "I'll come check on him in an hour."

I noticed that Nathaniel looked a bit pale. "Are you feeling all right?" I asked.

"I gave Jeremy my lunch when Poppa asked me to meet him here," he said. "That poison was meant for me."

Bonedale stopped in the doorway. "It's a good thing he didn't eat all the stew you gave him or he'd be dead by now." He turned to leave. "I'd say none of you should eat anything you haven't prepared yourselves."

I looked over at the tray of food sitting on the stand beside my bed. My appetite completely disappeared. Or so I thought until a growl from my stomach objected to my decision not to eat. I reached over and picked up the metal lid covering the plate. Seeing the liver and onions confirmed my decision not to eat. Maybe dinner would look more appetizing. I put the lid back down.

"What's on your mind?" my father asked.

"Not much," I said. "The past few weeks of not eating regular meals have turned me into a skeleton and now I'm afraid to eat."

He took my hand in his. "You're safe now."

I shook my head. "Tell that to Jeremy. None of us are safe."

The deputy made sure the back door was locked and then walked to the door that led to the waiting room. "I'll be out here if you all need anything." He looked at Nathaniel. "You should probably check out of the hotel and bring your things here. From now until you leave town, you're all in protective custody."

Nathaniel exited the room with the deputy and came back later with his bedroll and saddlebags. He claimed the bed across from me. My father also took up residence in the patient room and spent the rest of the day praying over Jeremy.

Chapter 38

At three in the morning, I woke up and looked at Nathaniel. He was awake, reading my journal. My father still knelt at Jeremy's side. The ten-year-old was breathing a bit stronger, but in the dim light from the lamp next to Nathaniel's bed he looked like a ghost.

I sat up and drank a glass of water while I watched Lance shift and squirm in a troubled sleep. Around four o'clock, Nathaniel closed the journal and walked over. He laid it on the stand next to me and took my hand.

"You're an amazing gal, Jo." His other hand brushed through my hair. "I'm sorry I was so cold to you about needing to remember that stuff."

"You have a job to do." I pointed at Lance. "Now let me do mine. Put him in bed with me." I scooted over a bit to allow room. "I need to practice being a mother."

He picked Lance up and gently laid him beside me. Lance immediately cuddled up against me and I put my arms around him.

When Dr. Bonedale and his wife arrived after sunup, they took Jeremy into the examining room and put him through another round of purging.

I felt Lance's tears fall on my hand where it lay under his cheek. "It's okay," I said. "Jeremy's a tough kid, just like you."

Jeremy was awake when they carried him back in. Mrs. Bonedale forced him to drink a glass of water every hour, but when she tried to get him to eat lunch, he refused. He was obviously just as afraid to eat as I. My father sat down next to him.

"Tell you what. How about if I fix us all some lunch? Would you eat something I made?"

"That depends," Jeremy said. "Can you cook?"

My father left and brought back such a masterful chicken

casserole that we all voted him in as our official chef until we left for Chicago. After three days of eating his cooking and receiving the care of the Bonedales we were all feeling well enough to make the journey by train to testify against Cain.

Nathaniel purchased a pair of knee-high moccasins with extra padding in the soles and a riding skirt for me to wear. Walking was painful, especially on that right foot, but my father helped me while Lance hobbled out of the clinic on crutches. An ambulance surrounded by eight guards took us to the train station where we boarded the private car.

George Tate and Paul were already on board. The boys rushed to their fathers at the best speed they could manage. Jeremy's father came up off the settee and met him halfway. Paul was still fumbling with his own crutches when Lance finished hobbling over to him. I took a seat in a high-backed chair and put my feet up on a footstool. My missing toes throbbed and my heel felt like it would rip apart if I stood any longer.

My mind turned toward the trip to Chicago. A home I no longer remembered other than in the memories I wrote in my journal. In many ways, I was anxious to get this whole ordeal over with, but also leery of going back to where it all started.

I watched Paul and Lance. They sat down on the settee together and shared their adventures. Their little two-bedroom house was what I wanted to call home. While I lived there, I felt like I was a part of their lives. Yet I still couldn't get over the guilt.

Paul looked at Jared's watch when Lance showed it to him and then across the width of the car at me. I looked away. I knew all too well how close Lance came to getting shot and possibly killed. To the boys, this was a big scary adventure that was slowly coming to an end. To me, it was a nightmare with too many lives lost, ruined, or in my case, all but forgotten. I wanted to forget the whole thing or at least take the calendar back to March and start down a different path that wasn't littered with so much grief.

Nathaniel sat in the chair next to me. "It's almost over, Jo."

"I'm sorry about Matt."

"Dad was right about him. I thought being his friend would keep him from following in his father's footsteps; I was wrong."

"No you weren't." I touched his cheek. "The last thing he said before passing out was that he only joined up to try to keep Dad from getting killed."

"Then why'd he try to draw down on you?"

"The more I think about it, I think he saw Deputy Frost coming up behind me and tried to draw on him. I think that if Lietz hadn't killed him, he would've testified against Cain."

He smiled. "I'd like to think that too."

The trip to Chicago took a day and a half, during which time I stared out the window of the private car's bedroom. The car also contained a small kitchen and a small room with a sink and privy. The men and boys slept in drop-down berths in the parlor section. That space also served as a dining room when a panel in the wall between the bedroom and parlor was dropped down. Four legs swiveled down to support the table, and chairs from around the sitting area were set around it while the men and boys ate. During meals, I heard them talking, sharing in each other's company while I remained in my room, refusing to see anyone.

Occasionally Poppa or Nathaniel came in to attempt coaxing me into joining the others, but I remained sequestered. Honoring my privacy, they brought my meals and kept everyone else out.

As we traveled, we passed crops, cattle, small herds of buffalo, and, until we reached eastern Nebraska, I occasionally saw Indians on their ponies staring at the iron horse and its train of cars crossing their ancestral lands.

Each mile took me farther away from Carol. Through everything, she remained the one bright spot in my life. My journal was full of sketches of her and I stared at them for hours, wishing I could hold her in my arms and touch the one life my surviving the accident saved from physical or emotional pain.

As I slept that night, a rush of images flashed through my mind. Many recollections were the episodes I already remembered, but others were new. I spent hours slowing the new memories down in my mind as I wrote them in my journal. Two dozen blank pages were left when I finished. Twenty-four pages left to write down what happened during the trial so that I could put closure to the journal's telling of the life I lost and found this year.

*****

A couple of hours before we pulled into Chicago, William Pinkerton entered the bedroom. I lay on the bed thinking about Paul and how I should talk to him and ask his forgiveness for not wanting to see him.

William took a seat in the chair next to the window. "The trial won't be for a couple of weeks. My brother, Robert, seized the rest of the gold from a warehouse belonging to a fake corporation going by the name Blue Mountain. You figured that one out pretty good. As a result, the attorney general thinks there's enough evidence to convict both Cain and Buford of stealing the gold from Sioux land with the intent to mint it into counterfeit coins. The boys will be able to substantiate the kidnapping charges. But to get the murder charges against Cain to stick, he needs both Nathaniel *and* you to testify." He rubbed his jaw and looked directly at me. "Have you remembered enough to testify or should I tell him to drop those charges?"

I sat up and handed him the journal. "I remembered it all. The night after the funeral, I went to Cain's house to find the jacket Cain wore the day of the train robbery. It was blue and green plaid and one of the witnesses said that the man who killed Dad was wearing a blue and green jacket. I knew that because they wore masks, the witness wouldn't be able to identify the killer unless the jacket was found and recognized.

"When Cain and Buford came through the back door and went straight to the bedroom, I hid under the bed. They undressed and crawled into bed together. While they were…um…making love, Cain told Buford he was the one who shot Dad and how he would make every effort to find me because I was the one who took the die plates. Buford told him the second shipment of gold was ready to be shipped to the warehouse. Cain was the one who beat Nathaniel, but he had to stop because he received a message that Buford arrived on the train. He was planning to take Nathaniel to the warehouse and finish him off by torturing him. After they fell asleep, I snuck out and broke Nathaniel out of jail."

William read the fuller details of what happened in my journal. When he looked up at me, he smiled. "Ely McDonald would be proud of you. I know your real father is." He stood up and handed the journal back.

He left and I packed the journal into my saddlebags. I was

ready to leave the train, but not ready to enter Chicago or the mansion I grew up in. I would prefer to go out to the farm, but the judge didn't want us that far away. Besides, the mansion with its high rock walls would be easier for the Pinkertons and federal marshals to guard.

Upon arriving in Chicago, the private car and the prison car were uncoupled and left on a sidetrack. I watched out the window. Cain, Buford, and thirteen other men were loaded into prison wagons. Cain tapped Buford on the shoulder and pointed at me. They smiled and laughed with each other.

I tapped the side of my head and then pointed at them. Their laughter stopped. The smiles turned into worried frowns.

I knew it all. Not only would the jury learn everything I saw and heard, but their fellow prisoners would find out that they were lovers and that they used two innocent boys as pawns in their game. I smiled because even if they didn't get the death penalty, their lives would be hell.

Riding in three coaches, eighteen Pinkerton agents and federal deputies escorted us to my childhood home. The limestone perimeter walls were covered with dormant ivy, and every twenty feet, a gaslight burned on top of a pilaster. The iron gate swung open and we passed light poles along the drive. I looked out at the snow-covered lawn and garden beds. It all seemed so foreign to me, so cold, so lifeless.

When the coach stopped in front of the house, William Pinkerton opened the door and Nathaniel stepped out before helping me down. Paul was looking at me from where he stood outside the second coach trying to get his balance on the crutches in the snow.

I gave him a humble smile before I looked up at the three-story mansion, which looked like a miniature castle. It was the home that Ely McDonald raised me in as his own daughter. The home that my mother filled with piano music. The home that survived the Chicago fire and became Dad's temporary stock brokerage office until the downtown business district was rebuilt. The home that would never be the same without my parents in it.

"Ma, is this really your house?" Lance asked.

I nodded. "Dad modeled it after the castle his ancestors owned in Ireland. In the 1640s when Ireland rebelled against England, Owen McDonald led a force of his countrymen against the British Army and lost. He escaped persecution by fleeing to the colonies and hiding among the Puritans. Dad traveled to Ireland when he was about your age, saw his ancestral home, and vowed to live there someday. His solution to doing so was to build it here."

Nathaniel laughed. "This one, of course, is only a third the size of the original."

He led the way inside and the boys spent the rest of the evening exploring Dad's castle. Jeremy did his best not to rush Lance from one room to the next, but like a horse chomping at the bit to run freely, he occasionally left his best friend a few steps behind. George Tate trailed along just to keep the boys out of trouble.

In some ways, I felt like an exiled princess coming home after a long banishment. I wanted so much for my mother to welcome me with open arms, but there wasn't so much as a maid, butler, or cook to greet us. Over the past nine months, they had all found new employment.

Yet, despite the lack of staff, there were no cobwebs or thick layers of dust. Someone was keeping the mansion clean. I looked at Nathaniel and he shrugged.

"Maybe Dad's attorney has a cleaning crew coming in once a week," he said. "I'll go talk with him tomorrow and arrange an appointment for the reading of the will."

"Do you think Kitty might be coming over?"

He shook his head. "She liked the idea of being married to a stockbroker's son more than to a lawman, so she went to New York and married a Wall Street tycoon twice her age."

I now understood the sad glint in his eyes each time I mentioned her name while we were in North Platte. "I'm so sorry."

Again he shook his head. "It's okay. I'd rather find out now that she was only after my money instead of after we were married." Then he smiled. "Besides, I met a nice gal while we were in North Platte."

"Really. Why didn't you say something?"

"I wasn't sure how you'd react."

"Why?"

"Because Poppa says Kimberly Talbourne doesn't exactly hold

a high mark with you."

My heart thudded. He laughed. I pretended to slap him across the face and he grabbed my wrist to kiss it.

"Actually, it was Chen Sue I met. She's a real nice girl and I like her."

"What was she doing in North Platte?"

"Visiting her uncle for his fiftieth birthday." He patted his stomach. "I sure could get used to eating Chinese food."

I gave him a hug and a kiss on the cheek before going upstairs to put my saddlebags away. It was getting close to dinnertime and apparently I was the cook since the staff was gone. Luckily, I was used to cooking for multitudes of people, and William's father arranged for the kitchen to be stocked with plenty of food for everyone including our security guards.

After dinner, I slipped into my mother's sitting room and sat down in front of the needlepoint scroll she was working on before leaving for St. Louis. It was a picture of a garden I remembered being in once when I was a small child. It belonged to a woman by the name of Annette St. Claire in Wilmington. Mrs. St. Claire and my mother often met for tea when we visited Wilmington and on one occasion Mom took me with her.

"Do you still love him?" Mrs. St. Claire asked.

"Yes," my mother said. "I always will." She kissed the back of my head. I was sitting on her lap and we were having a tea party in the garden. "I wanted to go to him after Barth died."

"Why didn't you?"

Mom hugged me closer to her. "Oh, Aunt Annette, it was terrible. Barth and I never made love the whole time we were married until the night he died. I never dreamed a seventy-five year old man could get a woman with child, but he did." She took a deep breath. "I wrote Joe a letter, telling him that I was carrying Barth's child and asking him if he would still marry me if I came to him." She toyed with the ruffles on my dress. "He wasn't at that church any longer and the current pastor sent my letter back with a note saying that he didn't know where the Methodist Ministry sent him. I tried to contact you, but you were in Europe."

She took a sip of tea and then stroked her fingers through my hair. "I was still waiting to hear from him or you or the Methodists when the house sold. Not sure what to do, I went ahead and sold the furniture and bought tickets to come here to stay on the farm with the folks. I was having difficulties with my condition and the doctor warned me not to travel, but I was only five months along and thought I would be fine."

Her hand came down next to my side and rested on her stomach. She remained quiet for a time while she sipped tea with a shaking hand. Mrs. St. Claire put a hand on her arm and that seemed to steady her nerves.

"Go on, dear. If I'm going to help you, I need to know."

Mom took a deep breath. "We were waiting for the connection in Chicago when I went into labor. I lost a lot of blood and the baby died just minutes after being born. They told me I'd be in the hospital for at least a month and wanted to know if there were any relatives to send the children to. They tried the folks first, but it was an election year and Mom and Dad were traveling around campaigning with Abe Lincoln. The only other relative I could think of was Ely. He was Barth's nephew by his first wife, so I asked the hospital to take the children to him. After the hospital released me, Ely and Barbara invited me to stay with them while I continued to recover. Ely took such joy in having Nathaniel and Josephine around that after Barbara drowned when her coach went off the bridge during that blizzard, I just couldn't take them away from him. He would've died of sorrow without the children there and I couldn't very well stay in the mansion alone with him unmarried, so since I still hadn't heard from Joe, I married him."

"Do you love him?"

She nodded. "But it's a different kind of love."

Mrs. St. Claire patted my mother's hand. "Are they sure you can't have more children?"

"Yes. They say it's because of the trouble I had carrying Barth's child."

"As much as I believe Joseph should have the right to raise his children, I think you made the right decision." Mrs. St. Claire handed Mom a piece of paper. "Here's his address. But you better write him soon because the ministry is sending him to Mexico to help children orphaned or left abandoned by the continued strife with war, Indians, and other pestilence there."

Mom took the piece of paper and slid it inside her purse. "Thank you."

We left the garden and went to the farm. The following day, Sossy wanted my roll.

I reached out and touched the needlepoint garden as if doing so would take me back there once again. But that was the only memory I pulled out of the stitch work my mother never finished.

Becker killed her and he died a slow death from the bullet I put into his arm. Poppa was right. There was no pride in taking a man's life, nor was there satisfaction in knowing Mom's death was avenged. I'd much rather have her back in my life.

"Can we talk?"

I jumped to my feet and turned to face Paul. Without waiting for my answer, he hobbled into the room, closed the door, and took a seat on one of the tapestry-covered sofas. I scooted an ottoman over in front of him.

"How is your leg?" I asked as I gently lifted it to the cushioned surface.

"Doc thinks it should heal up okay, but I'll always have a bit of a limp because there's a lot of muscle gone from it." He patted the cushion beside him. "Sit. We need to talk."

Guilt plagued my mind for ignoring him while we were on the train. I broke out in a cold sweat as I sat down. His arm immediately wrapped around my shoulders and he turned toward me as his lips took hold of mine. My fingers caressed his cheek and I felt a muscle twitch beneath my touch. My heart pounded as he drove the kiss deeper, so deep the aggressiveness hurt. I tried to break away, but his arm held me in place. After a few minutes, the buttons to my riding skirt came undone and his hand slipped in and pressed down against my abdomen.

I sucked in a deep breath and forced his hand away. "What'd you do that for?" I asked.

He pulled away and rubbed his face with both hands. "To let you know how my heart feels every time you try to run away from the love I feel for you." A tear escaped his eye and he turned his head away as if trying to keep me from seeing it. "Stop pushing me away." He stood up and grabbed the crutches. "I know what I can offer doesn't compare to what you have here, but if you'll give me a chance, I'll share with you the same kind of love your mother and father shared the night they made you."

I looked over at the needlepoint garden. "You may not believe this, but I was always more at home on the farm." I leaned my head back and looked up at the gilded ceiling. "But after everything that's happened, I don't think I could ever live there again either."

I stood up and slipped my arms around his waist. The dampness of his skin soaked through the fabric of his shirt. His muscles were quaking. He was nervous.

"I shouldn't have done that," he said. "I'm sorry."

I looked into his eyes. "I'm the one who should apologize for refusing to see you while we were on the train. But I needed that time alone without distraction to finish remembering what happened last spring."

"So you did?"

I nodded before I rested my head against his shoulder. "That wasn't the only thing I concentrated on while I was alone. The whole way here I felt homesick. Not for this place, not for the farm, but for your house. I want to go back there and live my life with you. I need you and Carol and Lance to make my life complete. I just wish the circumstances that brought us together weren't covered with so much grief."

His lips pressed against the top of my head. "We'll overcome that grief together." He slid a hand inside my skirt and let it gently rest against my abdomen. "I really am sorry I did that just now. It was stupid and wrong and…cruel." His hand came out and he buttoned my skirt back up. "I'd better go and pick out a bedroom."

Shaking my head, I pulled on his arm. "Come with me."

I led him up a secret staircase behind an oak wall panel to my parents' bedroom. The same bedroom where the man I called Dad loved two different wives during his lifetime. I pulled one of my mother's gowns out of the wardrobe, slid behind a dressing screen, and changed into it while Paul put on one of Dad's nightshirts. We heated water in the fireplace and bathed each other's wounds. We lay down beside each other, holding hands and talking about the future. Somewhere in the wee hours of the night I fell asleep, feeling safe, secure, and loved.

Chapter 39

A disturbance in the bedroom prompted me to open my eyes the next morning. It didn't surprise me to find Poppa standing at the foot of the bed, silhouetted by the sunlight coming through the windows. Even though I couldn't see his face clearly, I imagined him wearing one of those frowns that tugged at his responsibilities as both a minister and a father.

Nathaniel leaned against the left canopy post, shaking his head. "I heard that couples should kiss and make up, but this is carrying it a bit far."

I rolled toward Paul. He was sitting up with the covers pulled up to his chest. The look in his eyes was a mixture of apology and defiance. I felt the same way, but I was also thankful that neither one of them was holding a shotgun.

"It probably wouldn't do any good to tell you we changed behind the dressing screens and didn't do more than hold hands. Would it?" I asked.

Nathaniel pointed to Mom's dressing screen. "I put your clothes behind there."

I slid on the robe he handed me and walked across the room. Behind the screen I found a green velvet dress that felt three sizes too big because of all the weight I lost. The dress used to be one of my favorites, but like the house, it was another part of a life I no longer wanted. I slid on the moccasins and then stepped out into the room.

Paul was still in bed.

"Go downstairs," Poppa said.

I obeyed as far as going out into the hallway. Lance stood there with a grin on his face. I put a finger over my lips and put my ear to the door. He slid in next to me to also listen.

"I expected better behavior from you, Paul," Poppa said.

"She told you the truth," Paul said. "We changed behind the screens, helped change each other's bandages, and then did nothing more than lie here talking until we fell asleep."

"And just what did you talk about?" Nathaniel asked.

"Us, the children, what we're going to do once Cain and Buford are convicted." There was a pause. When Paul spoke again, it sounded like he was crying. "I'm sorry, but we've all lost so much this past year. If it wasn't for Lance and Angela, I'd be dead. The love I feel for them is the only thing that keeps me from putting a gun to my head."

My heart knotted up. Lance looked up at me with fear in his eyes. I put a hand on his shoulder for support.

The bedroom was silent for over a minute before Poppa spoke. "Who initiated this little rendezvous?"

"I hate to say it, Poppa, but Jo had to be the one," Nathaniel said. "Paul wouldn't have known about the hidden passageway."

"I swear that girl's going to test me to no end. Melinda always said she was such a sweet—"

"She was until all this started," Nathaniel said. "She taught Sunday school, sang in the choir, and never disobeyed Mom and Dad. It wasn't until after Grandpa died that she started wearing jeans whenever she helped out with the farm work. But even then she was very modest and except for a little sibling scrapping when we were kids, she was still very well behaved."

"Well, she did tell me that she didn't know who God was anymore," Poppa said. "I guess some of this immoral behavior comes from not remembering what's right and wrong." There was a pause. "But you should know, Paul." I could almost visualize him pointing a finger at Paul. "What happened to all that talk about doing things right this time around and not jumping the gun like you did last time?"

I felt sorry for Paul having to defend himself against my father and Nathaniel. It probably wasn't too unlike what happened when he faced his father after getting Rose with child.

"I love Angela, sir, and I'll do anything it takes to show her that my love is far deeper than the guilt she feels for my losing Jared, Wyatt, and Neil…If you knew the depth of the guilt she's carrying around in her, you'd understand why it was important for us to spend the night together last night…I also think it was very important for her to feel me next to her as a husband would sleep next to a wife, so that she knows we can be together whether we're ever able to join physically or not."

Nearly a minute went by during which time I held my breath. My lungs ached for air. I supplied them with oxygen while I continued to wait.

"I think the best thing we can do is marry the two of you this afternoon," Poppa said. "We'll pick up the license while we're at the courthouse this morning."

I heard footsteps approach the door, so I motioned for Lance to follow me toward the stairs. The grin on his face only meant one thing: He liked the idea of his father and me getting married whether I was completely ready to share my life with Paul or not. I loved him and wanted to marry him, but I still felt we should wait until this whole ordeal was over.

I wanted Lucille to be my brides' maid and Paula to make my wedding gown and Jarvis to play the piano and sing and Nathaniel to walk me down the aisle and my father to marry me to the man I love.

As I helped Lance down the stairs, I still couldn't get past the flickering thought that my love for Paul included the desire for him to have more children. I knew we could adopt more children, but he deserved to have children by his own seed. He was the last brother and needed sons to carry on his family.

Halfway down the stairs, I caught Lance and kept him from slipping. His crutches went tumbling to the bottom. We stood on that step a moment to let our running pulses slow down.

Our eyes met and he smiled. "Thanks, Ma."

I bent over and kissed him on the head. "You realize that it's your responsibility to make sure the Garrett family continues to have sons and daughters, don't you?"

"Yeah. Pa and I talked about that while we were on the train."

"Then be more careful."

"I will." He slipped his hands around my waist and hugged me. "I'm glad you're here to help me keep Pa from wanting to kill himself."

My hands moved up and down his back and arms. "So am I."

Nathaniel came down the stairs. His eyes quickly took in the fallen crutches and that "Lance nearly broke his neck" look on my face. Even inside a house, he could read the signs like a seasoned lawman. He picked Lance up and carried him the rest of the way to the foyer. On an impulse, I stepped closer to the banister, sat on it sidesaddle, and slid to the bottom.

Lance laughed. "And you were telling me to be careful not to break my neck."

"Go see if Jeremy's already in the dining room," I said.

He picked up the fallen crutches and disappeared down the hallway. Nathaniel sat down on the bottom step and I joined him.

His eyes focused on my abdomen. "How bad does it hurt?" he asked.

"You could probably compare it to a man getting kicked between the legs."

He tried to hide the reflexive pained look in his eyes by reaching into my hair and feeling the ridge. "And this?"

"Only when I think too hard. Sometimes the pressure gets so bad, I pass out. Other times, it makes me throw up. I'm hoping that once all this is over and I don't have to try so hard to remember everything, the headaches will go away completely."

He crossed his arms over his knees.

"Bonedale thought we should talk to a surgeon while we're here in Chicago about you having surgery to…uh…well…to remove your—"

"No." I rubbed my forehead. "I've lost enough."

"Still, you should think about it," he said. "Especially if you and Paul ever want to do more than just lie beside each other."

The front door burst open and William Pinkerton rushed in. "Nate, we've got trouble. Cain and Buford escaped last night."

Nathaniel rose to his feet fast. "How'd that happen?"

"Two policemen on the nightshift are missing. We suspect Cain bribed them." William looked at me. "I don't want any of you to step foot outside this house. A drunk in one of the cells says he overheard Cain plotting to kill you. All of you."

Chapter 40

I spent the day in my mother's sitting room trying to keep my mind busy by finishing the needlework garden. When I showed Poppa what I wrote about the garden memory, he wept. He felt ashamed for how bitter he felt during that time in his life. Bitter at my grandfather, bitter at Mom for marrying another man, and bitter with himself for running away without telling Mom where he went. For a while, he sat with Paul and me talking about loss, love, and marital responsibility. Around one o'clock, he and Paul went into my Dad's study to continue discussing Paul's torments about losing so many members of his family in such a short time. In many ways, Paul felt orphaned and alone after being shoved out of his father's house. It didn't help that a telegram from his father came after lunch telling him to quit trying to cover up his sins by trying to initiate a relationship between his parents and their illegitimate grandson. Paul threw the missive in the fireplace just before going into Dad's study with my father again.

Thankfully, the boys were off exploring more of the mansion under Mr. Tate's watchful eyes when that happened.

Except for the emotional wars going on, everything seemed quiet until shots and yells were heard from the front lawn. I started to reach for the Peacemaker, which was lying on the end table beside me, when I heard the double click of a Colt cock behind me.

I stood up and turned around. Cain and Buford stood there. Cain held a gun in his hand and motioned to an open passageway. The mansion was filled with hidden corridors, stairways, and tunnels. This particular one led down into an old abandoned portion of Chicago's sewage system. Most of the catacombs were caved in, but the tunnel leading from the house to a manhole in an alley two blocks away was still intact.

"My brother helped build this palace," Cain said. "I know all of its secrets. Now let's go before the diversion we set up outside subsides."

When we climbed a ladder into the alley, a coach waited. I no sooner sat down on one of the seats and Cain shackled my ankles and then my wrists. Even though I was wearing moccasins instead of boots and still recovering from the toe amputation, he wasn't taking any chances with my feet.

"You sure cost us a lot of money," Buford said. "But I'm sure your brother will make up for that by handing over your father's fortune to us for your safe return."

"You have no intention of letting me go."

"No, but we do intend to get something out of this."

When the coach started moving, the closed shutters prevented me from seeing where it headed. As we traveled, Cain and Buford held hands. That minor show of affection between them was enough to make me squirm.

Without a coat or a cape, I shivered. The green velvet of my dress did little to keep out the December cold. I rubbed my hands up and down my arms the best I could with the shackles on. The motion drew Buford's attention away from Cain's caresses to the emerald ring I now wore on my right hand.

"Where'd you get that?" he demanded.

"What do you care?"

His hand wrapped around my wrist and squeezed. "Where'd you get it?"

"Neil Jones gave it to me," I said. "It belonged to his mother."

A strange look came over his face as he released my wrist.

Cain laughed. "If you like it so much, why don't you just take it from her?"

"I can't."

Cain raised an eyebrow. "Why not?"

Buford rubbed a hand against his cheek. "It belonged to my ex-wife."

"All the more reason to get it back and keep it in the family." Cain laid the gun down and grabbed my wrist. I curled my fingers when he tried to take the ring from me. "If you don't give it to me nicely, I'll chop your fingers off to get it."

I kicked the latch of the right shackle against his shin.

He let go of my hand and slapped my face so hard I tasted blood.

I punched him between the legs with my left heel and then brought it up to knock him under the chin.

His face turned red as he choked down his pain and grabbed for my feet. He pressed hard against where my toes were removed.

I screamed.

He laughed.

I clasped my hands together and raked the shackles across his cheek.

"You bitch!" he screeched as his hands came up to protect his face.

I pounded both feet against his chest and heard a bone crack. His hand grabbed the gun, but Buford knocked his arm up. The bullet went through the roof of the coach and the driver screamed as he fell off the seat. Buford grabbed the gun and immediately opened the door and climbed up on top of the coach.

I continued to kick and stomp my feet against Cain. His attempts to defend himself became feebler by the second until he finally slumped into the corner, unconscious. I reached into his coat pockets and found the key to the shackles.

Just as I finished freeing myself, the coach came to a halt. I jumped out and ran until Buford caught up with me.

He tackled me to the ground, rolled me over, and kept me pinned there in the snow.

"Why'd Neil give you the ring?"

"He loved me and wanted me to marry him. He proposed to me just before Becker shot him in the back. After Judge Hayes tore up the marriage license between Neil and Kimberly, he married Neil and me. I was kissing him when he died."

"Becker's the one who shot him?"

"Yes."

"The bastard!" He rolled off the top of me and stared up at the night sky. "Roseanne kicked me out of the house not long after Neil and Rose were born. She found out about Cain and me. She was a widow with four daughters when I met her in Peoria and married her. She was older, but needed a husband."

"Neil was your son?"

"Yes," he said softly with a nod. He sat up and hugged his

knees to his chest. "My father knew I liked men and wrote it into his will that I couldn't inherit his wealth unless I married a woman, so I married Roseanne to keep from losing my inheritance. The marriage lasted long enough for me to get his money, but then Roseanne divorced me. She said she couldn't handle sharing her husband with another man. I gave her enough money to raise the children and then she moved to Omaha and started using her first husband's last name again."

It was strange hearing him talk so gently about a woman. It seemed so out of character for someone who cared little for other people, especially women.

"You loved her, didn't you?"

He shrugged. "A man like me doesn't love women, at least not for more than just pleasure. But the time I spent with her was the only time in my life I felt like I was doing something meaningful and worthwhile. If I could've put my other desires aside, I probably could've enjoyed being her husband for the rest of my life. I actually thought of all those girls of hers as my own."

"What now?"

He stood up and helped me to my feet. "As Neil's widow, you're my sole heir should anything happen to me. For now, I'll send you the deed to the restaurant and saloon. If Cain's still alive, he can hang for all this mess. I'm going to disappear." He walked with me back to the coach and unharnessed one of the horses while I checked on Cain. "Is he alive?"

"No. That rib I busted got him in the lung."

"Can't say I'm sorry. He was starting to get a bit too full of himself for my taste." I shivered when he took my right hand in his and looked down at the ring. "That ring belonged to my mother. It's been in the family for at least five generations that I know of. Take care of it. I can't think of a better woman to wear it than you, Angela. You've got grit."

He mounted the horse bareback and rode off into the night. I should have stopped him, but decided the Pinkertons could track him down. After all, I needed to get back to Chicago to attend my shotgun wedding.

Chapter 41

If I thought the pain I felt after the accident was bad, what I felt now was four times worse. Sweat dripped off my forehead and Paul wiped it with a cool cloth.

"Just relax," he said. "We knew this might happen. Dr. Miller warned us the pain would be intense given what happened to you."

I gasped for air and nodded. "I know."

"It's my fault, I never should've given in and let you talk me into making love."

"I'm your wife. You have a right to have me fully and completely. I just never thought this would happen, especially considering I've never had any monthlies after the accident."

"Ron will be here soon," Poppa said, as he finished putting the stretcher he and Nathaniel washed the blood off of into the closet.

I was in Dr. Miller's surgery with my feet in the stirrups. Mrs. Miller stood between my spread out legs feeling my abdomen.

"Her womb's split wide open, Paul," she said. "I don't think we can wait for Ron. She'll bleed to death and you'll lose her and the baby."

"Is there anything I can do?" Poppa asked.

She smiled at him. "What you always do, Joseph. Pray."

Poppa and Nathaniel led Lance and Carol out into the waiting room. Carol toddled along on legs that were longer than most for a two-year-old. She would definitely be tall like Homer, but her eyes and smile came from Margie. Nathaniel closed the door.

I looked at Mrs. Miller as she walked closer to my head. "Save the baby first."

She held a chloroform mask in her hand and placed it over my mouth and nose. "I'll do everything I can to save you both. I haven't been a doctor's wife for twenty-five years without learning a few things about doctoring."

I focused on Paul's eyes as the fumes from the chloroform filled my lungs. The last thing he needed was to lose someone else he loved. Rose died giving birth to Lance and I resigned myself months ago to the fact that the miracle of giving him another child was most likely going to kill me. It was the price I would pay for cheating death so many times the year we met. I just prayed the baby would live and give him a part of me to hold onto.

The last thing I remembered was a tear dripping from his cheek onto mine.

Pain and cold. Those were two sensations I knew all too well. For a moment, I tried to remember if I was at the bottom of the cliff or out traipsing through the snow to get away from Cain. I often woke up in the mornings trying to remember where I was and what was past and present in my life.

Looking up and seeing a ceiling let me know I was in neither place. I wasn't in the mansion or Granma's farmhouse either. It wasn't my room at Mrs. Chalk's or the bedroom at Paul's house where I clenched my teeth the night I told Paul to go inside me. That was on our first anniversary. I was tired of feeling guilty for being a virgin after a year of marriage. My jaws ached for two days afterward, but I took his seed and wound up carrying his child despite the damage done to my uterus when I fell off the cliff.

That was eight months ago and now my abdomen felt like it was on fire despite all of the ice surrounding me. I shifted my head and heard the fist sized chunks shift position. Being in that much pain, one thing was for certain—I wasn't dead.

My mouth felt dry. I coughed and could have sworn Jenny's cat left a fur ball in the back of my throat. I lifted my arm, found a pecan-sized chunk of ice and slid it into my mouth. The cool wetness felt good on my throat, as it melted and washed away the fluffy feeling. When the piece of ice melted, I found another.

I was sucking on a fourth chunk of ice when I heard the sound of an infant cry. My pulse surged at the knowledge my baby was alive. A door opened and Dr. Miller entered the room. It finally dawned on me that I was at his house. He smiled when he saw me awake.

"Good morning, Angela."

I spit the chunk of ice out. "Maw-nin'." I swallowed. "The baby fine?"

"Both of them are just fine."

I coughed. "Both?"

"A boy and a girl." He felt my forehead and checked my pulse. "It's about time that fever of yours went down. I removed your womb. It never should've carried one baby, let alone two." He lifted the bandages over my abdomen, which was the only part of my body not covered with ice. "The infection is clearing up. It's taken four days. You always were a hell of a fighter."

Four days. No wonder my hands looked like prunes. I've been lying in ice for four days.

"Paul?"

"I'll send him in after Chen Sue and Lucille finish feeding the babies."

My maternal instincts were jealous. "Why can't I feed them?"

He put his hand against my cheek. "You did your job by carrying them. Be thankful you survived that and have a best friend and a sister-in-law who can nurse them."

A half hour later, Paul came in and sat down beside me. His hand caressed my cheek. "How do you feel?"

I spit out a piece of ice. My mouth was so dry. "Like I fell off that cliff all over again."

"Speaking of cliffs. Nathaniel got a telegram from William. Buford was found dead last week at the bottom of a cliff in Utah. They think he jumped."

"The last letter I got from him did say a doctor told him he had syphilis. He probably decided to end his life quickly before he went insane."

He nodded. "I was thinking the same thing, especially since they found his will in his coat pocket naming you and Lance as the heirs to what's left of his father's fortune." He took hold of my hands and rubbed his thumbs over both the emerald ring and the wedding ring. "I love you, Angela. Have I told you that lately?"

"Not in four days."

"You just weren't awake to hear me blubbering it in your ear." He leaned over and kissed my lips. "Now, promise me you'll get well, so we can raise those babies *together*."

"What are their names?"
He smiled. "Joseph Neil and Melinda Rose."
I reached up and touched his cheek. "I promise."

Reaona Hemmingway resides in Topeka, Kansas where she is an active member of the Kansas Authors Club and Kansas Writer's, Inc. During the month of November, she participates in National Novel Writing Month (Nanowrimo) in which writers challenge themselves to complete a 50,000 word novel in 30 days. In 2009, her 2007 Nanowrimo novel, *Baseball Card Hero*, was published and received honorable mention in the J. Donald Coffin Memorial Book Award contest. Her published work also includes *September 11*, *Mariah*, *Home for Christmas*, and *Tillie's Marbles & Other Stories*.

More novels by Reaona Hemmingway

Baseball Card Hero

Eight years after Dr. Lorain Donaldson adopts a premature baby, an autographed baseball card found on the birth mother's body becomes the key to finding her son's biological father in the event a bone marrow transplant is necessary to treat his leukemia.

"*Terrific! A sweet love triangle--mother, son and father.*"
--Errol Anderson, author of *The Job Coach* (Golden City Books)

"*I...finished reading* Baseball Card Hero, *and assure you that you have every reason to be proud. You have created a good story and peopled it with believable, real characters. And...you make the reader care about them and the outcome.*"
--Max Yoho, author of *The Revival, Tales From Comanche County,* and *The Moon Butter Route* (Dancing Goat Press)

September 11

Since his birth on September 11, 1985, Kevin Stillwater has lost one family member after another on his birthday, including both of his parents at the Pentagon in 2001. After returning from Iraq, he meets Jeremiah Flint, a special agent with the Kansas Bureau of Investigation, who enlists Kevin's computer skills to find Jeremiah's missing nephew, Ivan. As Kevin's 21st birthday approaches, Jeremiah is fighting for his life, Ivan is kidnapped, and Kevin's last remaining brother is shot down in a helicopter. On September 11, 2006, the race is on to save Jeremiah, rescue Ivan, and stop Kevin from trying to end the family curse by committing suicide.

"*Ms. Hemmingway takes the reader on a cerebral and well-researched adventure with Kansas Bureau of Investigation (KBI) agent Jeremiah Flint.*"
—Mark Bouton, author of *How to Spot Lies Like the FBI.*

Mariah

In search of her mother, Mariah Wingate accepts a governess position in Elk Creek, Wyoming, where she quickly wins the heart of Deputy Brent Sawyer. While her relationship with Brent puts her in danger from cattle thieves and a rapist, she also stirs up long hidden secrets of the town's most prominent citizens.

"*I love the Christianity that runs through your books, and that the characters still act like we do in real life. It makes it seem so natural and right, and how it can fit into anyone's life.*"
—Christina Brown, independent proofreader

Short Story Collections
Home for Christmas
Tillie's Marbles & Other Stories

All titles available at your favorite online bookstore.

Made in the USA
San Bernardino, CA
27 August 2014